YOUTOPIA

**A "Youtopia" Novel
by
Joseph Rein**

YOUTOPIA
Youtopia – Book 1
Copyright © 2024 Joseph Rein

FIRST EDITION SOFTCOVER
ISBN: 1622535766
ISBN-13: 978-1-62253-576-7

Editor: Lane Diamond
Cover Artist: Kris Norris
Interior Designer: Lane Diamond

EVOLVED PUBLISHING™

www.EvolvedPub.com
Evolved Publishing LLC
Butler, Wisconsin, USA

Printed in Book Antiqua font.

Books by Joseph Rein

YOUTOPIA
Book 1: *Youtopia*
Book 2: *Youtopia Reborn*
Book 3: *Youtopia Infinity*

Roads without Houses: Stories [Press 53, 2018]

Dedication

For Colette, James, Johnny, and Olivia:
my Heroes.

Prologue: 2014

The Senator watched from below as Sonya Young's hand slipped. Her legs dangled suspended, as did her left arm and shoulder. Only the supreme grip of her right fingers kept her from a hundred-foot drop—from assured death.

It was lunacy, pure and simple. Sonya clung like a droplet of rain from the cliff's edge, and the Senator could only think: Sonya was insane. A woman with a death wish. And so he, too, must have been insane, trekking all this way just to witness her fulfill it.

It began earlier that morning at the tiny airport in a town called Devils Lake, where their plane circled the runway twice because some idiot in flight control mishandled the routine landing of their cramped plane. The terminal was no better, a meager space with one poorly-lit Americana restaurant and dead flies in the urinals. Then came the drive, a pugnacious sixty-two miles of aimless turns and signless intersections that took over two hours. Deer looking to die sprinted before them. Trees discarded their bedraggled leaves onto the windshield like rain. Each mile of naked foliage and dampness, each whiff of that corpse-like smell, pushed the Senator nearer to calling the whole thing off.

"Just a bit farther," his young driver and escort, just a boy really, said over and again. "We're nearly there."

When they'd finally reached the building—Sonya's headquarters, her business, stuck in the middle of nowhere like some goddamn ice shanty on a desolate lake—the Senator could only shake his head at the pathetic building, little more than a warehouse with metal siding that curled like unruly fingernails. Its fascia sagged beneath a dull corrugated roof. The place had all the aspects of an abandoned storage facility plunked in the middle of woods and small bluffs, a dumping ground where one discovers the decades-old chattel and rotting furniture of hoarders. The Senator blamed himself for having expectations otherwise.

Then, along a sand-colored bluff just beyond the decrepit building, they'd spotted the figure that turned out to be Sonya, clad in all white, her ponytailed hair midnight black. She scaled the crags without rope or harness, with only gloves and climbing shoes and a small pack affixed to her waist. She glided about the rock with an assured, steady grace. With a flippancy toward her own safety that he found despicable. Insane.

Then her hand slipped, and the Senator knew it for certain. Her fingers couldn't hold; she would shriek, would plummet to the ground, and he would have come all this way just to see an old acquaintance — no, not even that, just a potential donor — reduced to nothing.

She dangled for longer than seemed possible. He halted, realizing he'd been holding his breath. But her body didn't sway, didn't falter. The immense grip of her fingers kept her aloft. She lifted her left hand and probed the rock for surer handling. Once found, she pulled herself up, affixed her body to the protruding stone like a spider, and passed the challenging spot as though nothing had gone amiss — as though she hadn't almost lost everything.

"Whoa," the boy said next to him.

Though Sonya was too far away to hear, her head tilted. She stopped, steadied her footing, and turned to them. "You are early," she called, her voice draping down with a soft echo. "I'm afraid that at this point, up will be easier than down. If you will be so kind."

She returned to the cliff and resumed her feline-like scaling up the pocked wall. Her movements were deft, intuitive. Up and over, over and up, she climbed until, just minutes later, she stood at the top. She looked down to them once more and nodded before disappearing behind the bluff's edge.

The Senator looked over to the boy, who stupidly shrugged his shoulders in response. Nothing about this felt right. The Senator wanted out. If only he hadn't come this far already. If only he had stopped it before it began. But Sonya had sounded so elated over the phone, so full of flattery. She mentioned their high school with fondness, though they had attended a decade apart. She spoke with praise and pinpoint knowledge of his voting record on the Senate floor. Her start-up company stood on the precipice of a breakthrough; there would be a speech. She would be so honored if he were in attendance.

His instinct had said to punt it. Many people wanted him to attend company events, signifying their success simply by smiling to a news camera. Sonya appeared to be no different. But then she had proffered her end of the bargain — six figures toward his reelection campaign — and in truth, he let the dollar signs, the opportunity for a lifelong donor, sully his judgment.

As the minutes passed, his agitation grew. Beside him, the boy teemed with restlessness as well, his arms crossing, his feet dragging fallen leaves into piles. "You two knew each other?" he asked, a question the Senator had no intention answering.

Then, from a shaded copse just beside them, Sonya emerged, quick and surprisingly soundless. The boy sidestepped for her as she extended an effeminate hand. She had aged, the Senator had to admit, particularly well. She had only been a child when he knew her, but a youthfulness remained in her face and in her figure—still gaunt, too few curves on her athletic body, sure, but in her forties a woman could better afford such severity. Her almond-colored skin—from a Peruvian mother, or some other South American nation, he couldn't recall—showed little sign of wear. About her face radiated an effervescence. The Senator fixated on her. Against himself, he wished to know Sonya's secrets.

"I am so grateful to you for coming here," she said. "I have admired you from the very start. Inspiring, to see former classmates reach such pinnacles of achievement."

The Senator attempted to conjure an image of Sonya from memory, some gathering with his younger brother's friends, a moment just at the tip of his mind, but nothing came. "Thank you. But you can save the flattery. My time is precious." Then, constraining his sarcasm, "As I'm sure is yours."

Sonya looked for a long moment at the large-faced watch on her wrist, as though just now realizing the time of day. "Yes. If you would." Then she turned and led them to her derelict building.

His first step was deliberate, his tent pole into the earth, while his ailing leg followed like a dislodged stake. The red, tender flesh of his upper thigh—a staph infection the doctors seemed incapable of fully excising—called out to him like a warning signal. He trailed Sonya and the boy, fighting to conceal his slight hobble as the pain crawled from his leg up to his stomach, burning into his throat. He tasted a sticky, sickly uncertainty. Sonya's precarious climb, her headquarters in the middle of God knew where—he had the sense he was being deceived, though how or to what end he couldn't surmise. He felt part of some elaborate prank.

Everything felt backward. Take the entrance of her building, with an encrypted keypad into which Sonya entered twenty numbers with her delicate fingers, security overkill on a wood door that would succumb to a common sledgehammer. Inside offered much the same, with cheap industrial halogen lights and stains on the laminate floor. Even the air felt artificial. Her few employees—if that was indeed who they were, in khakis and untucked shirts—passed by with little more than a nod. All around him looked less the work of a genius than some arrested hermit. A person out of touch with the world itself.

Then Sonya walked him down the hall to a sliding-glass door, and outside, he finally saw some semblance of sanity: a modern, ostentatious outdoor amphitheater—the grandiose stage at which she planned to deliver her speech. At its head stood a presidential podium. Speakers large enough to broadcast across a space thrice its size rested atop wooden poles. Rustic and yet sleek, it bore the look one gets when pouring large sums of money into false authenticity. It appeared, fortunately, nothing like the rest of the place.

Sonya paused at the glass and, from the pack on her waist, removed a small snack wrapped in featureless packaging. Green, shaped like a granola bar, it smelled of dirty water. She ate in precise bites. In her eyes sparkled the aureate optimism of every person who had ever pitched an idea to him.

"I see," the Senator said. "With the right camera angle, you might hide the building."

"It is my vision board," Sonya said. "You are familiar with vision boards?"

"No."

"A belief-based concept. Create a board with images of your desires, and your faith makes it true. Some would call it confirmation bias, or a simple placebo effect. But in all my scientific studies, do you know what I have found?" She paused, wanting the Senator to take the bait.

He obliged, though only this time. He disliked questions, disliked the subservient position of asking them. "What have you found?"

Sonya turned to him, her eyes completely past the Senator and the boy. He followed her gaze down the deep hallway, where the lengthy shadow of some unseen person escaped into a room.

"Not everything can be explained," Sonya said. "Sometimes belief is everything."

"That is..." The Senator paused, picking his words carefully. "Fundamentally untrue."

"In your experience, perhaps. For me, the auditorium was always here. It is my living vision board. Today's speech will be the beginning. I see the world changing, right here."

He allowed himself a laugh he couldn't contain. "Sure." He made a show of looking at his own watch. "But I won't be in that audience unless you tell me what this—" He stopped himself from assailing her with myriad critiques. "What you plan to say."

"I'm sorry. I won't be giving the speech myself. We have a far more prestigious, more eloquent, speaker than me." She smiled. "But you are right. You must see, as I did. Please follow me to our next stop."

She continued down the broad hallway. The building, eerily absent of sound, felt to the Senator like some lonely country hospital awaiting death. They passed white doors, some with windows and some without, an office laid bare except for a desk and two file cabinets, a residential-style bathroom, a custodian's closet.

Sonya finally stopped at a windowed door marked with the word ONE in red letters. She peered in with her hands clasped before her as though in prayer. Similar doors lined the remainder of the hallway, all with similar marks, six in total. These doors, unlike the others, had no handles.

The Senator's body started. An acute premonition hit him: through this door, Sonya held some imprisoned test subject. He expected keypad entry, another lock from the outside. As if on cue, his leg flared up and he hitched. He steadied himself against the wall. The boy rushed to his side but the Senator shoved him away, thankful that Sonya hadn't witnessed his weakness.

His fears proved unfounded, as Sonya pushed and the door swung open freely.

"How is he today, Mrs. Haskins?" Sonya asked the person in the room, her tone an octave higher.

The Haskins woman didn't respond. Sonya waited, and waited, and ultimately Haskins replied, her voice congenial but exasperated. Sonya offered beverages, pastries, a full lunch plate, all of which Haskins declined. "I'm sorry to interrupt," Sonya said. "Please do let me know if you need anything."

The Senator peered in as Sonya returned. Haskins was younger than he expected, pale, with a stark line where she'd last dyed her hair. She sat at an unadorned table, water bottle and pad of paper and phone and clock in perfect order. Haskins paid no attention to any of it. Instead, her gaze fixated on an impressive floor-to-ceiling, concave, panoramic flatscreen, its near semi-circle bend unlike anything he'd seen, intended to encompass the woman whole. It broadcasted a frantic high-definition video, the camera turbulent, the peripherals disorganized. He saw balloons, a pack of unrestrained dogs, an inflatable castle on which scores of children bounced, a cake with five candles. It seemed to be some immersive home video, a queasy callback to childhood.

"The Observers must be allowed their moments," Sonya said. "I was hoping you could speak with Mrs. Haskins directly, but that must be for another time."

"What can she tell me that you can't?"

Sonya laughed from somewhere deep inside her, hollow and mannish—a laugh at his expense. "Everything."

The remaining rooms down the hall had identical interiors: the desk and untouched materials and curved flatscreen, all of which displayed different videos to similar effect. In *TWO* and *THREE*, a bearded man and an elderly woman watched in unremitting attentiveness, with paralytic stares that Sonya hesitated to break. *FOUR* and *FIVE* were unoccupied, their screens showing some rock concert and a police chase. At the end of the hall, Sonya stared through the final window of *SIX*, at a bald black man in his fifties, with the affection of a mother. She placed a hand on the Senator's wrist but said nothing, as though the sum of these rooms would explain.

"Miss Young."

"Their courage," Sonya said. "It amazes me still. I questioned whether to install windows at all. Since we are in a trial phase, it seemed necessary. Now, I find I cannot keep my eyes from them."

"Miss Young," the Senator repeated. "Have you drugged these people?"

"Of course not."

"Because this looks like some cockeyed mind control thing. Except those videos, whatever they're watching... they're ridiculous."

"No. No, they are the exact opposite."

"What then? You need to shoot straight here. You're trying to elicit some sort of sympathy from me. It's a juvenile ploy. It won't work."

"No," she said again. "I apologize for what you perceive as a ploy. I am, despite my best efforts, an asocial person. What you register as deception is simply apprehension. I have something unique to present the world. I want you to appreciate it as much as I do."

"How can I do that, when you won't tell me just what the hell *it* is."

"Of course," she said. "Seeing is only believing when one knows what to believe. The belief is here."

She raised a hand to the far wall, taking him aback by pressing a nondescript brick that enlivened into a palm-reading entry pad. Aside from the screens, this advanced technology appeared nowhere else, the door and room beyond completely clandestine. The door's edge separated from the wall with a faint puff of air. She ushered the Senator and the boy inside.

The room's interior was larger than any before it, the floor and walls a peerless white, so white that Sonya's clothes seemed to vanish within it, as if her exposed body parts floated in air. The glass desk shimmered crystalline, like freshly fallen snow. Beside the desk stood a life-sized statue of a Great Dane, harlequin black and white and taller than the desk itself, so lifelike the Senator began to think it was a taxidermized former pet. But then Sonya sauntered past and the statue's eyes shifted with her. The dog was real.

"Hello Kali," Sonya said.

The dog blinked in response. Even when Sonya ran her hand down its broad neck, across its arching back, the dog stayed still.

"An impressively patient breed," she said. "Reverent. Almost as though they experience time differently than us. And this one especially." From the desk, she picked up a short black object, like a stunted magician's wand. "This is what you must see."

She flickered the baton and the wall behind her, arched like the others, came alive. It broadcasted all six videos, divided in layers from top to bottom. The boy stared transfixed. Beside himself, the Senator found it striking, beautiful even, like the surveillance system of some strange world not quite their own, a world with a particular sheen. He watched all and none of them at once, the wave-like tumult of the videos hypnotic. Just beside his head hung an analog clock, its secondhand issuing an echoed tick into the room.

With baton in hand, Sonya seamlessly paused the videos, shuffled them until the child's one reached the apex, then rewound and stopped at the exact spot from the Haskins room earlier. Sonya's fingers moved purposefully about the baton, her deftness and mastery with the technology impressive. He had seen things like it, but this was distinct — her own.

She expanded the child's video and sound rushed through invisible surround speakers, filling the room with delighted squeals, with chattering parents and winsome children's tunes. A mother's soothing voice overlaid it all, clear through the cacophony even as a whisper: *We love you, Oscar. We love you so, so, so much.*

"What if," Sonya said, "you could live in your perfect world?"

She killed the audio. Into the sudden soundlessness flooded the monotone ticking of the wall clock.

"His name is Oscar Haskins," she said. "He's celebrating his birthday today. He loves birthdays. Loves seeing his life progress. Loves having his mother by his side, in everything. You see, there she is."

In the low corner of the screen, the Senator caught glimpse of a pale young woman with bleached blond hair. Haskins.

Sonya jumped to the next video. A pair of hands knitted a quilt bursting with color. People carouseled about the top, some pressing their faces to the camera. "This is Edna Gillespie. She loves to knit. Loves her family. The quilt is for her son Michael. He will cherish it."

THREE entertained a handsome young man at a Parisian restaurant. **FOUR** swayed amidst the massive crowd of a country music concert. At **FIVE**, a hectic video reminiscent of a chase, Sonya paused. "This is William Sanders. His desires are less... conventional. This is not a defect. In fact, he was chosen for this very reason, to prove that everyone — *everyone* — can live their own perfect life."

Sonya flipped to **SIX**, watched briefly, but did not comment. Then she returned the screen to white. "It is Youtopia. Y-O-U. Not just a perfect world, but *your* perfect world. Because, as both you and I know, our world is wholly imperfect. It is struggle: pain, death, intolerance, boredom and uncertainty. We contract diseases. We lose loved ones. We rape and kill. We crumble under the weight of societal standards. We falter."

She took a deep breath as if to steady herself. "However, within that world, all of us strive for peace of mind. Our own perfection. That perfection takes unique forms — a birthday party, a concert, and yes, even a police chase. Within our own minds, we can all *perceive* perfection. In that space, we can even achieve it. It's only when forced to interact with the outside world that perfection falls apart."

The Senator looked again down the hall. "Those people out there... they're not the subjects."

"They are Observers. Loved ones of Oscar and Edna and the others. Each Immerser is allowed one Observer."

"Immersers. Observers." He scoffed. "You know this sounds crazy."

"I recognize the difficulty in comprehending the process. This is why I needed to show you first." She leaned forward, lowering herself to his gaze. "It's akin to what a layperson would call *virtual reality*, if that metaphor helps. The Feeds are the mind's eye of each Immerser. It is their entire world."

"And these Immersers... they're imprisoned somewhere in this facility."

Sonya flinched at this. "That is the wrong term. Immersion is voluntary. It is a gift."

He stepped back to the screen and said, "Turn on the Feeds again."

Sonya waved her baton. The six screens illuminated, each in order, each much the same.

"The videos are recurrent," the Senator said. "Cyclical. They're trapped in time."

"Time is certainly relative, is it not? At moments, it passes swiftly, like breeze. But in others, it can stretch, refine, become nearly infinite." She moved over to the dog and passed a hand down its dense, black hair. "Of course, as you can understand, in a perfect world, an Immerser will often return to a favorite place. Take Mr. Nichols, for example."

She rubbed the baton, and a liquid glow enhanced *SIX*: sunshine, shorn green grass, fences and bleachers—a little league game. An announcer thundered out the name of a young boy in a turquoise uniform and stirrups as he strutted from the on-deck circle. Hooting, encouraging fathers filled the stands. In the distance, mothers played with younger siblings on a web of particolored slides.

"His son will drive in the winning run. After the game, Mr. Nichols will buy him a hot dog and popsicle." Sonya turned to the Senator. "Scientists have spent years, *trillions* of dollars, trying to understand the human brain—psychologists, pathologists, criminologists—all attempting to assimilate the inassimilable, to make the round peg of human consciousness fit the square hole of society. It is something they cannot do."

"And this Youtopia can?"

"Yes," Sonya said without hesitation.

An aluminum ting echoed about the room, followed by cheers. The boy rounded the bases with the speed and resolve of youth. As he crossed home, the fathers in the stand turned to the camera with clapping hands and raised thumbs.

The Senator shook his head. "I've seen enough." He stepped toward his boy, but in a momentary lapse forgot his leg—a fierce howl of pain ripped through him as his body stiffened. He leaned into the boy, breathed hard for half a minute or more, until the shriek finally subsided.

Sonya waited for him to recover. Then she stepped forward. "I hope that everything—"

"I said I've seen enough." He shucked the boy. "You believe in your work. Great. So does every moron with a start-up. But what you're doing here? There's no future. All I see are civil and criminal lawsuits. Human rights violations. I don't see success. I see chaos and ruin. There's no way I can stand in that crowd and—"

"I'm sorry," Sonya interrupted. "I haven't made my intentions clear. You will not be standing in the audience. You will be giving the speech."

The Senator bristled. Then he laughed, from somewhere so deep inside him that it overshadowed his leg, the cloying boy's skittishness, the clock's tick. The laugh made him invincible. He chanced a step, then three more, until he reached Sonya's side. He snatched the baton; Sonya did not resist. Its warmth startled him. He tried to locate a power button, some switch that would cut the asinine baseball game or at least freeze it, but the surface was smooth and featureless. So instead, he reared back and slammed it to the ground hoping it would shatter. But it only clanged, bounced, rolled to a corner.

He raised a finger in Sonya's face. "*I'm* giving the speech," he said, his voice caustic.

"I believe you will—"

"Just shut up now. You need to learn when to shut your mouth and just listen." He waved his hand in no certain direction. "When we show up, you're a slip away from death. You take us through this Frankenstein's monster of a building. You spin some melodramatic web that, for all I know, is covered in bullshit. Me give a speech? You truly are insane."

Sonya stepped back, but he pursued. He would not let her retreat. His blood ran hot in his cheeks, in his hands. He had delivered similarly warranted tirades to special interest group leaders, to junior senators and PAC endorsers, to his own wife. Some recipients apologized straight off and retracted into the shadows. Others held their indignancy, their desire to be right even when entirely wrong, until the Senator, as always, overcame. He felt the upper hand embrace him. Like a wild horse, Sonya Young needed to be broken.

"You're a savior to these people? This is a cult, and you, their demented leader."

The boy looked to him, discomfort in his squeamish stare. The Senator appreciated this—his words were working, even if they hadn't yet registered on Sonya's unflappable face.

"I'm leaving. But I cannot let what I've seen here today go unnoticed. I am alerting the authorities immediately."

Sonya finally lowered her eyes. She walked to the corner of the room, picked up her baton and stared at it wistfully. The Senator had, finally, struck her an indelible blow. The show was over. When she looked up again and resumed her erect posture, he felt relieved, reassured that this wouldn't go the way many of these disasters went, that she wouldn't kneel before him or cry on his shoulder. She would accept her failure with some dignity.

She breathed in, her neck elongating, her eyes unnaturally large. "May I show you just one more thing before you go?"

He turned to the boy. "Let's go."

"Please," she said, and in her brief pause, he heard, beside the clock's relentless tick, a soft whimper from the Dane. "You've come so far."

Before he could interject another word, she flourished her thumb across the baton, washing the room in a tsunami of sound. The screen alighted. The Senator turned to it. At first, he couldn't be certain what he was looking at. But as it came into focus, his pulse quickened and his eyes widened. Sonya's stare, the pain in his leg, the boy behind him... all fell away.

Finally, the Senator could see.

JOSEPH REIN

CNN Exclusive: Breaking News

OCTOBER 22, 2014 – 19:05:05 ET
Video obtained for exclusive dissemination by CNN; all rights reserved.
<BEGIN TRANSCRIPT>
[19:05:05 ET]

(An outdoor auditorium. Large crowd. Senator ███████████ *enters stage left to boisterous applause. Dons the podium)*

SENATOR: Thank you. Thank you. I am as happy to see every one of your faces as you are to see mine.

(Laughter)

SENATOR: But seriously. It is exceedingly rare to take part in a significant historical moment — even rarer to recognize, in that very moment, the magnitude of the history occurring. That day is today.

(Applause)

SENATOR: I will admit, when my good friend Sonya Young first presented this idea to me, I was skeptical.

(Murmurs)

SENATOR: Now, now... I know you're invested in Youtopia. But it's important to remember that you did not start there. You arrived at your enlightenment after recognizing the truth of this company's infinite significance. After seeing. We are here today to help those watching at home begin the journey to this very truth. To our vision.

Because Youtopia is the answer. An answer to a timeless human problem. A solution for depression and suffering, for the debilitating humiliations of illness and old age, for the scourge of crime and pain of war. I've had the honor of serving my state, and this, the U. S. of A., the best damn country in the world, my whole life. I've faced many adversaries, all of which seemed unique at the time. But now I see they were not. Now I see that these problems, every single one of them, will be solved by Sonya's creation.

I don't exaggerate. Every. Single. Problem.

For reasons that will become obvious, Sonya had to keep this confidential until this moment. I wish I could describe to you today, right now, exactly what Youtopia is. I wish everyone knew what I know. But I will have to leave that to its creator. Sonya, your territory, not mine!

(Laughter as his hand stretches out to the audience)

SENATOR: I'm sure she will do so with eloquence. And everyone will see, as I did, its importance. No, not importance: its necessity.

This necessity brings us here, because choosing Youtopia is a lifelong commitment. Once a foot goes in, we will not pull it back out. We will be decisive. And yet, I ask, what integral decision in our lives is not so? Marriage, faith, career path, having children, buying a home—these are all fundamental choices that forever change our lives. In that way, Youtopia is like everything that matters. Everything we hold dearest to our hearts.

You may see me placing my hand atop my tie and tapping gently three times. I do so not out of unconscious habit. With every decision I make, I look to three places: first, to my wife. Barbara, I love you, and know you will approve. Second, to my country. As your Senator, I vowed to affect positive change. My fellow Americans, I assure you that Youtopia is the improvement and change our country, and the whole world, needs.

And finally, to my God. *(Quoting King James Bible, John, Chapter 16, Verse 33):* "I have told you these things, so that in me you may have peace. In this world you will have trouble. But take heart! I have overcome the world."

Unfortunately, my words—even when I steal from the Holy Book!—are not enough. Not when action speaks so much louder. I didn't win your votes, and your trust, by talk alone. And so I have decided that, effective today, I will usher in a new era of human achievement. I will pioneer. Hell, I'll put my money where my mouth is!

(*Laughter*)

I will follow the longest tradition, the one that has cemented the greatness of man. I will be Moses parting the Red Sea, Magellan exploring the expanses of the world, Neil Armstrong stepping first foot on the moon.

I have decided that today, immediately following this speech, I will myself enter Youtopia.

(*Raucous applause*)

[19:17:59 ET]

JOSEPH REIN

Youtopia Promotional Flyer: Selected Excerpts

YOUTOPIA

Utopias are a dream. Youtopia is the Ultimate Reality.™
What is your best life?
Where do you want to go?
Who do you want to be?

YOUR DESTINATION AWAITS!

What if you could live *your* perfect life?

The key to Youtopia is our minds, which hold stores of wishes and desires far beyond our reach. We want to dazzle in Oscar-winning dramas but loathe the nonstop hassle of paparazzi. We want a World Series trophy but lack the physical skill. We crave an adventurous life on the shores of Alaska, fishing for prized salmon and halibut, but have trouble making even the minimum payment on our credit cards.

Love rigorous debate with colleagues? Binge-watching your favorite '90s sitcoms? Whatever your dreams—from Nobel Peace Prize to family life on an inherited farm, and anywhere, *anywhere*, in between—Youtopia can and will provide it for you.

PEACE OF MIND

The world of 2024 can be a scary place: the threat of another global virus outbreak; riots and social injustice; endless wars abroad; a political landscape so polarized that we can't agree on the simplest things; a crisis in our world's climate destined to get worse.

The truth is simple: the world is indeed getting worse. It is not what we once knew, what we loved. Most of us wonder if we can ever get back to the good life. Will it ever be safe to do so? Is it even possible?

There is hope, because in Youtopia, the answer is: yes. Yes. So many times, yes.

THE SCIENCE

We could bore you with the science behind Youtopia (and in fact, our Science Team, headed by visionary Sonya Young, would love to do just that. They are geeks to the extreme!). But the truth is, happiness isn't a scientific equation. There exists no special key to unlock a giant treasure chest of contentment. The answer lies in each of our minds, where hopes and dreams clash against concerns and nightmares, where the drive to *be great* fights the never-ending battle against the fear of *not being good enough.*

To simplify: Youtopia is a complete mindscape experience that supplants your reality with one of your mind's own choosing. Your deep, beautiful mind is your guide. It takes you where you want—no, where you *need*—to go.

PRICING

You're likely wondering:

> 1) How preposterously expensive must a perfect world be? and;
> 2) Can only the top 1% afford such luxury?

The answers are, simply:

> 1) Not as much as you would think, and;
> 2) Absolutely not.

Unlike some medical options, Youtopia is meant for everyone, not just those with accumulated or generational wealth. We have an incredibly talented Finance Team to ensure that everyone who wants to be a part of Youtopia can live a perfect life.

FAQs

You have questions. Of course you do! Any lifelong change is scary. Think of all those recent technological advances we live with every day: voice and facial recognition, smartphones, drone delivery, chatbots and other automation technologies. Unlike those other ubiquitous lifestyle changes, however, Youtopia is completely your choice and completely yours.™

You keep mentioning Youtopia like it's some vacation island. It sounds more like a virtual reality headset.

Okay, so this isn't exactly a question. And on the first one! But the virtual reality analogy can be useful. Youtopias are places of permanent suspension that exist within each Immerser's mind. Our technicians do not create the landscapes within Youtopia—the only limitation is the mind itself.

Can I choose my Youtopia?

In a way, that's exactly what you do! Your unconscious mind is the pilot. It takes you where you want to go.

Can I bring my dog into Youtopia?

We all love our pets! And rest assured, they're likely to join you in Youtopia. In fact, any beloved pets that have passed may well return. It all depends on your mind's desires.

Can my wife and I enter Youtopia together?

We love our spouses too! And you both may enter your own, unique Youtopia. However, Youtopia by design cannot be a shared space. Think of it this way: you both sit on the couch one relaxing Saturday evening and can't decide on a movie. You want the cool new superhero action flick, while your wife wants rom-com. The very notion of Youtopia posits that we cannot have a perfect world when simultaneously attempting to please ourselves and others. Perfection lies in singularity.

What kind of quality control does this thing have?

A lot. More than we can tell you, in fact. Our system has built-in regulators and monitors to keep your experience secure 24/7. You may also designate one Observer, a person who has access to a local, safeguarded Youtopia Office to view your Feed and ensure we are always meeting your needs.

There's so much in my life I would have to square up before even considering this. Does Youtopia help with this?

Yes. Many times, yes! We help with 100% of your move from the corporeal world to Youtopia. This phase, your Evolution, begins with alerting everyone in your life of your impending Immersion—a task that seems Herculean but, thanks to social media, is often the easiest part of Evolution. From there, our Legal, Finance, and Medical Teams assist you and your loved ones in preparing for the future. You create a will—or utilize a current one—to secure your assets. But think of this: instead of drearily considering your demise, you will be celebrating the start of your best life!

Can I cancel Youtopia?

The short answer is yes, though the question is more complex than it seems. Youtopia relies on complete Immersion. In other words, for Immersers, Youtopia becomes reality. It is your world, through and through. Because it is perfect, you will experience no moments of discord or discombobulation. Thus, no Youtopia Immerser has ever had reason or desire to "cancel" the program and Reintegrate into society.

I have a debilitating illness. Will my health insurance cover part or all of the costs?

Or you might be asking, why would insurance cover this at all? But consider the average medical costs of a typical American. In 2023 alone, we spent *3.9 trillion dollars* on health care. Most of us will spend more than half a million dollars alone in our lifetimes. Keep that same adult Immersed in Youtopia for 100 years, and you could significantly reduce that cost.

An added bonus: since Immersers' bodies are entirely shielded from pathogens or preventable illnesses, and are under constant medical observation, we have discovered that those with preexisting conditions actually *increase* their life expectancy in Youtopia. So in a way, we are literally saving lives!

But we haven't answered the original question. And it is, as of right now, unfortunately: no, not yet. But sunshine peeks its head on that horizon. Sonya Young and her team are working diligently with Washington to enact a bill that would make Youtopia covered by all major insurance providers. Watch the news, watch Congress, and check with your insurance company.

TESTIMONIALS

Still unsure? We get it. Hearing from the company itself can only take you so far. So here are some unpaid, unprompted testimonials* from Observers of current Youtopia Immersers:

"My 77-year-old father was a jovial man throughout his whole life, but he suffered greatly when my mother died. They grew up together, married in college. After fifty years together, they still held hands during Wheel of Fortune every night. They prayed twice daily. It's hard to believe, but my dad hadn't made a single meal on his own in half a century! After Mom passed, he spoke of little other than dying himself so he could see her again. It is hard, unspeakably hard, to see a man you so revere reduced to such violent depression. He spoke of nothing but a "better place" awaiting him. Well, he's found that better place, and it isn't heaven. It is what Sonya Young created. We would pay ten times what you charge for this. (Though please don't make us!) From our family to yours: our deepest, deepest gratitude."

~ Melinda, 52, of Ann Arbor, Michigan

"Of course I was skeptical at first. I mean, a perfect world? Bro. But then my buddy Lane tried it out, and he asked me to be his Observer. I was like, what? But now I see he was giving me an amazing gift: the gift of erasing my doubt. I mean, when I saw Lane in his *[content deleted to protect privacy]*, I was immediately hooked. Once I get my affairs in order, I'm going straight to Youtopia myself. I'm literally counting down the days."

~ Henrick, 25, of Huntington, Indiana

"I suggested it to Carol the minute I saw the Super Bowl ad. She had chronic back pain, and then an opioid addiction, and then more pain. Pain was her life. But pain is in the mind, right? That was my immediate thought when I heard Sonya. If you can live in your own mind, you can live pain-free. And sure enough, Carol is now finally living the life she deserves, her full life, because of you all at Youtopia."

~ Justine, 44, of Asheville, North Carolina

*Testimonials included are unsolicited emails written to feedback@lifeinyoutopia.you. Since every Youtopia differs, the specifics herein in no way represent the entirety of the Youtopia experience.

<u>CONTACT US TODAY</u>

Scan the QR code, email us at info@lifeinyoutopia.you, or call 1-555-YOU-TOPIA for a free, no-hassle consultation to find out if Youtopia is right for you. (Hint: it is!)

Chapter 1

"Funny you should ask," the man across from Ana said. "I've never given it any real thought." His nametag read Brad, though in his rushed handwriting the B looked decidedly like a P. His body was muscular but squat, his neck as wide as his face. And yet he was handsome, strong. She wondered, as she did so often with attractive, seemingly well-adjusted men who sat across these tables from her at the Copper Rock Pub, what lurked beneath. They likely wondered the same.

"Not once?" Ana said. "Come on. Impossible."

Prad sipped a dirty martini, the mossy liquid swaying in the low light. He admired the glass like a lover. As he set it down, he adjusted his sleeve cuffs to just such a length. "Never. Youtopia is for suckers. People who can't handle the real world." He reached out a manicured hand and placed it atop hers, steadying the fidgeting she hadn't even known she was doing. "I mean, you agree with me, right? You're here."

His hand gave a pleasant squeeze, his workout calluses abrading her in the right places, his face beaming with youthful honesty, and so she decided to take him home. To let him stay the night. She imagined his body would look good awash in the moonlight spilling through her window. She imagined his breath, hot and sharp with olive.

Then the bell sounded. All the men along the line stood and began their awkward leftward shuffle. Prad retrieved his hand. "It's been nice. Ana, is it? Best of luck. These things are so hit or miss." He offered a curt smile, and then dove headfirst into the waters of the buxom brunette next to her.

The next man up—older, teeth with uneven gaps, patches of gray like feline spots in his full beard—introduced himself and then immediately launched into an earnest, exhausting sales pitch on why they should skip the formalities and begin the necessary work of determining their sexual compatibility. If she didn't mind, he would go first. He began with his tastes, in order of preference—a sliding scale of what he needed and what he enjoyed but could do without. If it helped, she could think of it numerically, like that pain meter hospitals use. Ana envisioned him delivering his speech in some business conference room, presentation slides on a projector, handouts for reference. With minimal participation from her, he continued on, and so Ana focused on things in her peripheral vision, attuned her body to her other senses. She'd acquired this skill early in life, when she recognized that authority figures — most always male — were going to demand that she listen, especially when they had nothing important to say. High school teachers spouted arcane psychology, and film professors explicated the male gaze while staring at her chest. Finally, her inept FBI superiors droned on about superfluous minutiae when, all the while, the crime scene whispered its own secrets, singing to her clear as a canary.

To Ana's right, the next and final man in the loop was even older and less enthusiastic about himself. He wore a beret and a sad mustache. To her left, Prad let fly the deep, guttural laugh of a man who had made his mark. The Copper Rock seemed darker than usual, its non-speed-dating crowd minimal, its music uncharacteristically subdued. She'd never eaten here, but at times enjoyed the intermixing, pungent smells of charred meats and brown mustard, fry grease and beer. Now, all she could smell was the redolent florals of the candle on their table, and the warm spice perfume she'd applied just below her neck. Her bearded man mused on his ambivalent feelings toward anal sex, his uneven brow suggesting that he'd surprised himself here, that he was feeling out this part of the presentation. He stopped mid-sentence, and in the pause, Ana recognized the stilted conversations, the slim tables, the candlelight, as the final vestiges of a dying ritual.

"Just do it online," her best friend Lonnie had said to her again and again. "Do people even go to bars anymore? There are literally a hundred apps. Ugly? Swipe away. That simple." Lonnie had found a handful of boyfriends this way. "You can only fight the future for so long, Ana."

The man looked at his watch. He knew his time was almost up. He hadn't asked a single question of her, of her own preferences, what she couldn't do without in bed. He had placed his sexuality before her like a murder victim, ready for her investigation. The bell rang, and he paused for a moment, awaiting an answer Ana didn't deliver.

Beside them, Prad stood with the woman he had effectively wooed, leaving the bearded man with no more options. He harrumphed in defeat and stomped out of the Copper Rock.

Ana watched him go, but then the next man called her to attention, and she was grateful, because if the bearded man had delayed, if he had pouted hangdog across from a vacant final seat, if his loneliness had dominated her peripheral vision for even a minute more, she might have offered to take him home.

***

She awoke to five messages. Two were texts from Lonnie — *Find Mr. Right?* and *This ignoring me dog won't hunt!* — but three voicemails straight from D.C. and urgent. Bruce's voice quavered more than usual. He ended each message with a light admonition for not answering his twilight calls. When Ana returned them, Bruce confirmed her suspicion that she would be gone from her apartment, from Chicago, for a good while.

"It's hard to explain," he said, his tone curiously uncertain. Bruce, like all his counterpart males at the Bureau, rarely admitted that he didn't have the answer. He took this to his social life: he accepted no advice when shooting pool or darts, two games at which he was notoriously average; he answered every restaurant recommendation with two of his own. His wife Leann found few points on which her opinion was salient or needed.

"Give me a little more, Bruce."

"It's a murder. But not in the conventional sense."

"Our murders are never conventional."

"I know. Don't you think I know that, Ana?" He paused for emphasis. "This one's exceptional."

Ana's mind flashed through the eleven-plus years of her time as Special Agent, recounting the most conventional murders — single bullets through torsos with small, whispered wounds — and the least conventional — bodies splayed in ungracious piles, blood both dried and not, smells of iron and rot. Missing limbs, grotesque ceremonial remnants. She recalled, as she often did without any prompting, the Villalobos murders, the horrific case that saw eight children dead and brought her a national prominence she may have wished for, but not that way.

From under her bed, she pulled her prepacked travel suitcase containing three pairs of work shirts and slacks, workout clothes, and toiletries.

"Estimated time of death?" she asked.

"Just last night," Bruce said. "But—" His throat caught in a cough. She heard him drinking water across the line. "That doesn't exactly matter. Not like it usually does."

She lifted the suitcase, lean and light enough to carry, from her bed. From deep in her closet she retrieved the heavier case, the one with her pressed business suits and Kevlar gear, her gun and badge. "What does that mean? Don't be cryptic with me, Bruce."

"It's Youtopia."

"Shit." She shifted the phone from one ear to the other. "An employee?"

"No. It's more complicated. Just... call me from the road. I'll explain then."

Twenty minutes later, she pulled from her underground parking lot and headed north. Mid-morning neared and, for April, it was still cold. The temperature had dropped overnight and now, under a full overcast sky, the earth struggled to regain her body heat, dispelling a drizzle that stuck to the car like snow. Still, the streets of Park West ran lively, full of workers with umbrellas, ambitious joggers and dog walkers, and young service industry workers replete with reusable mugs and earbuds and dreams. She loved that about Chicago while growing up, and still loved it now — the city's inability to be quiet, its dogged execution of life even against nature's recriminations, its resistance and waywardness. At any hour, she could step from her apartment doors and see somebody, anybody. At any moment, she was not alone.

She hit the Kennedy Expressway and lurched through thick but advancing traffic until she reached I-94 toward Milwaukee. Tolls and rail stops and interloping careeners gave way to sparser traffic and the open fields of northern Illinois. She headed toward Racine, a city just across the border in Wisconsin, strategically chosen between two of the Midwest's largest metropolitan areas for Youtopia Towers.

She called Bruce again. He tried to explain the specifics of the case, which he clearly struggled himself to understand. "You won't be going into a crime scene, least not as you're used to. It's more of a cybercrime... but not really."

"A cyber murder?" Ana waited, but Bruce didn't follow up. She could hear the repeated banging of a small basketball against his floor, his way of dealing with stress. "Bruce, if someone was able to—"

"I know. But cyber can't lead this. They're geniuses on Russian espionage, but they wouldn't have a clue how to handle a murder."

"I'm no computer expert."

"I want you on this, Ana."

A silence followed, in which Ana allowed herself to revel. At the outset of her career, she'd had difficulty convincing superiors that she could contribute to any challenging case. She was both female and a

Special Agent, with emphasis always on the former. Many thought her best as an undercover prostitute, and said as much. That Bruce chose her now over his many other male lapdogs felt like a pleasant, if spiteful, slap in all their faces.

"Your video expertise will go a long way here," Bruce said. "And you know more about this Youtopia thing than any other agent."

To this, Ana didn't reply. She sped past one eighteen-wheeled delivery truck and then another, their tires spitting slush onto her windshield.

"You name your team," Bruce continued. "Especially from cyber."

"Sergio. I'll need Sergio. He just transferred to Jacksonville."

"Done. You know what, just make me a list. If they're available, they're yours." Bruce let out a long exhale that whistled like wind through the phone. "Look, I know it might be... things might come up. You need to keep your head."

"You just told me you wanted me," Ana said. "Now you're trying to protect me from myself?"

"All right," Bruce said. "Just keep your phone on. I'm overseeing a dozen other cases, and you know what? I still answer. Every time."

"Got it. No more missed calls."

He hung up abruptly, as he always did.

Her console replaced his voice with the cutting static of a vanishing radio signal. She scanned, landed on an oldies station playing songs even her grandfather disliked. She let it play.

***

A mile from the address proper and she saw it: Youtopia Towers. Sky-high, imposing, a picture of modern impossible architecture, the three-pronged building stood like a warrior in a wide-open field. It should've been in downtown Chicago, some metropolitan marvel, but instead they chose this site, tucked away and yet, in its resemblance to nothing else around it, completely standout.

The first gate stopped them half a mile away. She needed to show her credentials at three separate checkpoints. At the final one, a mustachioed guard pointed her to a vacant parking spot along a ten-foot-high wrought-iron fence that stretched the entire premises. "Shuttle will get you in a few," the guard said. He looked straight out of college, alabaster shirt and argyle tie. Then, as an apology, "We're putting in a parking structure in the fall."

To her left, two-dimensional wolf silhouettes on sticks encircled a manmade pond. Employees walked the surrounding paved track, each with their head in a phone. They laughed and spoke but not to one another. To the right Ana saw only cars, rows upon rows, whites and reds and blacks and the occasional blue or orange, but all eerily similar in their compact body design. They seemed like a massive fleet of electric rental vehicles, all newer and shinier than Ana's own. Beyond the cars, the towering structures loomed even larger. Three thirty-story high symmetrical buildings, all slightly slanted like Ys, held up a long platform that looked like a cruise ship ready to set sail. Though they were difficult to see, Ana noticed people walking atop it, weaving in and out of the trees that inexplicably grew so far up. Like a civilization itself, a city in the clouds.

As she waited for the shuttle, Ana read the reports Bruce sent to her phone. A 911 distress call had come from the Towers at 11:22 the night before, from a frantic technician who mumbled about unstable levels and peaks of light. A Racine PD report showed more confusion than Bruce's, from an officer, captain, and then chief of police, each flummoxed by the bigger picture. The only thing she could glean for certain: a Charles Fowler died suddenly by the hand of an unidentified, digital assailant.

The shuttle arrived and Ana boarded. The driver, another young man, this one a surfer-blonde, escorted her with caffeinated gusto through the monotonous car lot. He chattered like a dental hygienist, upbeat and without need for response. His face alighted in pride as they approached the first of the three Towers. As they dismounted the shuttle and came to the heavy glass doors, he took on the mannerisms of a magician ready to reveal a particularly inspired trick. A small, barely detectible sensor glowed blue.

"Hello again Mister Falcon," an automated voice said. "I take it you've retrieved Miss Downer?"

"Facial rec," he said with undeniable pride. "And I know what you're thinking—what if it's wrong? It never is, but even if it was, it cross-verifies with three other points, one of them being the cell in my pocket."

"What are the other two?"

He just shot a childish grin. "Nobody can pretend they're me. These babies are the most secure buildings in the world."

"And yet someone was murdered inside," Ana replied.

The driver looked at her nonplussed. "But he wasn't even..." he began, but then shook his head, tossed errant bangs from his eyes. He was used to awed guests, to field trips of wide-eyed grade schoolers ready to swoon at Youtopia's every technological marvel. For a moment he seemed to consider whether to speak further, to drum up a potential argument with her. But then he turned and continued through the building, though now as a less eager guide.

He weaved her through a front desk area, down a long hallway to the elevators. Twelve of them, all glass domes, shot up and down the thirty floors with nauseating speed. They waited for the one farthest from the entryway. When it arrived, a sensor similar to the one on the door glowed red.

"Mr. Peterson is high security," he said. "So is Central Control." He took out his phone and scrolled, taking obvious pride in his personal level of access. "Here we go. Override code four-two-alpha-nine-eight-kilo-seven-Romeo-four."

The elevator doors parted. Her guide waved his hand inward in a gesture meant to say, *Impressed yet?* Ana entered, followed by the man she couldn't wait to shed.

The fast ride felt surprisingly natural, like riding on a light rail. When the doors parted to the penultimate level, just below the urbanscape of the rooftop Terrace, Ana's wish was finally granted. Her guide stopped at the first open area and wished her well. She watched him shuffle back to the elevator, hoping the rest of the employees were not as ingratiating.

The lobby area on this floor was a sunken living room of sorts, with couches surrounding a central hexagonal desk. Ana approached the woman behind, young of course, brunette hair done up, business suit with a shirt opened one button too low. She both typed on a laptop and spoke into a Bluetooth headset no bigger than a dime. Her voice was deeper than it seemed it should be. "Ms. Downer?" she said. Ana already knew she would like her more than the guide. "Dr. Peterson would like you to know he will be out shortly. And that he's sorry for making you wait. It's been...well, I guess we're all still shaken."

"I bet," Ana replied. The woman smiled with half her mouth. "Never expected this to happen, I imagine."

"Oh no, no no." She pouted in the way only young people could. "We save lives here. We don't..." She stopped herself just short of saying, *destroy them.*

"That's what I'm here to find out," Ana said. "To get to the bottom of what happened."

The woman's face lightened, even if Ana hadn't intended the comment as solace.

Ana sidled to one of the sectional couches and perched on its edge, the leather giving a soft squeal beneath her. The woman left for a moment and returned with a coffee Ana hadn't requested — it was good, dark but not bitter. Ana took out her phone expecting to find firewalls, access blockages, various restrictions to the internet, but got only a standard sign-in page with minor legalese. The Youtopia logo filled the screen, a simple, slanted U against a cloudscape background. She accessed the web, opened a general search where, amidst her usual stops — the New York Times, Pinterest, and FamilyMatch — she finally saw Youtopia's footprint in links to sponsored pages, all with favorable headlines:

Youtopia Immersers near the half-million mark.

Your dreams just became attainable.

Sonya Young named Time Magazine's Woman of the Year.

A PEW survey cited growing support for insurance coverage of Youtopia. This last topic led down a rabbit hole of headlines, all of which grappled with the idea of Youtopia becoming not just a refuge for the pained and wealthy, but a health necessity. At first, the op-eds were predominantly negative. It was absurd, they said — costly, immoral. Why, they asked, when some Americans couldn't even afford their own healthcare?

But in just a few short weeks, the tide shifted, as certain medical professionals and university professors and human rights groups emerged with an alternate narrative. Why not? they asked. How was it so different from therapy, or rehab, or certain medications? Wouldn't more people in Youtopia mean less people to spread the next coronavirus? X threads sprouted with hashtags like #freeyoutopia and #healthforall. Ana followed the trail like a sociological experiment, where both the *Washington Post* editorialists and the @bitchinmomof4s of the world began so vehemently on one island, and then gradually, through a tidal wave of public scrutiny and opinion, washed ashore on the island opposite. The most recent news spoke of a pair of bipartisan representatives who presented a bill to the House Speaker. It was named, simply, the Healthcare Bill. A vote was expected within the week.

On a whim, Ana typed *anti-Youtopia* into her search engine and hit enter. She knew of the religious zealots, the doomsday theorists and troll factories, all eager to claim Youtopia as the first phase of the rapture. She had heard of the hacker VikkarAll and his movement, X-ACT, who spouted conspiracies like Youtopia being a cover for alien abductions, or that all of Youtopia's clients were either manipulated, coerced, or even kidnapped into Immersion. Ana imagined X-ACT and the like would be blocked on Youtopia servers, but to her surprise, she got millions of hits, the first of which prophesized a date, some two months from now, for Youtopia's cataclysm—an X-ACT countdown to the end.

"I'm so sorry you have to wait," the woman said. It had been, at most, four minutes.

Ana smiled. "I have immaculate patience." She looked over the woman—late twenties, beautiful—and wondered if, by living in the daily orbit of Youtopia's gravitational pull, young women like her considered Immersion. Behind that desk, the woman interacted with the lure of a perfect life constantly. She lived it. She likely didn't have access to see the Feeds, as Ana would. But then, what was stopping her? Indeed, what was stopping Ana? Everyone? She wanted to know, just for this one employee, just in this moment. She wanted to understand why. The desire was so intense that she rose and approached the desk.

The woman's face shined with enthusiastic pep, but then a man— this Dr. Peterson—entered and offered a rushed hand.

"Unfortunate we have to meet under these circumstances," he said by way of greeting. He wore a perfectly tailored suit. Across his head, his hair was parted so scrupulously that the thin white line of his scalp gleamed. He wore a watch the size of a child's fist, and designer thick-rimmed glasses.

"Under no other circumstances would we ever meet," Ana said.

Peterson offered a pained smile. "Right off, I have to tell you that we've never needed outside intervention before. Aside from inspections, of course. We're painstakingly meticulous. Local law enforcement, government oversight, are, shall we say, lacking. Even the FBI—pardon my saying so—but it's not exactly the FBI of Hoover's time."

"Hoover's FBI wasn't Hoover's FBI."

"I don't mean to insult you. It's just that our processes are, as I'm sure you understand, incredibly complex."

"I'm a fast learner."

Peterson nodded and placed a weighty hand on Ana's shoulder. She stepped to shake it away, but then in his face she saw, beyond the unwanted gesture, an earnestness, a paternalistic feeling. A decent, if misguided, intent.

"We want this to be resolved quickly," he said.

"We have something in common then."

Peterson led Ana down an ornate and luminous hallway. Framed contemporary paintings from artists both obscure and infamous, from a young upstart named Garek to a Basquiat, hung under bulbous track lights. Peterson stopped at a closed door in the middle of the hallway. It was highly protected: in addition to facial and voice rec, Peterson also had to scan a thumbprint and enter a twenty-digit code into a keypad.

"Is this Sonya Young's office?" Ana asked.

"Her office is in the second Tower," Peterson said. "But she hasn't been there much. She's needed in many places. Drifts so much she's hard to catch."

"But I will," Ana said. "Meet with her. She should be here now."

"She does not need to be here," Peterson said, "for me to show you what you need to see."

"The murder scene. Mr. Fowler's body."

"No. His body is—well, was—in its Nest. Which, by coincidence, is also nearby. Just a few hours north."

"Its Nest."

"Holding cells. Where corporeal bodies of the Immersers lie in stasis." A heavy thump issued from the door, a final lock unlatching, and then it opened of its own accord. "You will be given access to the Nests, I'm sure. But we try to keep their location as secret as possible, for obvious reasons. And besides, this person—this murderer—never accessed the Nest." He pointed down to Ana's hand. "You'll have to leave your coffee."

The two entered the square room, twice the size of any other and in line with Ana's imagination of the company: three crisp white walls, and a fourth with a floor-to-ceiling concave screen. The air in the room possessed the lofty, pumped-in quality of airplane cabins. The room dwarfed them, making her feel miniscule. A wave of lightheadedness hit her, as though she'd just stood up too quickly.

"This is Central Control," Peterson said. "There are twenty security cameras focused on this small space alone. So to answer the first question you will have: no, nobody unauthorized has ever been in this room before."

"Okay," Ana said. "But don't presume to know what I'm going to ask."

Peterson reached into his inner suitcoat pocket and removed a black baton-like object. When he waved it, the screen enlivened in a burst of lucid silver. He flicked his wrist, tapped the baton with his fingers as though picking a guitar, as file folder images flittered past in a frenzy. He opened and dismissed files within files within files, all named with happenstance combinations of letters and numbers. He entered a dozen passwords.

Ana watched him work, trying to make out the controls, the functions of each movement—his baton, his steady hand, his focus. It all moved with the cadence of a symphony, with Peterson a deft if rigid conductor. Despite herself, Ana was impressed.

He finally stopped as a red triangular warning flashed.

"We're about to enter the Feeds," Peterson said. "The system wants to make sure you're authorized personnel." He offered the baton to Ana. "Point it at the screen."

"Slow down," Ana said. "I wasn't expecting a normal crime scene, but I need a little more—an autopsy, for one, and a tox report on—"

"We know how Mr. Fowler died," Peterson interrupted. "He suffered an overdose of duratonia bifetanol. What we call KaliSerum."

"He was drugged. But you just said—"

"If you'll just allow me." Peterson gave the baton a placating shake.

Ana took a deep breath. "I'll take it if you stop interrupting me."

Peterson conceded.

In Ana's hand, the baton felt surprisingly heavy, warm. She sensed an alluring current running through it, a small pulse of life.

"You get used to it," Peterson said, recognizing the quizzical look on her face. "Oddly enough, you miss it when you pick up a TV remote. A book. Any old object."

The red triangle disappeared, replaced by a smattering of information on Ana: employment history, car loan applications, copies of her first and subsequent driver's licenses. Her wedding certificate. They flashed and then assembled into a file. It moved on to her social media posts, restaurants she frequented, lists of favorite movies, her most played songs on Spotify—nothing she would consider useful. Then her public photos appeared, starting with the most recent, all from some years ago. She tried to look away, but before she could, one sprang onto the corner of the screen: she and her husband Paul together, on vacation in Barbados. He wore a dress shirt: his shoulders had burned within the first few hours, forcing him into sleeves for the rest of the trip. Ana had donned a bikini top with a locally-bought shawl across her arms. Paul smiled in the photo; she didn't. It was their final vacation, one last attempt to make it work. It hadn't.

Then she watched too long, too many years backtracking within seconds, and she saw what she shouldn't have: Charlotte on her fourth birthday, Charlotte in pigtails, Charlotte holding onto Ana's hand as they waited in line for an ice-cream truck, her little blue eyes lucent with anticipation.

"Just a bit more," Peterson said.

Ana closed her eyes. After a minute, she heard a soft ping, and like that, the book of her past closed into an invisible folder. The baton cooled in her hand.

Peterson took it. "That was a one-time thing."

He accessed more files, more flying folders. "This is it," he said, more to himself, as he opened an indistinctive file and the screen blossomed in an enveloping expanse of sight and sound. The room darkened in quivering candlelight. A gruff, baritone voice panted, *"Hmmmm, hmmmm,"* until it was abruptly punctuated by a woman's scream, shrill and painful.

Ana shivered. The video showed only a sparse, dim room, rocking as though afloat. But then it panned down to show a bed. On it, a young woman was bound by meaty hands that shoved a cloth into her mouth.

"Shit," Peterson said. He cut the Feed. "Sorry sorry sorry... I must've transposed a number." He gripped the baton in two hands, his gestures measured now that he'd made a mistake.

"Turn it back on," Ana said.

"We have a good deal of unsavory content in Youtopia. It can be — jarring."

"I've seen worse. Turn it back on."

Ana stepped forward, into the hemisphere of the screen, to punctuate her point. She had heard of Youtopia as an alternative to prison, as a more humane means of incarceration, but the company kept tight control of its records in that regard. She was curious to see the depths of the human mind into which Youtopia Immersers plummeted. But more, she knew how men underestimated her ability to handle the grotesque aspects of her job. It had been a daily occurrence in her early assignments, but even now, they casually stepped in front of Ana at crime scenes. They told her, with words or their bodies, that she might not want to look. That it was nothing for a woman to see. She wanted to tell — often, to scream at — each of these well-intentioned men that she grew up on true crime television, that she directed intense noir films in college. That, for her first job in the Bureau, she'd filmed the vilest crime scenes in the Midwest for evidence. She'd analyzed home videos of serial killers dancing about their victims for clues of their whereabouts, studied their weapons cutting through flesh for brand or signs of wear, analyzed their satanic laughter for echo and voice recognition. She had seen and stomached and learned to deal — in one way or another — with more than the imaginary worlds of Youtopia could throw at her.

Peterson needed to drop the fatherly act. He needed to know she was unafraid.

Raising the baton, Peterson reluctantly plunged them back into the flickering flames of an Immerser raping a young woman, perhaps a minor.

Ana matched her sightline with the Immerser's own, forced herself to adopt his vantage. Peterson was right—it was jarring, difficult. She felt the strange weight of it, of being taken to a place from which you could not return, like diving headfirst into an old well. She knew none of it was real, and yet, standing there, she couldn't deny its tactile quality, its authenticity. The details she spotted along his peripherals—the fire-red digital numbers of a clock, the weathered grain of the barn-like walls— were arresting in their complexity. The woman's muffled cries were overcast only by the distinct male huff that issued from some unseen place behind Ana. As a cinephile, Ana had always frequented the newest theater technologies, 3D and 4D and Omnitheaters. Just a month back, she'd dragged Lonnie to an IMAX film in full first-person POV, an insufferable shoot-em-up affair that left a ring in her ears for two days. 'You are the hero' was the tagline, but aside from the slightly clever use of the camera, everything else—the acting, the lighting, the green-screen lack of depth—felt entirely perfunctory, staged. Even if she wanted, she simply couldn't envision herself as the impervious hero who saved his damsel in distress and subsequently all of New York.

Now, as she watched the victim beneath this rapist, the tufts of hair on his outstretched hand and the vampire-red of the clock, Ana finally felt the intended effect. This, she thought, might be the future of film— wholly, harrowingly immersive.

Then, into the voices came a knock. The view shifted to a small door. The video became spastic as the rapist further gagged the girl with his hand.

Beyond the door, an older woman's voice called out with concern.

Then the rapist's voice boomed: "Everything's fine!"

The lingering echo in Ana's ears gave the effect of hearing her own voice, even more disconcerting than the video. Half a minute passed as the rapist waited for the woman outside to leave.

"This is paradise," Ana said. "Rape a teenager and almost get caught by your wife."

"For him," Peterson said. He continued on, musing about Youtopia and its complexities. How it was not stasis as some would believe, not Immersers doing the same thing over and over in some manic or lethargic stupor. He spoke of how Immersers, like all people, got tired of beaches eventually. Sure, there was a lot of sex, much of the aggressive variety, but the mind's experience of perfection included so much more. He cited Freud and Jung, and all the while the rapist panted in concert, his breath unnervingly reminiscent of before.

"The truth is," Peterson continued, "our desires, and what satisfies them, are too multifaceted for anyone to pinpoint."

She stopped herself from reminding Peterson again of her position, and that she needed no lecture on the desire for deviancy, for doing destructive deeds.

"Take, for example, our many artists," Peterson said. "Painters and writers and musicians who toil and struggle for years while perfecting a project. For every sex-crazed maniac, we have someone whose mind will only accept success after adamant labor. Desire is a complex thing—if something comes too easily, our brain will either reject it as unreal, or will feel it isn't worthwhile."

"That's a strange way of equivocating sexual assault and Michelangelo."

Peterson didn't reply to this. On screen, the man had returned his attention to the young girl.

"You can guess how this will end," Peterson said. "Do you mind if we—"

"Yes," Ana said. "Show me the murder."

He again conducted at the screen, erasing the rapist's world in a single swooping gesticulation. Everything went black for a moment. Peterson squinted to double-check his numbers, and with a turn of his wrist a large crowd filled the screen, thousands of people seated on blankets and lawn chairs down a grass hill. A waft of bluish smoke hovered above. The crowd swayed and thrummed in a cadenced, cult-like unison. After a short while, a singer in a Hawaiian shirt emerged from backstage, and the room filled with rowdy applause. The singer strummed a few notes on his acoustic guitar, sending the crowd into jubilant throes. Just below the scene, where the Immerser's mouth would be, a joint bobbed like a limb itself. Before them, women climbed on shoulders and coquettishly removed their shirts.

"Oh, I can't forget," Peterson said. In the bottom corner of the screen appeared a small blue number: 0.08. "Quality control. It measures how acceptable one's reality is to the Immerser at any given moment. As you can see, Mr. Fowler is right near baseline. Content as a clam."

"What happens when the meter rises?"

"You're about to see."

Amidst the sea of heads, a man turned to them, the effect jolting, immediate. The tall figure had a swath of wispy brown hair sticking out from a white hooded sweatshirt. He walked with intent against the mass.

Fowler's gaze narrowed on the figure. His meter raced like a stopwatch above 2.

"Mr. Fowler is elevated here," Peterson said. "And that's natural. Necessary even. For the mind to accept its world, it can't completely erase fear."

"But you have ways to mitigate it."

"Of course." Peterson's eyes fixed on the figure. "The scale goes up to ten, but that number is misleading. As with a speedometer in a sedan, you should never get close to top speed. Before Mr. Fowler, the highest ever was in the four-aughts."

The figure slipped around an elderly couple twenty feet away. Fowler's meter stuttered at 3.5.

"It shouldn't go any higher here," Peterson said, "because the system has kicked in. Anything above three and we introduce a small dosage of KaliSerum."

"Explain to me this KaliSerum."

"It's a concoction made specifically for meditative sedation. It stimulates the brain and releases endorphins. The closest correlative is opioids, but that has all sorts of stigmas."

"So your Immersers live in a drugged state."

Peterson scoffed at her description as an accusation, and retaliated with any number of drugs the average human consumed daily: pain relievers, hypo-allergenics, and even the caffeine in Ana's coffee outside the room. A single glass of wine. All of them, according to Peterson, did more harm than did the common dosage of KaliSerum needed to restore balance.

"In every single situation before this," he said, "the Immerser's reality has positively altered, and the meter has dropped instantly. With a shot of Kali, the offending stimuli leaves, or at least loses its edge. Turns friendly. Here, the level remains around three and a half, and the hooded man continues forward. A sure sign that this guy, whoever he is, is not a natural part of Mr. Fowler's Youtopia."

"So this is our murderer."

The intruder confronted Fowler, his face blocking the stage. He had a manicured beard, green-blue eyes, and a burn scar on one cheek—

menacing, but an unhelpful likeness. Peterson assured Ana it was a caricature, a composite, a digital rendition only. Youtopia had run their own facial recognition without a match above twenty-five percent. He suspected the FBI would turn up much the same, an opinion with which Ana wished she didn't agree.

Without hesitation the intruder shoved Fowler with both hands. The whole screen shook as his meter jumped to 6. Around them, the concert continued in rollicking merriness.

Ana expected Fowler's flight response to kick in, for him to run, to cover himself in the cloak of the crowd. But nobody around registered this intrusion. Fowler even cried out, his voice swallowed by the acoustic guitar and cheers.

"This is where it gets interesting," Peterson said.

From far off, a woman dressed in all black bounded. She shoved away other patrons with considerable force, her gait workmanlike, her strength superhuman. When Fowler saw her, his meter plummeted.

"You have a built-in defense."

"We call her Nikita. She's our safety net. A reset button, so to speak. In tests she removed offending stimuli within seconds. Sometimes the Immersers didn't even notice her. But that was all beta phase. This is her first appearance in an actual Youtopia."

The bearded intruder landed a blow to Fowler's midsection, ticking his meter up again.

Nikita neared striking distance, her legs churning ferocious and soundless, like a pouncing leopard.

Ana held her breath. The packed stadium, the sheer antagonism of the intruder, the otherworldly entry of Nikita, all played out like an action film itself, like a video game she felt determined to win. She reminded herself that she was here to investigate, that, though what she saw wasn't real, Fowler was. Somewhere, his body lay on an examination table, awaiting autopsy.

Nikita shucked the last of the concertgoers and stretched out arms that seemed impossibly long. But then, even faster, the intruder released Fowler and was on Nikita, flipping her broadside. He constrained her hands to her back. His body elevated in sync with Fowler's meter. He removed a knife and stabbed Nikita behind the neck so quickly, so effortlessly, that Ana needed Peterson to replay it.

She watched the hand, the swift and practiced kill it executed. "How did he know she was coming?"

"We don't know."

The intruder rose over Nikita's bleeding body. He slowly turned to Fowler. The music grew distant now, drowned out by the thunderous drums of Fowler's own heart in his ears. Ana felt the pulse press on her like heavy hands as the spastic twitch of his meter continued, the fear elevating and the drugs suppressing in a relentless war.

"As you can see," Peterson said, "he's passing the point of no return."

"You didn't have a cutoff? A level where the system said enough is enough?"

"That was Nikita."

The intruder raised his chest ape-like. He poked at Fowler with a determined finger. There was little else he needed to do. Fowler's world was shocked into vibrant, euphoric color, the sky above a permanent purple, the grass neon green. Everything sharpened, shimmered, and became the harshest version of itself. Then lines began to melt, to drip, as his world slipped farther and farther away. The concert no longer played, its twangy guitar plucks lost to a soft, throaty wail. Peterson said something about new precautions, about an added failsafe they installed just that morning, about more vigilant monitoring, but Ana stood transfixed, watching the brilliant rainbow slowly transform into a dazzling, all-consuming emptiness. A fade to white. A passage into light. Fowler's end. And she realized, as the sound dropped away, that she had shared Fowler's experience intimately. That she had just experienced a sort of death.

***

Ana dined at a corner joint known for buttered hamburgers. She ate one even though it was saturated, slippery and willfully sinful, even though she had, in the years since Charlotte's death, become a reliable vegetarian.

She'd left the Youtopia grounds soon after taking in Fowler's Feed — for all Peterson's talking, he had nothing else to give her — and still felt shaken. When she called Bruce, her descriptions of the incident lacked order. She tried to recreate it in her mind, but the vision of pure whiteness snow-stormed her memory. Bruce told her to write it up and then to get some rest, that she had a long day ahead of her tomorrow. Before he hung up, he asked her the likelihood of another murder.

"The same way? Probably slim. They say they've fixed the glitch. But..." She sucked the stale air of her car through her nose. "Today I saw *how* he died. We haven't even scratched the surface of *why*."

"Write your report. I've got Sergio on the morning flight."

She held her phone in her hand for a minute after Bruce hung up, staring into its glossy blackness, the silhouette of her face like a ghost somewhere inside. She needed to steel herself against her feelings, against this subtle fear. She closed her eyes and, as the waitress brought her check, tunneled into herself—the first step in her regaining control, in continuing forward. Her calm, her ability to detach, was why she'd gravitated toward film studies in college: through the lens, the world was all fiction, all subjects and sets and shade. Effect and affectation. Her first Bureau job as an A/V Comms Specialist had been the same. Crime scenes were a vision, and her job had been to either capture or recreate it. To find the lens. Even when she married Paul, and then Charlotte was born, she'd recognized the need for detachment, for seeing through filters, for not seeing in the faces of the countless victims her own husband, her own child.

The nearest hotel was a small two-story chain, the décor brown and decidedly rustic, with a cow pasture painting above the king bed and a wagon wheel nightstand lamp. Bruce would tell her to stay somewhere nicer, somewhere with concierge and valet underground parking. But when Ana lay on the bed atop the comforter, the weight of the day affixed her down until, still in her suit, she drifted off.

Her night was fitful, her sleep shallow. She was haunted not by Fowler's death, but by Nikita—the blackness of the woman's attire, the vagueness of her features, the intensity of her movements. Ana abandoned sleep and unlocked her tablet, intending to delve into Youtopia's social media mentions in the hours leading up to Fowler's death—hashtags, trends, high volumes—but Youtopia talk had taken over the internet since the news of his death broke. On X alone, it dominated the top five trending topics. To even start seemed exhausting.

Instead, she hovered over and then clicked the FamilyMatch bookmark in her browser, knowing where this was going, knowing she should stop herself, but she didn't. She clicked straight to her matches but, of course, in the two days since she'd last checked, the number meeting her criteria hadn't risen—more likely to go down, the chosen ones vacated, the grapes ceremoniously plucked from the vine.

She found, tucked beneath her suits and workout clothes, her reserve bottle of zinfandel, useful for such sleepless occasions. She poured a heavy drink into the hotel's plastic water cup, ready to survey the thirty-two candidates again. Candidates like the young lothario with an unfortunate family history of epilepsy, or the middle-aged, average man whose inability to sell his average qualities in a world of spectacle had left his average specimen on the shelf for three years. His early enrollment in the program wore poorly on his profile, like an expiration date for overripe produce.

Then Ana found a new face, a new profile. The number thirty-two was deceptive: there had been a swap, one out, one in. Enter Evan, whose specimen was a 79% fit with the profile FamilyMatch created for Ana two years ago, when she'd first met with their consultants. She filled out numerous questionnaires, but they also mined her medical records, online data and purchasing habits, providing what they called a superior, comprehensive overview of her life. Her donor match would ideally have a college education, an athletic build. No record of criminal or domestic abuse, no history of heart disease — that was a non-starter, with Ana's mother having passed in her early 50s — and talent in visual arts, perhaps music. Evan's 79% was just below the desirable range. But his face was symmetrical, his features proportionate. He looked kind.

She dug further. He managed a bed and breakfast in Vermont for two years, founded a few fledgling bands in the early 2010s. As she finished her wine, she clicked on a tab requesting more information, knowing that doing so would bombard her email and browser ads with photos of Evan from youth to adulthood, from skinned soccer knees to unshaved cheeks to business suits. Her computer itself would push Evan upon her like a haughty salesman, and this was not the time, with her highest-profile case since the Villalobos murders. She needed, as she had in times past, to shut out her personal life completely, to give herself to the job. To sideline her own pain and, like a machine, take to Fowler's death with clinical focus.

Then again, in reality, no time was a good time. There hadn't been, might never be. If she was serious about FamilyMatch — if she wished to justify the money she'd already spent, the money she'd saved to raise another child — then she had to stop fixating on faults. On the why nots. She couldn't continue to feel each profile, each potential child their sperm might bear, as a minute but palpable tug on the fraying, unraveling ball that was her heart. She had to keep the strands from lengthening. She needed to find the right thread with which to sew her heart anew.

***

Before eight the next morning, her mind still in a haze, Ana walked across the street to a family diner specializing in overstuffed breakfast burritos. The slush from the night before seeped into her tennis shoes. The full parking lot and overcrowded waiting area surprised her. The host told her thirty minutes for a table, so she asked him if they could make her a quick something to go, briefly explaining herself and flashing her badge. He spoke to a supervisor, who spoke to another supervisor, who said yes, they would get her something as soon as they could, if she had fifteen minutes.

She sat on a bench between a teenage couple and a family of six, all with heads buried in their phones. Ana pulled hers from her purse and found a message from Lonnie, asking how Ana enjoyed her first night in her Wisconsin paradise.

Seriously though, Millennials aplenty working for those guys.
Snag one you cougar.

Ana again ignored Lonnie and opened a message to Bruce detailing her agenda for the day, starting with setting up her team. She wanted Jade and Michael, both from Chicago and both great at scouring the internet and datasets for days without stop. She'd meet with Sergio, then visit the coroner and Charles Fowler's corpse. She needed to start the victim profile. When he'd been in the real world, Fowler lived a few hours north, in a town called Crivitz, and so Ana would begin interviews there. All this she planned to do today.

And Sonya Young... she needed to meet with Sonya Young as soon as possible.

She texted all of this to Bruce. His simple reply came seconds later:
Sounds good.

Another five minutes passed, and so she logged back into her FamilyMatch account to find six notifications related to Evan. She regretted marking his profile, but then, as she began to delete the notifications, each a different picture of Evan, one caught her. She stopped. He crouched on one knee, tossing softballs to a cadre of adolescent girls wearing matching pink jerseys. She never would have imagined this side of him. Deviously clever, she thought, forcing her to preview the notifications before deleting them — show interest and you must absorb the donor's entire repertoire, the full proposal. It was a theft of her individual will. An entrapment of her heart. And it worked.

The notification invited Ana to take the next step: an online interview via webchat, FamilyMatch's largest draw. They strictly regulated it—

thirty minutes only, and a limited number of interviews, depending on her monthly plan — but this was Ana's chance, as they advertised, to see beyond the profiles and truly decide for herself, to look into the man's eyes. It was what drew Ana, the same reason she speed-dated and conducted victim profile interviews in person: the ability to see beyond the presentation, to stare into the real. She had never before taken it this far, never found a candidate worth such consideration. She wanted to shut down her phone, to stop herself, but the unexpected silence of all those awaiting a table unnerved her — the couple, the family, and thirty-plus people all standing, all staring at their devices, all somewhere else. All lost to their own digital worlds. The interview request button shined green on her screen and seemed to pulse; either that, or her sleeplessness played with her vision.

She clicked it.

In less than a minute, Evan responded:

> *So great to hear you're interested! I'm free this coming Thursday, between noon and four your time. Would you like to schedule the interview?*

JOSEPH REIN

Chapter 2

Sergio arrived at Ana's hotel at quarter past ten. He was thinner than when she'd last seen him, the result, she assumed, of his third marriage. Ana thanked him for being available. In their last case together, Sergio had in minutes created a digital suspect profile broader than the one Ana put together in a full day of interviews. She hoped for his brand of lightning to strike here once again.

He wore a wool peacoat that appeared crisply new, as though he'd just purchased it. He had an aversion to the Midwest but didn't hold it against Ana. His thinning hair was littered with gray, stark white in some patches, belying a rather youthful face with a stark black mustache. "Got ourselves a doosie, eh, Downer?" he said as he pulled out a laptop. "This hotel is a shithole."

"I thought we might be going to Youtopia Towers."

"Better to start here. We're like a random person with a random internet connection — a thief in the night. We'll see how high we can climb before their defenses knock us down."

He plugged in and set up on the small desk. As his computer booted up, he whistled a familiar tune Ana couldn't place. He opened a web browser, but almost immediately his next moves eluded Ana. He typed in code, a dizzying blur of symbols and letters foreign to her. His fingers clicked with a controlled belligerence, like some master on a piano. He attempted to describe some of it to her, but when he saw none of it registering, he turned to Medieval metaphor: "Like an underground tunnel, but you can't dig just anywhere, you need to find the soft soil," and, "Imagine a moat. You can't walk, you can't swim. Basically, you have to create a huge catapult and find a safe landing."

He stopped multiple times to point out names to Ana, asking if she recognized any of them, and she realized this was her purpose: to make connections between any potential gems Sergio might unearth. Many were Youtopia employees, mostly higher-ups like Peterson and Sonya Young herself.

"The guards of the castle," Sergio said. "And boy, are they packing the heavy artillery. I haven't even scratched the surface and already they're hacking back."

"Hacking back?"

"Going on the offensive. Wrong paths, sending viruses our way. All the big players — including us — do this. Better than being a sitting duck." He stopped, put his hands together as though to crack his knuckles, but instead placed his thumbs under his chin and craned his neck until it let out a soft pop, the sound sending a shudder down Ana.

"How did our guy get past all this?" she asked.

"There's always a way in. Sure, they've got the usual firewalls, data encryption to the nth degree, as top of the line as it goes, but the code necessary for it — it's..." Sergio clasped his hands together and then widened them, as though stretching some invisible object. "The bigger the wall, the bigger the chance for holes. Your average code has thirty errors per thousand lines. Youtopia's will be cleaner, but their programs still have something like *one hundred million* lines of code. That's a *lot* of room for error."

"We can find the error, right? Find the hole, find the person who crawled through it?"

"Easy. But that won't actually tell us much. We used to spend time tracing servers, locating the physical location of the hack, but even your average teenage punk can reroute his signal. Our guy likely bounced through hundreds of servers, and not just in the US — London, Istanbul. Cape Town is a favorite. No way to know the true source."

"So the attack could have originated abroad."

"You shush now, Downer," Sergio said, raising a finger to his lips. "You start talking China or Russia and we'll have some stiff from Homeland Security up our asses."

He reached into his satchel, but instead of some tech gear, he pulled a plastic zipped bag with tobacco and papers. When he opened the bag, the piquant smell wafted out immediately, and he began a methodical process of rolling his own cigarette. When he finished, he put it between his lips but didn't light it. It dangled below his mustache like a piece of wayward food.

"No," he continued, "tracing the source won't help. You remember Sony? Or that Target shitshow? We *still* don't know the architects. The best we can do here is find the hole itself — find where the weakness started. Most times, it's some gullible worker with an insecure flash drive backing up his shitty TikTok videos."

Sergio returned to the computer, typing lines of code no different to Ana than the others. His fingers danced on, but this time they stopped more often to hover, flutter atop the keys in uncertainty.

Ana checked her watch as ten, then twenty minutes passed without a word.

Sergio finally stopped and smiled. "Hello beautiful."

"You've found it?"

"Classic Trojan. Nothing too sophisticated. I'm actually kinda bummed."

"Trojan?"

"As in Trojan horse. Our guy slips in and disguises himself, hides out, goes undetected by assuring the system everything is tip-top. This could be days, months. If he was patient enough, years. All the while he's reconning the system for vulnerabilities."

"It's possible he's still here?"

"Unlikely. Criminals online are like criminals everywhere—they don't stick around the scene of the crime too long. But as for other entry points... like I said, one hundred million."

He attacked the keyboard again, this time in patterned bursts, typing feverishly one minute, contemplating the next. He gave no expression, no indication he was getting anywhere.

Ana's phone buzzed on the bed beside her—a notification from FamilyMatch—and she went to silence it. When she returned, Sergio sat back.

"Afraid to say," he said, the cigarette gamboling about his lips, "we've reached the end of the road here. Any more and this laptop becomes a prisoner of war."

He returned the laptop to his satchel and retrieved a king-sized candy bar. He placed the rolled cigarette behind his ear, then peeled down the candy bar's wrapper like a banana.

"So where do we go from here?" Ana asked.

"I'll pinpoint the entry date. Bruce will clear my schedule, I'm sure. My wife will demand I quit, if I find time to call her." He chewed loudly, his lips smacking. "But the truth? Whoever did this, I wouldn't count on finding them virtually. Besides..." He waved the candy bar like a wand. "Well, there's nothing I can do for motive. That's your department."

Ana thought of Fowler, of her pending drive north. She pondered past murders and motivations. For the Villalobos murders, the killer's reason was little more than convenience of the victims and a crazed obsession.

"What are common motives for cybercrimes?" she asked.

"A hack this size? Sometimes they want the tech. Or control. But most are just displays of power. A digital pissing match."

"None of those lead to murder."

"Yeah, well, that's why us tech guys don't pound *that* pavement too often." He snapped his fingers. "Message boards. Check the most prominent hacker message boards. Thousands might try to claim this, but one might actually be our guy. Hubris is a potent drug. If he has some message he's trying to send, it might be there."

"Maybe the murder is the message."

Sergio gave a solemn nod, then patted his pants pockets. "You have any matches? No, forget it. I'll make a stop."

Before leaving, he turned to her, slinking in the final bite of his candy bar. "Buckle in, Downer. Got a feeling this rollercoaster's just getting started."

***

Lonnie's pestering accelerated, so Ana relented and agreed to meet her for a quick lunch before her drive north. Ana chose an old restaurant on Lake Michigan, and sat along a glass wall overlooking a weathered patio and the water. They served Italian but seemed in the midst of some larger transition, with Asian-fusion specials and drinks. It needed a facelift to pull off the transformation, new tables and leather, new sconces — new everything. The place smelled of age, of salty wear. A young waitress refreshed Ana's diet soda. Lonnie messaged that she was still thirty minutes out, blaming her two Persian cats for the delay. Ana ordered a bowl of miso soup and started reading published articles related to Fowler's murder. The big news outlets stuck to the facts, but the fringe sites didn't hide their hysteria. X-ACT linked Fowler's death to the Kennedy assassination. Terrance Martin of ReaLife Church called it an intervention from a higher power. Ana saw her own name, and sometimes her stock Bureau photo taken in her early years, her hair tight against her head, her lips unsmiling. She wondered if, anymore, she looked so severe.

Thirty minutes more and no sign of Lonnie. Ana needed to leave. She needed to see Fowler's body, to interview his surviving family and friends. She needed to meet her team members and start delegating. She needed to focus.

Just as Ana typed an apology message — *Had to run, so sorry you drove this whole way* — Lonnie stormed into the restaurant. She waved off the hostess and smacked her purse and then herself into Ana's booth.

"Kitschy," she said. Her dyed blonde hair was up, her eyeliner and mascara heavy. "When you told me Racine, this is literally what I imagined."

"You never know. It might grow on you."

"Like a wart."

Ana laughed, and felt her shoulders loosening, her body responding to the particular brand of carousing and comfort that was Lonnie.

Lonnie ordered a bottle of red and three meals to split—Ana took only a few small sips and, as usual, Lonnie finished the rest. She probed again about the men of Racine, and Ana deflected. All those years ago, Lonnie had introduced Paul and Ana—Lonnie and Paul were friends first, had in fact dated for a brief, ill-fated stint. Now Lonnie felt it her permanent trade to matchmake for Ana—this guy, that guy, most any guy—as though she knew Ana better than herself. Because Lonnie was a good person at heart, Ana humored her.

"Well," Lonnie said, "whatever guy you find, make sure he's willing to move to Andalusia." Then, with a wry wink, she added, "And that he's into threesomes."

Lonnie and Andalusia. Andalusia and Lonnie. Ever since Ana mentioned that her grandmother was born and raised there, just outside of Seville, Spain had become for Lonnie the immovable symbol of the life they should be leading, some exotic, grandiose wonderland of luxury and the erotic encounters for which Lonnie constantly fantasized. "What's holding us back?" was Lonnie's refrain, willfully ignoring the intense focus Ana had always given her career, even before the accident. Lonnie was a workaholic of sorts herself, a proprietor of a home-selling business called *Doing It Right*, which sold tasteful erogenous toys, one of those top-down sales schemes for which a person like Lonnie was uniquely suited. She could sell her wares anywhere, even through a language barrier.

But moving abroad, especially with someone like Lonnie, seemed to Ana a step bred of desperation, of starting over, something to do not at 41 but 21, when the world seemed conquerable. When she had visions of becoming Spielberg, the next Agnés Varda. When life seemed infinitely possible.

"I counted at least seven bars on this street alone," Lonnie said. "Think we can hit them all before happy hour ends?"

"I have to run," Ana said. "I have a drive ahead of me."

"And I have one behind me." Lonnie looked longingly at her empty wine glass, as though someone else had finished it. "Before I release you, you need to spill one thing."

"There's nothing to—"

"One goddamn thing! I drove oh so far."

Ana watched Lonnie overtly sulk and pout, her shoulders sashaying in flashy repartee. At times she was too much, at times the exact right amount, but never not enough. This time, her faux-peevishness made Ana laugh, and so she let slip Evan's name.

"Evaaaaan," Lonnie said. "You dog! Knew you were holding out."

"It's nothing," Ana said. She didn't mention FamilyMatch, the incorrigible desire not for a man but a child, a life she had lost. "I don't think it'll go anywhere."

"Mmm-hmm. Pictures. Gonna need pictures."

Before she thought to lie about not having one, Ana pulled out her phone, downloaded one of Evan's profile pictures, and flashed it to Lonnie.

Lonnie's eyes narrowed. She grabbed Ana's hand and brought the phone closer to her face, like an elderly woman attempting to read fine print.

"Well?" Ana asked.

Lonnie leaned back. "Really?"

"What? He's handsome, young. I thought you'd be thrilled."

Ana looked at the picture, a close crop of Evan from the shoulders up, his hair short, his smile knowing. He was better looking than any of the suitors Lonnie had presented her, and certainly more youthful.

"You think he's too young for me," Ana said.

"Sure. That's it." Lonnie grabbed the check before standing. "Enjoy the northwoods."

***

"Totally fried," the coroner said. He popped citrusy gum that Ana could smell from across the table. "As you can imagine, we get fentanyl ODs like clockwork here. But this..." In his mid-fifties, he appeared more frat boy than doctor. Ana imagined some ironic band t-shirt under his scrubs. It was possible he'd been elected to his position, that he had no real medical experience, though the hospital and the city—Appleton, near but not too near Fowler's Nest—felt big enough to lure someone with a bit more heft than this man.

Ana walked alongside the body while awaiting her forensic pathologist from Chicago. She'd seen enough dead bodies to never be shocked, but Fowler's was unique. His skin was exceptionally sallow and smooth, like porcelain, but his hair and beard had grown gargantuan, thick and gnarled, lying about his chest and the table like unruly vines. His fingernails too had softened and curled, some pressing against his thighs. He seemed part pallid child, part unkempt geriatric. The only signs of abuse were the incision marks from the coroner himself, all around his forehead and in a precise X over his heart.

With hesitation, Ana reached out to touch Fowler's pale wrist. Something inside her expected the body to twitch, or to slowly rise up planate off the bed. It had some magnetic, fountain-of-youth pull to it. She realized that, beside company employees at Youtopia and this coroner, she was likely the only one to ever see an Immerser's body.

"The guy's heart is," the coroner continued, unable to simply wait in silence. "It's just a mess. It's like... I don't know... meth plus speed plus coke, but not really. It's hard to explain."

"And yet it's your job to do so."

The coroner stunted, his face souring. Ana enjoyed the brief silence before the forensic pathologist entered, her suit pitch black and her hair up. Her first name escaped Ana, though her workmates had shortened her last name Fitzgerald into the nickname Fitzy, and it stuck. Like Ana, she was early forties, and moved with the purpose of one who had invested herself into her career. Before even addressing them, Fitzy found an open table space onto which she unloaded her equipment.

When she shook Ana's hand, Ana felt the warmth of constant use. "Glad to have you on this," Ana said.

"Glad to help," Fitzy replied. "Though it sounds like this might be a quick visit. We'll see if he's holding any secrets."

The coroner stepped in and explained his findings to Fitzy. Fitzy listened with full attention, never breaking eye contact with him, until he reached his end. Then she thanked him and asked him in a voice much more polite than Ana could muster if he would stand aside. Gloves on, she delved into Fowler.

Fitzy removed the skull, opened the chest cavity a much wider berth than the coroner had, and pressed with a gentle precision on every inch of Fowler's skin. Her face gave nothing away, no sign of surprise, understanding, or even interest. The coroner left and returned with a Coke, the smack of the opening can echoing through the room. Fitzy didn't react, and after twenty minutes, she finally leaned upward and craned her neck to the side. She closed and opened her eyes, as though awaking from a deep sleep.

"Atypical," she said as she moved one of many scalpels to the wash basin. "That duratonia bifetanol is clearly not meant for such high doses, but I don't see any reason to doubt their account."

"Atypical how?"

"Overdoses generally happen to people with altered consciousnesses. This duratonia bifetanol, though, is designed to keep the senses intact. As more and more flooded his system, likely the effect was heightened. It was—"

Fitzy stopped for a moment and looked down, a rare break in her composure. "It's not a pleasant way to go."

***

Ana drove the two hours north to Crivitz, Fowler's hometown. Along the way, she tried the listed number for Fowler's wife Carol, to no success. She pulled a bird's-eye map of the house that Carol and Fowler shared, the house she still occupied, a quaint, secluded place off a forlorn county road. As she reached such snaking roads, held together only by thick tar and pea gravel, she got a call from Bruce.

"Jade and Michael say they haven't heard from you," he said before Ana could even say hello.

"I've barely just begun myself here."

The dribble from his basketball resonated into the phone. "Congress called a special session for this afternoon," he said, revealing the real reason for his call. "They're going to vote on the Healthcare Bill."

"You're kidding."

"They want to get it passed before anything else happens."

"They do realize that the Healthcare Bill might be the reason for the first murder?"

"Preaching to the choir. Either way, our clock is ticking."

"I won't rush this, Bruce. You said it yourself: we can't afford any mistakes."

The basketball stopped. "Just use your team. Sometimes quicker and better are the same damn thing."

She drove down a thick, winding gravel driveway and arrived at a house both bizarre and impressive. The entire side yard, and what Ana could see of the back, was lined with teak planter's boxes in perfect geometric order. Carol had left herself the thinnest slice of grass on which to walk; Ana imagined the woman tiptoeing between boxes like a mother in a sleeping child's bedroom. She counted hyacinths, bearded irises, and as many as seven boxes of budding tulips wrapped in small plastic bags to prevent overnight freezing. Half the boxes sat empty, likely awaiting a stronger upturn in the weather. Beyond the boxes, in the far corner of the yard, from the awning of a large shed hung a sign that read:

Start Each Day with a Grateful Heart.

The house itself had recently been renovated, modern and yet rustic. The doorbell played the opening of an oldies tune. Despite the fact that a pickup truck sat near the open garage, nobody answered. Ana knocked, waited, rang the bell again. She returned to her car, considered waiting until Carol either emerged from inside or returned home in a different vehicle. She considered sleeping there, stakeout style, though her body no longer responded well to such subtle cruelties. A half hour passed, and as the sun disappeared behind decades-old maples and pines, she realized she hadn't eaten since lunch with Lonnie.

Then Ana saw, in her peripheral vision, the beginning blurry rainbow aura of a migraine. It was small, bean-shaped, and unless she looked away, it rested just above the Fowler home. Like many of life's ills, Ana's migraines emerged at inopportune times — for her, often when cases weren't going well. Frustration may not have been the cause of the migraine, but they did feed one another, frustration growing migraine growing frustration growing. In ten minutes, the rainbow would blossom into a full circle; in thirty minutes, if she didn't pop the potent painkillers in her glove compartment, the screaming throes of the migraine would press against every edge of her head, front to back, temple to temple.

She gathered as much saliva as she could and shuffled down the two oblong pills in struggled waves. Ten minutes passed. Her blurred vision peaked and then subsided, leaving a hazy film with it, like the effects of a hangover. When the headache came, it was strong but thankfully subdued, the pills staving off the worst. Still, as the sun dropped behind the trees, she recognized the migraine as a portent. As her call to end the day.

The sign on the nearest motel advertised free wi-fi and off-road quiet. It was worse than her one in Racine, with burnt-out light bulbs and a stiff flannel comforter. A spiderweb crack emanated from one corner of the television. A doughnut-sized lime ring circled the bathtub drain. It would have to do.

After lying on the bed for a long time, too early to sleep, she called a local pizza joint and then finally reached out to her team. Jade, a twenty-something just years out of graduate school, her voice high and cheery, thanked Ana for taking her on. Ana assured her that she had earned it, that she would be invaluable. Michael was mid-thirties, single, steady. His voice boomed confidence through the phone. She asked him to scan dark web message boards for anyone claiming the murder.

"Sounds fun," he said without a hint of sarcasm. "I'm on it."

The pizza arrived. Ana overtipped the deliverer. It was deep dish, thick with cheese and crust. Despite her Chicago roots, Ana preferred thin, New York style, and yet she forced herself to eat two pieces. The rest she put into the small refrigerator beside the sink, knowing that she likely wouldn't return to it, knowing that tomorrow would be another long day, if not longer. Knowing she had only just begun.

***

She dreamed of geese. They opened their vast wings as they took flight. Those still on the ground pecked and bickered. She inhaled the damp, earthy smell of spring. Yes, the smell—her first sign this was more than a dream.

Paul walked ahead on the dirt path, with Charlotte holding his hand. Though it was afternoon, he sang Charlotte's favorite lullaby, a hand-me-down from Paul's mother, one about a train entering some heavenly station. *Night will fall too soon, choo-chooing under the moon.* In his other hand, he held a cannister of oats for feeding the ducks, one of Charlotte's favorite pastimes.

She was four, nearly as old as she would ever be.

Paul halted near a gaggle, just two adults but many yellow goslings—ten, twenty—that appeared from the river and behind buckthorn patches in droves. He opened the oats and handed some to Charlotte, who sprinkled them like seed on the ground. The adult geese rushed in to steal away their own children's snacks. They hissed, looked poised to snip.

Ana wanted to warn Charlotte to keep her distance, wanted to scold Paul for his recklessness, but she could not speak. She could only observe.

Eventually, they reached the duck hangout along the river, mallards and gadwalls and even a solitary wood duck, but the geese far outmatched them in number and aggression. No matter how far Paul threw the oats, the ducks received little.

Then Anna felt a tug at her side. She looked down, saw her daughter's face illuminated in a harrowing glow. Her eyes were crystalline blue.

"Mommy," her singsong voice said. "Move the geese."

Ana looked into her own empty hands, then to Paul, who had mysteriously disappeared. The can of oats lay tipped on the ground.

Ana drifted here for a minute—or ten minutes, an hour, she couldn't tell—between the images of the can and her hotel bed. The room felt clouded in a stifling heat. Part of her wanted to stay with the dream, a dream that adopted her past like none before. When she finally stood and looked outside, she saw it was dawn. She didn't remember lying in this dull hotel bed, falling asleep. She checked her phone to make sure an entire day hadn't passed. To make sure she was still where she needed to be.

***

She pulled into the Crivitz High parking lot before six. Teachers and administrators arrived in waves, greeting each other as they entered. A handful of students came early in athletic gear, their morning sports practices awaiting them. Ana crossed the parking lot, the sun and warm air promising a temperate spring morning. She entered the front doors, pressed a buzzer that was shockingly loud, reminiscent of the first alarm clock her mother bought her when she was a teen. The woman behind the desk poured herself a coffee before engaging the intercom. Ana was here to speak to the principal. A flash of her badge gained her entry.

His office was strangely located at the back of the building—the woman walked Ana through halls covered in posters and stunted lockers. Inside the office, felt banners from decades ago littered the walls. The man himself, late 50s with a paunchy stomach and cheeks, wearing a sweater vest in the school's navy and yellow colors, greeted Ana with assurance. He smiled like an old friend.

"I must say, I never thought a real federal agent would sit in that chair," he said.

"If it helps, I never thought I would be here either."

He issued a soft chuckle. Then his jowls sank. "I was sorry to hear about Charles. A good man. No, great man. Great."

"Yes, I'm sure he was. But great men are murdered just as often as bad men."

The principal bristled at this. "How exactly can I help you?"

"I need to pinpoint why Mr. Fowler was singled out. What might have made him a target."

"Oh," he said, "I wouldn't know about any of that."

Of course he wouldn't, Ana thought. She pried with generic questions about their relationship, trying to get past the praise reserved for the recently deceased — kind, patient, great with kids, excellent volleyball coach — and into the seedier, real parts of the victim. The parts that made a profile.

"What did people think of his Immersion into Youtopia?"

The principal took an industrious drink from a water bottle. "Well, before all that he was pretty well liked, but after... let's just say the whole town had an opinion then."

"Any particularly negative ones? In the school perhaps?"

The principal looked upward. The answer was yes, though Ana knew he didn't want to tell — didn't, as leader, want to snitch on his own.

"The only way Charles Fowler receives justice," Ana said, "is for me to know the truth."

The principal nodded. "I know, ma'am, and I'd love to help, but people get angry about, you know, the littlest things. Mr. Fowler singled out my son in class for this-or-that reason. He's not playing my daughter enough, because we think she's D1 material. If you liked him or didn't like him, either way, his leaving for that place... I guess it just made whatever you already felt stronger."

Ana scribbled on a notepad: *Favoritism. Playing time.* These weren't useful, but she wanted the principal to know she was listening. She asked him to continue.

He obliged, but his answers went no deeper, and Ana jotted down words that wouldn't make it into her report. When he finally ran dry, the principal escorted Ana to other teachers who prepared for their soon-to-be hectic days. They were of two sorts: those of near-retirement age, who'd taught at Crivitz High for decades, fueled by the sunset awaiting them; and those fresh out of college, new to prepping and authority, fueled by caffeine and youthful optimism. All the teachers were kind, painfully so, offering Ana seats and coffees from the teacher's lounge, but nothing of substance on Fowler.

The dull remnants of yesterday's migraine lingered in Ana's temples. She was getting nowhere here. She had to go. Finally, after speaking to an old social studies colleague of Fowler's about their shared penchant for cribbage, Ana excused herself to seek answers around town.

She fared no better there. At City Hall, nobody had thought of Charles Fowler in the ten years since he'd fled. Local law enforcement were the same — Fowler was a nonentity to them now, as he was then. At Silver Spur Saloon, his favorite jaunt and the location of his weekly dart league, those who remembered Fowler glorified him as a pillar of their community, offering vague praise, as one might about a politician. Only one man, a twenty-something in a ReaLife t-shirt, held any hostility, but it was aimless, directed at Youtopia and not Fowler specifically. He recited a Bible verse about the sanctity of life between pulls of Bud Light. The consensus seemed to be that, friend or foe, Fowler was simply not worth another thought.

At lunchtime, she returned defeated to her motel, and after a greasy fast-food meal that left her queasy, in the stained shower, water smelling faintly of iron draining from her, she attempted to make sense of the morning's failure. Many of Fowler's acquaintances simply would not trample on a fresh grave, especially here in his hometown. But then, profiles took time, she reminded herself. Fowler died less than seventy-two hours ago. She was here, and not Gilles, or Hatch, or any other qualified agent. Bruce chose her.

And yet, as she opened a file to begin her victim report, it all felt relatively futile. In past cases, Ana sensed when interviewees withheld things from her — the dubious eyes, the overabundance of praise on small details, the sudden silences. Here, it felt like people gave her everything they had, which amounted to so little. Their pictures, incomplete as they were, might have been the best these people could do. After all, it had been a decade since any of them had seen, or probably considered, Charles Fowler — the man, the coach, the neighbor, the village board member. Ana thought to 2014, to the people with whom she'd lost contact, and could hardly recreate their faces, let alone the nuances of their personalities. She would have been of no help in inquiries about their deaths. So, what good was the profile of a victim ten years removed from the real world? No wonder she failed today: of these people, she'd asked the nearly impossible.

***

Carol Fowler's house was the same as before. Ana planned to wait her out this time, all afternoon if she had to, but only five minutes in, from behind the house, Carol emerged.

She wore denim coveralls and a bandana over her white hair. Deep-brown soil covered her hands and knees. She didn't look up, not at Ana's car, not at her door closing, not at the sound of her feet on the gravel driveway. Instead, she bent down to the base of a gangly lilac bush, its dry branches snaking from the ground like crooked fingers as she attempted to resuscitate what seemed destined for death. She wore thin glasses adorned with a gold chain that hung around her neck.

Ana nearly reached her before her voice suddenly called out, "I'm not interested in talking to you."

"I can understand," Ana said. Carol turned, her face dirtied and her eyes entirely vacant. Ana saw in them an exasperation born of wizened wounds, of dealing with her husband's loss all over again. "And I hate to be the bearer of bad news, but I think that bush is on its last legs."

Carol turned back to the failing bush. "Anyone with eyes can see that." She gently crumbled a browning leaf in her fingers. "Over a decade now I've had her. This winter was particularly tough."

"You could cut it way back, see if it grows anew."

She shook her head. "Better to just let go."

Ana moved to Carol in timid steps, as though descending a steep stairwell. She crouched next to her and admired her work with her eyes and soft praises. This trick — getting to eye level, showering compliments — Ana learned from one of the many college-age helpers at Charlotte's daycare. Ana remembered feeling belittled, belittling, but when she took the advice, Charlotte would immediately calm from one of her frantic tantrums, her shouts turning to whimpers, the threats in her eyes to pleads. Adults, Ana had expected, would be too wily for the trick, and yet she often found it effective.

Like now — after a few minutes, Carol's humanity, her Midwestern hospitality, overcame her grief. She removed her gardening gloves, offered Ana a seat on a wicker porch chair and tea. She entered her house and returned with a pot and two cups on a tray.

"Nice to be outside again," Ana said. Carol only hummed in reply.

And so, Carol served and Ana sipped. She gave Carol the time and silence she needed, the time and silence no other investigator or reporter, or anyone else asking about her husband's quixotic death, had likely given her.

***

"To be honest, I'm not really sure why he did it." The searing peppers on Carol's stove spat a satisfying hiss. Ana politely drank her second tea, ate the crackers Carol laid out. She remained silent, allowing Carol her tangents, interjecting only to show she was still listening. So far, she had heard much the same about pre-Youtopia Fowler: high school social studies teacher, classic car aficionado, avid outdoorsman, Catholic but only in name. The pictures about the house confirmed this, displaying a man with varying facial hair on boats, in red overalls, beside classic Mustangs and Roadrunners. He had wanted children, many, but after their fourth miscarriage his heart had had enough.

"No illness, no great sorrow," Carol said. "One of the jolliest men you ever saw. He had a child's heart in him, that's for sure. Like that Rod Stewart song—forever young, he was."

Ana thought immediately of the body, its paleness. She needed to use the bathroom but didn't want to step out of the conversation just now, right when Carol had opened up. She needed to get as much as she could about Fowler's social habits, his health, his stressors. "So what made him choose Youtopia?"

Carol's roving hands paused for a moment. "I asked myself that. A lot. For too long. Was there something I wasn't giving him? Something he needed that I couldn't provide? Other than children, of course."

"I didn't mean to suggest you were the cause."

"The truth is, I was as surprised as anyone. He had a few meetings with Sonya Young, but he never told me much. Half the time, he'd be giddy as a kid on Christmas, the other half he'd be reserved. Closed off. I told him, 'You gotta quit this thing, Chuck.'" She tossed the peppers. "And then I blink, and... well, he chose to go the other way."

Ana considered her next words with care. "Did you ever consider Immersing?"

Carol pushed up her glasses with a single finger. "Of course I did. Who hasn't? But there's this..." She looked out the bay window at a squirrel acrobatically scaling one of her many birdfeeder hooks. "I think of it like I think of laser eye surgery. Would it improve my vision? Make life easier? Sure it would, and maybe millions of people do it safely. But you're still messing with the eyes, right?"

Ana nodded. She found that, sometimes against her own will, she asked people this question. She asked it of every speed dater she considered taking home. She would soon have to ask Evan, if she planned to continue down that haphazard route. She gathered people's justifications for remaining in the world, especially when loved ones had entered Youtopia, and stored them like profile information, somewhere deep inside her. She found them a comfort.

After eating the peppers, Ana went to the bathroom. She opened the cabinet drawer in search of a spare roll of toilet paper, but instead found a worn shoe box, cover open, overflowing with old Polaroid photos. Each one had a date indicator labeled in permanent marker beneath: July 4 1992, Conference Championship 2001, Carol's 47th birthday. The older pictures had the wear and whitened fade of clothing left in the sun. Ana shuffled through the photos, knowing she was taking too long, searching for something, anything. Whatever it was, it wasn't Fowler's countless trophy deer horn poses or annual volleyball team photos. It was not in house renovation time lapses, not in Carol's sewing phase or Fowler's body cataloguing phase. It wasn't here.

Then, suddenly, it was—a fishing photo, with Fowler at the tail end of a massive muskie. Holding the fish's head was a man with a face so familiar Ana almost recalled a name. She envisioned the man in all black, hands outstretched. But just as quickly, her vision cut. Ana couldn't yet place him. She slipped the photo into her jacket pocket.

Carol was already cleaning up when Ana returned. Ana offered her a business card. "If anything comes to you. Your husband deserves justice."

Carol continued wiping the counter, so Ana placed the card on a damp patch.

"Appreciate it, dear," Carol said. "But Charles... I moved on, you know? I had to. I don't think there's anything else I can give you."

A half-mile down Carol's labyrinthine road, Ana stopped, pulled out her phone, and took a photo of the photo. The result was somehow both grainy and glossed, and when she tried to upload it into her facial recognition program, neither face took.

Back at the hotel, she requested the use of a scanning machine she knew they didn't have. The teenage clerk mentioned a copy place just down County Road X, toward Main. Ana begrudgingly thanked him and retired to her room. She called Bruce, informed him about Carol, the odd garden, and that she might have found something in an old photo.

Bruce asked about meeting Sonya Young.

"I'm working on it," she said.

"Work harder," he said before hanging up.

***

Her FamilyMatch interview with Evan was scheduled for four. She'd planned on skipping it—had secretly hoped that she would be staking out Carol's house, that the interview would go on much longer. She hoped her cheap motel's promise of wifi wouldn't hold. But here she was, and it had, and so she had no excuse.

At five-to, Ana sat in front of her screen, web browser open to the FamilyMatch video chat website, chewing at the meaty inside of her lip until she tasted blood. The company logo, a thick oval encircling a nearly distasteful cartoon fetus, glistened in the corner of the site. In the center, a black rectangular screen waited latent. Then it flickered. The blackness immediately gave way to a couch, a kitchenette, and Evan's face.

"Hello?" he called out, his eyes scanning the corners of his own screen. "Are you there?"

As his hands moved to remedy the disconnect, Ana took the moment to watch him, to study his eyes, his slim nose, the way he tilted his head, tongue in one cheek. She looked at the apartment around him: the undersized refrigerator, the running shoes atop the kitchen table.

"I'm gonna have to... maybe..." Evan said.

Ana took a breath, then clicked on her own camera. He saw her, and smiled as she apologized for the trouble.

"You'd think the world would have this down by now," Evan said. He was less handsome than in the picture, and many years older, both of which she found endearing. "So, you're Anabel, yes?"

"Ana for short."

"Ana it is."

A beep sounded somewhere in Evan's apartment. "Sorry, that's just my coffeemaker shutting off. The thing's more obnoxious than a roommate."

He stood to unplug it, walking the few steps to his counter in a sauntering, deliberate gait, and Ana finally recognized it. How did she not see it? She understood now why she chose Evan, why she reached out, why Lonnie was so skeptical at lunch. Ana saw in his height, his tussled hair, in the way he ambled about the room: he was a younger version of Paul.

Evan returned and his smile, even that, carried hints of her former husband, with the uniform and prominent teeth, the curved upper lip. Ana felt in her ribcage an immense tightening, her heart retreating into itself. She realized all the ways in which this entire effort—FamilyMatch and the services before it, the avid, scrupulous selection, the hesitant outreach to Evan and this very interview—was her attempt to have a child as close to Charlotte as possible.

"I'm sorry," Ana said as Evan centered himself on her screen. "I think this was a mistake."

Evan let out a surprised laugh. "What, because of the coffeemaker?" When Ana didn't respond, he leaned toward his camera. "Look, there's no obligation here. We're just talking, trying to see if this is a good fit. You haven't even asked me any—"

"I think I should go," Ana interrupted. "I'm terribly sorry."

She reached out a hand and Evan's body jittered, his hands waving on either side of the screen. "Wait wait wait," he said, leaning back. His face lost its cordial veneer. He looked soft, vulnerable. "Let me level with you. I'm not supposed to be telling you this, but..." He glanced around him as though someone might be listening. "The stipend we receive for donating is—excuse my language—shit. It's piddly shit. But the commission if we actually sell... it's why we have to do these interviews, why we have to parade ourselves in front of you."

Evan spread his fingers wide as he combed them through his hair. "If you hang up now, you won't respond again. They never do."

Ana's cursor hovered over the hangup button. She sighed. "Okay."

They spoke for the remainder of the half hour. Evan detailed his life, from a California childhood to failed attempts at colleges on both coasts. Then his multiple failed entrepreneurial enterprises, mostly arboreal. He was surprisingly candid in admitting his own faults. He liked surfing but had a tenacious fear of sharks. He found wakeboarding on lakes an unsatisfactory compromise. He had two cats who did not appear but, he assured Ana, were omnipresent in his apartment, with the ridiculous names Muffles and Tootles. He played piano. He had always wanted to earn his pilot's license but could not overcome the acrophobia either. Ana listened, all the while attempting not to see Paul.

He stopped speaking to drink what must have been cold coffee. "I've been prattling," he said. "Do you have any questions for me?"

Ana ground her molars against one another. Then she said, before her mind could stop herself, "Have you ever considered entering Youtopia?"

He blurted out a small laugh, sending dribbles of coffee down his chin. He wiped at his lower lip. "That's... kind of heavy for a first question." His eyes roamed about his apartment. "Okay, you're serious. Yeah, I guess. Who hasn't?" He raised a hand deliberately to the camera and rubbed his thumb against his forefinger. "But that costs."

"Soon it might not."

"True. But then I wouldn't have met you, right?" He let this sit, as though their interaction, as though every encounter happenstance or planned, bore the proof of life's significance. "Maybe I'm needed here. Maybe there are some astonishing things on the horizon. Who knows."

Their time was nearly up. Ana thanked him. Evan attempted to schedule a follow-up call, but Ana balked. She would contact him when she was ready. His disappointment was palpable. But what could she be expected to give him, a young man whose stakes were so simple—a commercial transaction, money, just the money? What could he expect of her, who had lost so much?

***

She immediately drove back to Racine, feeling the failure of Crivitz weighing on her. Her tactics, her detailed profiling, felt more and more like relics of a distant past. She admonished herself for the interview with Evan, for dining with Lonnie, for spending even small amounts of time on herself when her processes themselves were already so time-consuming, so — she hated the word, but had to admit it was true — slow.

Meeting with Jade and Michael did little to make her feel better. They arrived just after nine, both with thumbs swiping intently on oversized phones that glowed in the night. They barely looked up from them and yet they hopped the curb and navigated the winding walkway to the front door. Jade even sidestepped the sidewalk cracks with intention. Ana marveled at their ability to navigate life in such a way, their attention doubly focused and still sharp. It was impressive, and yet it gave Ana a sinking feeling in her stomach.

At the door, they pocketed their phones and greeted Ana with veneration. Jade especially held onto her hand for longer than necessary. She wore a full business suit and Adidas tennis shoes. Michael was tall, upright, his dark hair slicked to one side with pomade — the son of two former agents, and it showed.

Ana let them inside and, in lieu of chairs, they sat on either side of the king bed. "I'm not much for field offices," Ana said by way of apology.

Michael pulled his phone again, but only to include Sergio, who had returned to DC to utilize the FBI's powerful servers there.

"I need facial recognition on this photo," she said, handing it to Jade, who looked at it briefly before Michael took it from her. "The man on the left is Fowler. The right... probably local. I need to know who he is."

"A suspect?"

"No," Ana said. "For his profile. It's coming together, but as you know, building a life takes time."

Michael looked at the polaroid again, flicking it between his fingers like a baseball card between bicycle spokes.

"Let's talk about what you've found," Ana said.

Silence ensued as Jade and Michael glanced to each other. Then Sergio's voice boomed into the room. "I guess I'll start. The answer, if you can't tell, Ana, is not much."

"Not much is better than nothing."

"Sometimes," Michael said. "But with the internet, there's a thousand possible strands and nine hundred ninety-nine of them are dead ends."

"For example," Jade said, her tone high, attempting to buoy the conversation, "I crossed all social media mentions. Taking out what we consider bots, we still have over five million people talking about the Youtopia murderer. Even zeroing in on dangerous language, we're in the hundreds of thousands." She rubbed the toes of her tennis shoes together, then looked up at Ana. "Once it's out of the news cycle, we could get a clearer picture."

"Michael," Sergio said, "anything on the message boards?"

"Too much. Roughly fifteen hundred hackers have laid claim to the murder already. None of them knew Fowler personally. None had any meaningful ties to Wisconsin." He turned directly to Ana. "With a job of this magnitude, you get a lot of bullshit chest-pumping."

"Any crosses with the most wanted list?"

"No. So far, all the major players are silent."

A low hum resonated from Michael's phone, though whether it was feedback or Sergio, Ana couldn't tell.

"We'll keep monitoring," Sergio said. "Watching for a slip. Profiling this guy has been near impossible, circumstances as they are—possibly white, male, reclusive... the usual. With the Healthcare Bill, our best bet on motive is a fight against Youtopia itself. In that case..."

Sergio paused, and into the silence Ana considered all the things he could have said, but likely wouldn't. It was the same irritant that initiated her migraine: the lurking sense that Fowler himself was unimportant to the investigation—a stooge, chosen simply because of his initial connection to Youtopia. The sophistication with which the intruder worked was flawless and instantaneous. He—or she, as they couldn't rule out that possibility—defeated the machine, not Fowler. It meant Ana's work in Crivitz was indeed futile, outdated. It meant the case could be beyond her.

"If that's true," Michael jumped in for Sergio, "we'll hear from the killer again soon."

Jade looked to Ana. Silent moments passed before Ana realized they awaited her instructions. They needed motivation, momentum. A leader.

She stood. "This is the first murder of its kind. That means we're writing the script as we go. It may be a needle in a haystack, but the needle is there. It's our job to find it."

***

Just before midnight, she checked her FamilyMatch account, where Evan had already sent two thank-you notes. Before she could stop herself, she replied to set up a second interview. Just as she sent the request, a different one came to her, directly onto her phone's calendar, for the following Monday at Youtopia Towers: a meeting with Sonya Young.

This revelation, so quick and unexpected, caused her to nearly overlook the message from Michael that immediately followed.

It was urgent. Its relevance beamed at her from the exclamation point encompassed in a thick red triangle. He got a solid facial recognition match on the photo. The man on the other end of the muskie was Holden Martin, father of Terrance Martin.

Terrance Martin. The flamboyant leader of ReaLife. And one of Youtopia's fiercest enemies.

JOSEPH REIN

Carry That Weight

Or: How the Beatles Saved Me from Youtopia (and Consequently Saved My Life)
By Terrance Martin
Originally published in *Barbed Wire Magazine*

WE OPEN ON a young man, late twenties, gaunt to the point of sickly, hair perpetually disheveled and awash in various dyes, this time a mix of purple and a fire-engine red, the effect as though his head is perilously aflame. He sobs to himself in the dark, the LED glow of a charging phone his only light. He has twelve missed messages, both text and voice, from the only two people in the world he might still call friends. They worry because they know. The studio apartment surrounding him is scantily furnished, his refrigerator bare, his unwashed clothes strewn about like roadkill. He is clearly unstable.

He cocks and presses to his temple the .22 held in his right hand. He switches from his right hand to his left, an arbitrary move and yet, his right side is his good side, his side of devil-may-care. At least, this is what his mother always told him, before things went cataclysmic. It has been an unbearable fourteen months, the cap of a trying ten years. He wants to think of something, anything—the mild rain outside, the pain of cracking skin on his fingers, the unfamiliar song on his Bluetooth speaker—but his mind cannot abandon the people he has lost, either to suicide or to Youtopia. John, Winnie, Becks—all now reduced to memories and callous social media reminisces. He remembers Vincent, yes, Vincent, his nostrils inhaling wide as he touched the young man's penis for the first time. So they are all gone, the young man thinks. Soon he will be too.

BUT THEN, PERHAPS that isn't our open. The young man's life hangs in the balance with that .22, but it does similarly at the Atlanta branch of Youtopia just a year later. He has completed Evolution, is scheduled for Immersion in mere hours. The Atlanta branch, he can tell you, seems intent on surpassing the rumors swirling about it: industrial décor, hipster down to its exposed beams and repurposed wood desks and artificial pine smell. It's pristine as well, not an errant pen or stack of papers—no paper anywhere, in fact. He signs innumerable electronic legal documents that float with his touchscreen finger like digital feathers, words and words he does not care to read. He just wants the pain to stop. In the year since the .22, Clint and Rose, his remaining friends who are also in Evolution, have convinced him that Youtopia is preferable to suicide. As if, for exiles like them, these are the only two options. At the time, he agrees.

His technicians open a new door for him this time, the pure white one that says only, omnisciently, *Waiting*. The door leads to a hallway of decade-themed rooms, the first being the 1940s—the earliest decade, the designers have decided, that any soon-to-be Immerser may remember—and goes all the way to the aughts. He passes the '50s, replete with leather jackets and pastel furniture and ash trays with real stubbed butts. The jukebox transitions clunkily from Elvis to Patsy Cline. With just a few steps, he passes history he knows but not intimately, not until the '80s, when the stark neons and Atari tings of his youth shock him into memory recall. The '90s room—the most populated by far—is shockingly reminiscent of his bedroom as a teen, part flannel grunge and part kitschy electric pop, the juxtaposition of moody angst and its bubbly denial. Stacks of *Mad* sit on a side table, accompanied by the smell of Preferred Stock cologne. A Cranberries CD plays from a boombox. It is so clever he almost laughs. He recognizes the ingenious play to his nostalgic desires— these rooms will, in effect, be the places to which he will now devote the remainder of his Youtopian life.

But something is off. His sense memory elicits not a fondness, not a gentle pull, but instead a forceful, unsettling shove of un-belonging. The room recalls to him the oft-forgotten worst of the '90s, the racial turmoil and Princess Diana and AIDS, always the lingering threat of AIDS, even as a closeted teen. He feels that, if he has had a happiest time of his life, this is decidedly not it.

So instead, he retreats backward and, inexplicably, with some determination that he can only later describe as kismet, he turns into the '60s room. It sits mostly empty and welcoming. On a muted television, the Professor begins the Sisyphean climb of explaining one of his illogical creations to Gilligan. The couches are draped with wild, illusory patterns in tangerine and aqua. The tiered coffee table's top shelf attempts to defy gravity. He steps around the ruddy shag carpet to the center of the room.

The three people here are all older than him, and two are visibly ill. One, a woman with poorly-dyed black hair, lets fly a phlegm-filled cough. One of the other men offers a handkerchief that she accepts without word. In that moment, that very act of non-recognition, the young man notices the downcast eyes, the shuffling hands of those *Waiting*. The melancholy. Strangers in a strange place, sharing a strange, twisted, similar and yet all too separate fate. The Supremes slowly fade, vacuuming with them all sound, all motion. It seems as though the room, like the décor itself, sticks in time.

The young man—and if it's not painfully clear by now, that young man is me—trills in desperation, a trembling echo sounding from a depth within him that he has never before summoned. His fear surpasses any he felt with the .22, and it is into this feeling that he hears, through some undeniably divine providence, the first dynamic piano notes of a forgotten song.

I WAS NOT an unhappy child. Despite childhood's challenges, its confusions and isolation, I felt adequately loved. My parents were regimentally Evangelical but otherwise kind. My father collected our vacationing neighbors' mail; my mother donated canned goods weekly to a rotating list of shelters. I had no siblings, but was involved in many charity events and sports gatherings with kids my age. My largest adolescent tragedy involved my dog Buster and the pickup that crippled him. Into all this normality, then, trounced puberty, and the stark realization that I was not normal, that when my parents and pastors spoke of the union of a man and woman as primal, as essential, my wanton desires allied to the unholy and grotesque. Simply put, I wanted to touch men, and wanted them to touch me.

I stumbled into my first sexual encounter with Vincent in the high school locker room after a junior varsity baseball game. It was awkward and suffocating, and after, I only wanted more. Ultimately, Vincent turned on me, flogged me in that very same locker room, left my face battered like bruised fruit.

I don't blame him.

I do, however, blame my unsympathetic father. After seeing my face, he called every official at our school, demanded a meeting with Vincent's parents. He wanted an audience to hear how, yes, his son may have been effeminate, but he was as much a man as anyone. He needed to set this Vince kid, the entire record, straight. Our principal offered to connect my father with the superintendent, and since I saw the exact destination of *that* hopeless road, I decided, in the flash of a second, to instead steer us over the guardrails.

"It's because he fucked me," I said. I remember the words, my deadpan inflection, so clearly. I thought that the harder I threw the dagger, the likelier chance of it piercing straight through his ideologies and hitting his true, true heart. "A few times. But then he couldn't handle his own shame, so he beat me up."

For a minute, my father stood in a predictable paralysis. When the superintendent's voice murmured from the phone, my father hung it up in a flash, as though it were hot to the touch. He stood so long that I was able to circle through every possible response, from total expulsion from their house to — as implausible as it seemed — extreme acceptance and love. "I never want to see your queer face again," intermixed with, "I just want you to love someone the way we love you." His eyes seemed to suggest that his own thoughts fluctuated along this axis as well, undecided on where to land.

I was wrong.

Instead of speaking, he turned to me and, faster than I'd ever seen him move, struck me clear on my temple. I fell to my knees and he pounced atop me, let the brunt of his bearish weight crush my body into the hardwood floor. One arm moved, deliberately and with a menacing purpose I will never forget, to bind my hands above my head. With his other he thundered down on my face, his mealy fist connecting in the same places Vincent's had just hours before.

My eyes felt aflame. I smelled only metallic blood pooling in my nostrils. My vision blurred and then cut completely. I feared he blinded me. I don't know how long this continued, because I lost consciousness.

My face ultimately healed, though I still have wispy scars along my eyes and a crook in my nose. What never healed, though, was the gay. No amount of psychiatry and medication and months of conversion therapy — countless hours subjected to the female form and its degradation — could cure me of my disease. It was the devil that my father, and Vincent, could never beat out of me.

TEN YEARS LATER, I was twenty-seven and gay in a world that seemed on the up. My then-boyfriend Raul and I had our vestiges of acceptance, our restaurants, our clothes shops and parks. We lived on the fringes and reveled in the sheer rebellion of ourselves. Being alive, loving, was a political insurrection, and it felt good. But then Newton's insufferable third law kicked in, and of course our enemies became more emboldened.

To wit: a hirsute man on the street accosted me and Raul to say, "Listen, you gays can do what you want. Really. Fags are cool with me. But take it inside. No one wants to see that shit."

Though our proposed marriage would be legal, we could not find a suitable religious entity that would perform the ceremony inside its walls—Raul's requirement, not mine. On one side of the argument, there was me: "I don't give a shit where we marry! It could be in a puddle of piss in some redneck's basement!" On the other side, Raul: "This is important to me, to my family. You can't even see past yourself to understand that." Then repeat the track. Eventually, Raul left.

And with him went all of our friends. This was a much more devastating loss to me than were my parents, for obvious reasons. I spent three weeks in a grief-stricken, alcoholic torpor. When I emerged, the rose-colored glasses smashed from my eyes, I discovered the world as it truly was: under the guise of religious freedom of speech, that hirsute man and his ideologies had gained massive ground. Rejection of my basic humanity again became normalized. A small-town coffee shop refused me service, and the whole place went mum. They agreed with the bigoted barista. Or if they didn't, they were unwilling to speak out.

I retreated to alcohol, then even harsher substances. I spent days in dim-lit bars with strangers, losing contact with anyone worthwhile to me in the process. I was alone, more than ever before. Inevitably, I had a breakdown.

Of this I am no longer ashamed—one shouldn't be—but at the time, staring into a urinal filled with ice and my own vomit, I saw nothing but the deep, yawning hole down which I was falling. It seemed impossible to land. It's one thing to recognize one's own endless pain; it's entirely another to overcome it. In many ways, I still haven't. But living on the edge does one thing: it helps you recognize its presence, and to recognize when you've finally, finally stepped back from it. When the pleasures of small moments reappear and life begins again to matter. Raul's overconfidence and religious piety were petty. The barista was a prick. My life wasn't yet worth living, sure, but at least I saw that it one day might be.

BACK IN *WAITING,* the young man's body is pummeled with the vibrant yet simple treble clef opening of "Golden Slumbers," the leadoff gem of a trio on the B-side of the Beatles' *Abbey Road*. The inaugural lyrics suggest a path home that no longer exists. You can see this immediately resonating with the young man. McCartney then follows with a request for his pretty darling to sleep while he sings his lullaby, and in a complete and utter heart shock, in the way only great art can do, the words feel as though they are written just for the young man. It is no longer a song admired by millions. It is a simple lullaby from a parent the young man has never had. Terrance. Yes, you. Sleep, pretty darling.

This all might suggest that the song is actually easing the man's transition to Youtopia. After all, many people have compared Immersion to a waking dream, to an eternal nap—Youtopia itself as the most golden of slumbers to ever fill an Immerser's eyes. But then McCartney wails— absolutely wails out—about the smiles that will be there, awaiting you when you rise, and that notion of rising, of simply waking up, has a second but just as equal shock. The young man realizes that, if he enters Youtopia, he will have no smiles outside of his own mind. He will have no one. He will never wake. Suddenly, McCartney's lullaby becomes a harrowing caution against the very thing he is about to do. He looks at the older people around him; they ignore the music, not experiencing an ounce of the spiritual transcendence he feels. They are on a march not to some perfect world, but to death.

As "Golden Slumbers" seamlessly transitions to "Carry That Weight"—as John, George, and Ringo join the anthem that might as well be the young man's life—he has already transformed. He recognizes that, when writing, John and Paul must have been filled with some fantastic, phantasmagoric foresight into his own future. They chant to him some half a century into the future that, yes, he will bear his burdens, but he must do so—he must always—and despite that, he must persevere.

As a final gut punch, confirmation of what he already knows, he hears the first lines of "The End" among the hammering guitar strings. Will McCartney be in his dreams tonight? Who will he dream about tonight? Raul? Vincent? His father? Someone infinitely more deserving? What of the hundreds, the thousands of people he has not yet met? New boyfriends and mentors and loves, people whose lives with which he is destined to intersect? Or people whom, some fifty years later, his own art may touch in some profound way? People to whom he may appear in an unknown premonition?

THE FINAL WORDS on love, like a Proustian madeleine, open a repressed memory of his father. He recalls with lucid clarity one of his father's many lectures on rock music, the only subject on which the surly man ever read a book. At the time, his father's words bounced off of him, like so many tennis balls off the well-strung rackets of Pete Sampras on their television. The smell of his mother's puff pastry wafted in from the oven, the sound of splashing water echoed from the sink, and from his father's Yamaha receiver, he heard McCartney's painfully eloquent voice amidst the piano.

"You know, Terry," his father said, using the nickname the young man had never, ever preferred, "this was the last album they recorded. They all wanted out. Shit, there were times they could barely sit in the same room!"

His father scratched the chest hair spilling from his collar like potato vines. "Despite it, they still made one of the greatest rock albums of all time." He held his hands in the air as though they might capture the music hanging there. "They made *this*."

Sitting in that faux-'60s room in Youtopia Atlanta, the young man finally sees wisdom in something that came from his father's mouth. He sees that the Beatles recorded their most complete, symbiotic — in a word, their best — album even when they knew they were finished with each other. Out of the conflicts surrounding their very existence came the hard-hitting trebles of "Golden Slumbers," the recall in "Carry That Weight," and the solemn, peaceful crescendo of "The End."

The young man has always hated the Beatles. They are his father. Yet here they arrive, at the most crucial of moments, to keep him from making the biggest mistake of his life.

YOUTOPIA IS THE most effective antidepressant the world has ever seen. This comes from someone well versed in them — Prozac, Fluoxetine, Escitalopram. I've tried them all. Just like these, Youtopia is meant to take our pain, our struggles and strife, and minimize their importance. It's meant to create a complacent, drug-induced white noise over one's mind, a perpetual hum. The thing about antidepressants, though, is that you never stop hearing that hum. It reminds you that you're just left-of-center. Your life isn't exactly *this*. You lose the lows, yes, but you also lose the chance at incredible highs, at frantic leaps on the heart monitor, at actual fucking living.

I knew, in Youtopia, I would never again relive moments borne of spontaneity. I would never again be thunderstruck by masterpieces like "Golden Slumbers/Carry That Weight/The End," or other storm clouds of art that shot down lightning at just the right moment. My tongue would never appreciate the foods I'd never before enjoyed: uncooked onions, quinoa, blue cheese. My life would be full of happy moments with Vincent, or Raul, or worse, with my father, forcing my mind to forget that they are the villains of this story. They are not my saviors. I would never meet someone new, someone I may very well need. That person is out there somewhere—of that, I am certain. My only fear is that he is lost to Youtopia. That he already is gone.

Put simply: life in Youtopia is, I recognize now and forever, the end of chance. It's the "All Thumbs" of existence. You get what you want and nothing else. This pigeonholing is just one of the ways in which our society, and Youtopia, attempts to present the idealized world through a microscopic lens, a television tuned to only one channel. We rarely stop to consider why we tuned into it in the first place.

Put another way: Youtopia closes our already shrinking minds. We become insular. We become my parents, or the man on the street who demanded Vincent and I hide our intimacies. We become the very people who drove me to consider Youtopia in the first place. I implore you: the world has too many of these assholes already. We need less, not more, of the intolerant, of the awful, of the real Devil.

To all those people, I say: maybe you should be the ones to fuck off to Youtopia. You can have your locked fantasies, your close-minded whims. You can piss on your subconscious all you want, without causing harm to any of us left who truly care, who truly want to live.

For the rest of us, the survivors, the real people: we are living! We are creating! We are open to changes in the world and ourselves. We have golden slumbers in our eyes. We do not know who will be in our dreams tonight. And in the end, we'll take all the love we can possibly make, our love and the love the rest leave behind. It belongs to us now. It is ours, and ours alone.

***

*Terrence Martin is the founder of ReaLife Church, a national non-denominational religious group that endorses the sanctity of natural human life.

Chapter 3

"This your first time?"

Ana turned to the younger, overweight woman standing at her side. She wore narrow black glasses, a shaved head, and a tranquil look of expectation.

"Yes," Ana answered.

"Knew it. I can always tell the newbies."

They both looked to the massive, impressive walls of the ReaLife Ministry of Los Angeles. From the outside, the building had appeared conventional, a repurposed Catholic church with grandiose entryways and spiral cathedrals, and few changes other than new paint and rearranged stained glass. It was nothing grander than the refurbished hundreds spattered across the East coast, the architectural equivalent of an aging woman under heavy makeup and plastic surgeries. But inside, the building became vibrantly alive. It had been completely gutted, its walls whitewashed and spotless, its original hardwoods shimmering with lacquer. From the ceiling hung innumerable candelabras, ones Ana swore were electric until a candle flame shuddered and then blew out. Lighting them alone must've taken hours. There were no seats, just runners indicating where one might not stand so as to leave an aisle.

Past the throngs of people—all who'd arrived early like Ana—stood the altar, which was cleared out as well, more theater stage than pulpit. At its heart, a ponytailed man in a tie-dyed shirt and brown corduroy pants wielded an expensive guitar. He strummed a few chords, tuning mostly for show, and then launched into a folksy version of Elvis's "Devil in Disguise."

"Follow me," the woman said, taking Ana's hand with a quick, unearned intimacy. She introduced herself as Gertrude. "Get ready for your life to change."

Ana wanted a feel for the place while stagnant, without the thrum and hullabaloo, but scores of people had already taken root, and more arrived by the minute. The doors proved a roving carousel of the young and old alike, of people spanning the ethnic gamut, of the formal and the absurdly casual. Just beside them, a man in a full suit offered his phone up to a woman in a one-piece bathing suit. Ana wondered briefly at this naked intimacy, so shortly removed from a world pandemic, but also undoubtedly influenced by it. Separation from human contact for such a long time had caused people to flock together now, to enjoy the bumping of bodies, the casual passing of sweat and breath — a willed, forced proximity.

"Is it always this busy?" Ana asked, wondering at what point they would stop people from entering, what fire codes they must've routinely broken. She wondered with skepticism what control they, or Terrance, had over the burgeoning crowd.

"Yes and no," Gertrude said. "It's never dead, that's for sure. It's the murder, probably. And the government crap. Terrance will have plenty to say about *that*."

"I'm not sure it matters what he thinks," Ana said.

Gertrude looked at her as though betrayed, but then seemed to remember they were strangers, that they had only just met moments earlier. "Another sign of a newbie," she said. "Once you see, you'll understand. With Terrance, it *always* matters."

Gertude continued through the crowd. She waved at various people and engaged in brief, giddy conversations. Ana stood behind, introducing herself by first name when necessary, simply listening when possible. Through the conversations, she gleaned that Gertrude was a regular but newer herself, a lavish follower with views too devout for many other congregants. She wore her *carpe diem* sentimentality like a jumpsuit, tight and revealing. Ana understood this galvanized sense of renewed purpose, especially for those who had found a new religion. But listening to Gertrude's falsetto enthusiasm brought about a pressure in Ana's forehead, the threat of another migraine. More and more, she had difficulty enduring people who denied the simple fact that yes, some days were to be seized, to be won, to be lived to the fullest, days like the opening miles of a marathon, where one was filled with gusto and energy and the early, jittery stages of possibility, of believing one could simply run forever, but that in all reality, more days were like the middle miles, strenuous but more tedious, more foot-to-pavement repetition of the same, always the same, or those days, especially as one aged, that resembled the final miles, the body fatigue, the mental weariness, the fight for enough air, the desire, ultimately, to grit one's teeth and just get through it, to just reach the finish line.

As they waited, Ana noticed many solicitors pacing about with ease. Two Gideons in suits handed Ana a mini-Bible; a bearded man offered her a pamphlet on gun control advocacy. In succession, as though planned, two women proffered pamphlets with opposing views on abortion. Many parishioners seemed accustomed to this mass of paper, turning the glossy pages into fans or makeshift flower bouquets for their children. A few performed impressively detailed feats of origami. Against all the paper, Ana began to yearn for her phone, where messages could be extricated with just a swipe, where the opinions of others could be sorted, filed away, or even relegated unseen to junk folders. She looked at her phone, where sixteen such notifications awaited, four of them from Evan. In each, he apologized for taking so long to reply. Another interview, he said, would be fantastic. Consequently, he planned a trip to the Midwest, to visit a relative, and to finally see Wrigley Field. He wondered if, instead, she would like to meet up in person.

"I hear they're just waiting for the murderer to strike again," Ana overheard Gertrude say. "I mean, this killer's clearly smarter than the authorities."

Gertrude's small circle of spectators looked around them. Ana's face was spread about the internet, and so she wondered if any of these people might recognize her, if Gertrude's words were themselves a passive-aggressive slight. A thin, freckled woman eyed Ana with mistrust, but before the conversation could go any further, the guitarist's heartfelt solo on the Rolling Stones' "Sympathy for the Devil" was abruptly cut by the booming, intense first chords of a pop song. Gertrude's face illumined as she brought her hands together, and all turned to the stage. At first, Ana couldn't place the song. The crowd clapped in unison; Ana couldn't tell if this was common, couldn't place what about this religious ceremony was ritualistic and what improvised.

Just as Beyonce's vocals kicked in, as Ana recognized the song, a lithe, powerful man burst from behind a black paper screen, colored theater lights bespeckling him in cadence with his choreographed steps. He wore leather pants and a collared shirt unbuttoned past his chest, his hair spiked and unmoving. Terrance Martin.

The crowd pressed forward as though caught in the gravitational pull of Terrance's orbit. They cheered and fawned as, all across the stage, Terrance jumped and fist-pumped, shouting the chorus of "I'm a survivor!" when it arrived, encouraging his spellbound audience to join.

Ana spotted Gertrude a few rows ahead. She slid, pried, forced her way through, earning scowls as she went. She finally reached Gertrude and tapped, then shook, her shoulder.

"Is this normal?" Ana shouted.

"Pretty much!" Gertrude replied with jollity. "Isn't he just the best?"

After more fluid dance steps, Terrance approached center stage and the song faded out. He raised his hands in the air like a priest and, with more control but still full of latent enthusiasm, he boomed into his headset microphone, "It's time to dream..."

"In ReaLife!" the crowd finished.

Terrance clasped his hands together, his demeanor assuming that of a caring relative, his posture all unctuous performance, his smile knowing. "What a joyous day to celebrate being alive, being here with you. Today is particularly special for all of us. But look at me, getting ahead of myself as always." He stepped back now, indulging in a self-deprecating smirk that the crowd ate up. "I'm very excited about today! Can't you tell? First, let us engage our Higher Power."

Close to twenty minutes of scripted actions followed. A string of young men and women brought Terrance texts to read from, not just a Bible and a Koran but also Plato's *Republic* and Descartes' *Passions of the Soul*. Another handed him a tablet from which he read jarring newspaper headlines, enumerating the week's atrocities worldwide and the lack of action taken upon them. Ana expected scathing Youtopia editorials, but those related to the company only speculated on when the Senate would vote on the Healthcare Bill.

The guitarist returned and delivered a slow, preening rendition of the Beatles trio of songs that Terrance referenced in his now infamous *Barbed Wire* article. The unique ceremony, unlike any other religious service Ana had attended, included much that Terrance stole from his Catholic surroundings. As he asked the congregation to give thanks to our ancestors, to all those humans who suffered and persevered in life, he requested that those who were able kneel.

The curtains drew down. It seemed an intermission would follow, but Terrance stepped in front of the curtain as the stage was blanketed behind him. He extended a hand to those closest to him, made and held eye contact as though greeting old friends. A few rows behind, the scratch of a lighter came, followed by the unmistakable smell of marijuana. Many around her pulled out their cellphones to record video.

"My friends, here in the crowd, watching us at home, at work, wherever you are..." He crouched, sat, draped his legs over the edge of the stage. "I know exactly how you are feeling. Uncertain. Confused. Frightened even.

"You may already know someone who has thrown away their life, has decimated their soul by abandoning us, by abandoning real life. This may be a loved one, an old acquaintance, a friend of a friend. Or maybe you've simply read the stories, and are heartsick just imagining that such abandonment may soon hit closer to home. As of this moment, thirty-seven percent of the United States population knows or has met someone who now resides in that living Hell. That number, in itself, is staggering.

"But when this Healthcare Bill becomes law—and it will, I assure you—that number will skyrocket. In less than a year, the projections are as high as ninety-seven percent. Ninety-seven! That's you. That's me. That's all of us."

Terrance paused, looked down into his cupped hands. He sucked in the deep breath of a stage actor inhaling some great grief. Ana looked down her row and behind her, taking in as many faces as the cramped space allowed. They all, each one, still retained the same jubilance they had when Terrance first arrived, some even more. They awaited the positive spin Ana expected to follow.

"It's easy to blame our politicians for the scores who will join the ranks of the ignominious *Immersers*." Terrance pronounced the last word with a seething hiss. "Easier still to blame those who ignorantly stand by, accepting Youtopia as just another part of life. Remember: we all have had trials and tribulations, traumatic losses. We are told that life doesn't have to *be* like this. We all know the allure.

"For Youtopia is not just a company, my friends. Not just a maleficent parasite of life. Let's consider, for a moment, a celestial entity who seduces people in whetted whispers. Who promises wealth and carnal pleasures and all of those hedonistic luxuries that appeal to the basest human desires. Who promises to deliver to man powers only available to the Higher Power. Who promises relief from worldly hardship only to inflict it eternally on his duped prey.

"He is none other than Lucifer. Beelzebub. Shaitan. Mara. And those who follow him, damned as they may be, are all cast under the same spell. The Devil lives among us, my friends. Her name is Sonya Young."

The crowd erupted in jeers, louder than any previous response. Terrance allowed the anger to build, encouraged it by closing his eyes. Half a minute later, it finally reached a crescendo. Then, as it declined, Terrance lowered his hands, commanding the crowd.

"Perhaps you still doubt. You think, Youtopia is bad, sure, but the Devil? Terrance, you're reaching a bit, aren't you? A bit off your game today?"

A few audible shouts followed, all unnecessary reassurances. Terrance thanked them with a smile, but he was on a roll now, his blithe talk fixed and his questions rhetorical. He talked over them, not responding to the calls or cries, allowing others in the crowd to reprimand the fractious.

"I say, look to history. Whenever the world does something so against the Higher Power's will, They respond in kind. Is it science only that can explain Covid, that causes raging wildfires and hurricanes and floods that consume the Earth? If you need a more pointed sign of such pestilence, for proof that Youtopia and this Healthcare Bill are indeed under attack by the Higher Power, then look no further than its first plague: the murder of Charles Fowler. That the Higher Power would rather see us dead than give our lives over to that Devil, we already know. But now, They have sent a messenger to wrest back the lost. They have bestowed upon us an archangel, a Gabriel, a Muhammad. This messenger has taken Charles Fowler's life, it's true. But he has done so in the service of the Higher Power. *And do not fear those who kill the body but cannot kill the soul: but rather, fear him who can destroy both soul and body in Hell.*"

The room took on an eerie silence. People looked from Terrance to one another and back again.

"And on this day," he continued, "a wonderful day to rejoice in life, we have a special visitor to our congregation. She is a law enforcement agent of the highest caliber. You may recognize her name, if not her face. Now you will know both."

Ana felt a weight press down on her shoulder, a sinking feeling that turned out to be the broad hand of a large, slightly hunchbacked man behind her. Ana slipped from his hand, but the man smiled disarmingly and pointed behind them to a large flatscreen against the back wall on which she saw herself. She immediately scanned the ceiling for the camera, tried to match her sight line with the screen, but all she saw were chandeliers and curved white peaks. Those surrounding Ana battled between turning to her and watching her on the screen. In the bottom corner of the screen, Gertrude silently mouthed *Holy shit!* to her neighbor.

"Anabel Downer. FBI agent leading the charge against our archangel, and our esteemed guest. Anabel, won't you join me on stage?" Terrance stepped to the edge nearest Ana, and immediately the crowd parted. The camera panned back.

Ana recognized the move, common with nearly every powerful man she had met: an attempt to knock her off-center. As a powerful woman, she was belittled, proffered illegal substances, sexually harassed, all in the name of gaining some predominance without which these men couldn't seem to communicate. She wanted to laugh, to sigh, to invite all these men past and present into a confined space, if only to show them, like a funhouse mirror, the absurd and grotesque reflection of themselves. But in this moment, she needed to react, to decide whether or not to play into Terrance's power grab.

"Mr. Martin," she called in as loud a voice as she could muster. "Our discussion is surely a private matter."

The congregation turned to Terrance, wondering how he would respond. A showman, a performer of the highest caliber, he possessed the improvisational skills to turn any situation into a heartening one. He laughed, clasped his hands together as though Ana had responded exactly the way he intended.

"And nothing could be less private than this moment! We completely understand, don't we? I look forward to our discussion. And we—I mean all of us, everyone in this room—are very much rooting for you. Because this Gabriel, whoever he may be, has every right to be exposed, to show his face to the world. Authority figures like yourself may not treat him so kindly, Anabel. But history surely will."

***

The hunchbacked man guided Ana through two guarded doors before reaching Terrance. At the second, her guide said something muted into a minute earpiece, some archaic, Gaelic-sounding phrase that let Ana through.

Compared to the cathedral, Terrance's dressing room appeared simple, bland even, its furniture threadbare, its walls and carpets beige. It smelled of expensive cologne. Terrance stood at its one oval mirror, wiping away cheek rouge with a towel.

"That stereotype about gay men loving makeup?" he said, tossing the towel to an indiscriminate spot on the ground. "Not this gay man."

"I rarely wear any myself."

"I noticed," he said, though his eyes never moved from himself. "A sign of confidence. You don't bow to social norms."

"I don't have the time."

Terrance presented her a seat on a ragged sectional couch patterned in vines and roses long since drained of their original red. "It was my father's," he said of the couch, sitting on the end opposite, sidling into the armrest with familiarity. "Contempt and nostalgia are an oddly potent concoction."

As she sat, the guard exited and closed the door behind him. Taped to its backside were a slew of newspaper articles, many printed from online sources, all with headlines about Fowler's death. From mainstream to dark web, the *New York Times* to Pushnet, many of them showed photos of Fowler in his middle age. Ana couldn't help but picture his smooth, pallid corpse, like an aged porcelain doll.

"You have a fascination with Mr. Fowler's killer," she said.

"How can I not? ReaLife is shaped by the fate of Youtopia." Terrance draped one leg across the other. "Oh, I get how it looks. Documentation. Souvenirs. Serial killers do so love to see their work in print. But let me ask: does that little FBI file of yours pin me as a killer?"

Ana didn't reply.

Terrance lowered his chin, shot out a mocking hand. "Please. You have profiles on *every*one important. You had your claws into me way before Chuckie Fowler."

"I'm not here to talk about that," Ana said. "I just want to know about your connection to Fowler. Did you know him when you were young?"

"I knew *of* him. One of my father's many fishing chums. All cigars and Windsor Canadian and the Green. Bay. Packers."

"Did you ever speak with him?"

"Likely. The man made no imprint on me whatsoever. I was a closeted teen in Podunk mutherfucking America. I had no time for my father's vanilla friends."

"Unless those friends imposed."

Terrance sighed. He pulled out a phone and took a selfie with an exaggerated look of boredom, replete with pouted lips and rolling eyes. "This will go a lot smoother if you say what you mean, honey. What you mean to say is: unless Chuckie F. got his rocks off on some friend's queer son. Unless that."

Again, Ana stayed silent.

"First," Terrance said, "not all gay people were sexually assaulted as kids. Most of us are just gay."

"I didn't mean to—"

"Secondly, I wonder if you—"

"This will go a lot smoother," Ana said, rising, "if you stop interrupting me. And if you drop the victim act."

Terrance typed into his phone. Within a minute, the hunchbacked man returned with a cafeteria-style tray of food: a kale salad, a bowl of granola, and a bottle of kombucha.

"Jimmy John's has nothing on my man here," Terrance said. "You want anything?"

"I would like to take a look at your phone, your tablets, any other devices you might have."

"Ha!" Terrance said, bits of granola spitting from his lips. "Not unless you have a warrant in that hideous housewife satchel of yours."

"If you have nothing to hide, it shouldn't matter."

"I never said I had nothing to hide." He took a long drink of his kombucha, then belched like a teenage boy. "We all do, don't we? Things we don't want popping up in FBI files, even if they have nothing to do with murder?" Without eating any of the salad, he rose with the tray and carelessly tossed it on the dressing table. "Will you be staying in sunny Cali for a while?"

"No."

"A shame. You'd like it here. We have the most enthusiastic people, more money than we can spend, and men. Jesus triple-jumping Christ, the men. I didn't start this for them, but I tell you: to the victor go the spoils."

The hunchbacked man stood beside Ana as though she might suddenly attack. Terrance rolled his neck and popped his knuckles. It was entirely possible that he harbored no real ill will toward Youtopia, that he had built ReaLife only for his own self-aggrandizement, for fortune and fame. Religious figures worldwide had swindled the same. But there was something underhanded, something slippery in the way he'd anticipated Ana's arrival, her questions. He could have taken down the newspaper clippings. Or he might have put them up just for her, with the intention of obfuscating her case. With performers like him, it was nearly impossible, from a brief interview, to know how much of the person was surface glitz, and how much was real.

Ana stood to leave. "I'll be in touch. Please do inform me if you plan to leave the area."

"I'm leaving the area in T-minus..." He pantomimed a long look at a nonexistent watch on his wrist. "I'll give you my itinerary, if that'll float your boat."

The hunchbacked man opened the door as Ana approached. She was nearly gone when Terrance said, "It's not me, love, but I sure as shit am rooting for the guy. If he can take them down from the inside, then all the better. But if not, well..." He paused for effect, his eyes adrift in an illusory, idyllic future. "Our numbers grow by the second."

***

Fowler's funeral was held a week after his death. The weather turned for the better, the wind warm, the buds blooming and grasses sprouting, the spring sun high and penetrating. The Crivitz cemetery was arranged in concentric circles, the oldest graves inward and the paved path spiraling toward its edges. Few spots remained, and soon the lots would abut the adjacent roads—no place left for the dead. Fowler's lot landed near the center, bought decades ago alongside his parents and a plot for Carol. The rectangular hole into which Fowler would be placed seemed smaller than it should have been.

A high canopy loomed above the spot. The mortician had shaved Fowler's face and returned his hair to its former short wave, though his body still lacked the creases, the extra weight of the ten years he'd been Immersed. The time for Fowler's service—high noon—passed, and yet the priest, an elderly, bald man with sunspots on his head, did not begin. He drank from a bottle of water and awaited mourners who never arrived. Carol was there, and the high school principal, but only two others, both in-laws attending more in support of Carol than Charles.

Ana had only returned in hopes of profiling some of the attendees: often, killers would frequent the funerals of their victims to witness the finality of their work. In this case, the impulse would be particularly strong, since the killer never came in physical contact with Fowler. Ana sneaked photos of the two family members, but feared nothing would come of them.

When the priest asked if anyone would like to say a word about Charles, the ensuing silence pressed upon them all, even Ana, with a strange weight. When they closed the casket, Carol did not cry. As they lowered him down, Ana's mind inexplicably flashed to visions of her own eventual funeral, to a similarly sparse affair—Lonnie, certainly, maybe Sergio and Bruce, alongside a few former mentors and local agents. She imagined not a single shed tear.

***

Back in Racine, Ana opened her tablet to an email from Michael. He tabulated the news stories from the day, in case there was anything relevant. The funeral got no headway in national news circles. Like Fowler's body, the case itself was subsumed, buried, by the weight of the Healthcare Bill and other world news. Sonya gave one interview, her quotes pointed and perfect. Ana found her own name mentioned in only one article, and they misspelled her first name, adding an extra *n*.

Social media turned its focus as well, directing any Youtopia mentions at senators from swing states. The speed at which Fowler's death both entered and exited the news cycle felt impressive and staggering.

On Facebook — and against all her professional impulses — Ana typed into the search bar the name she probably should have long before: Evan Lancaster. A common name, but she found him under the same profile picture as his FamilyMatch account, the one with the seductive half-smile and controlled tsunami of black hair. His account, and others on Instagram and TikTok, were unsurprisingly public. His photos varied from slapdash to professional, from uncentered selfies at concerts to serious headshots with blurred natural backdrops. He had a sister who appeared in many; she seemed a softer, less pointed version of him. He liked coffee shops and skateboarding — with numerous photos of scars to prove it — and soccer and rum drinks. He read young adult novels. In 2021, he posted a string of hyper-critical, politicized rants about mask mandates, but seemed otherwise reserved. He seemed a decent person.

***

The smell of the cheap American restaurant lambasted her first: an odd mixture of old leather and burned bacon. Past peak hours, the waitstaff bare, the restaurant had only a few patrons who sat untended in booths along the window. Empty tables lay unbussed of their half-eaten oval plates. Salt shakers were tipped, water spills unwiped. One booth leaked coffee creamer onto its bench.

She'd invited Evan to a late dinner, a choice she now regretted. At this moment, she could think of no worse place in which to plan her future.

A woman appearing to be the hostess approached, but instead of greeting Ana, she pulled a *PLEASE SEAT YOURSELF* sign from behind the podium.

Ana turned to leave, to flee back to the safety of her hotel room, to write Evan an apologetic note. She would thank him for his consideration and then say a final goodbye, would drop FamilyMatch altogether because this just wasn't right. The halogen lights and noxious smells of this festering restaurant exposed all the problems in her foolish endeavor. It all felt off.

But before she could escape, the door's overhead bells jingled and Evan entered.

He stopped, set his feet, shed his spring jacket and smiled, showing dimples Ana hadn't noticed before. He stood shorter than she'd imagined. She immediately registered other things she couldn't get through the screen: a scar just below his bottom lip; faint shimmering streaks of near-blue in his hair; the piercing green of his eyes. To her relief, he looked less like Paul in person.

Ana expected formalities, niceties, the sales pitch from the outset, as his appearance, his manner, did in some way suggest a jewelry salesman. Instead, he placed his coat on the wooden hanger near the carnival-red gumball machine, pointed to the sign the hostess had just placed, and said, "Don't mind if we do."

He wandered toward the middle tables, excusing himself past curmudgeonly patrons with a politician's flair. He waved, finger-gunned, and yet somehow, the place warmed to his charisma. An elderly woman snickered behind her coffee. He seemed ready to occupy the middlemost table, center stage, but Ana hurried ahead and redirected him to the only clean booth across the room. She slid in as far as her bench allowed. Beside their table hung a black-and-white photo of the very same booth, dated 1968. The upholstery was the same faded maroon, the napkins folded in the same tented triangles, as though the booth itself had frozen through the decades.

Evan immediately grabbed menus from behind the condiments and scrolled a finger down its glossy pages. He peered at the descriptions with a devout interest, turning the ingredient lists about in his mouth as though the sound of the words themselves — dried cranberries and refried beans and buttermilk — would somehow foretell their tastes.

"Were you ever so hungry," he said, head still in his menu, "that every single thing sounds good?"

Ana contemplated this. "No."

Evan laughed. He looked up and around them, as though surveying the restaurant for the first time. "How did you land on this place? From your profile, you seemed... I don't know... different."

"Not a family diner person?"

"Classier, I guess. This is one hundred percent a dive."

As she passed by, the hostess from before — who was apparently a waitress, the only waitress — snickered in agreement. She took their order; Evan chose two separate plates, Ana a salad.

"I've done this a few times before," Evan said as the waitress fled. "The other women all chose bars."

"I don't know what I'm doing."

"No, no, it's not like there's some script we have to—"

"No," Ana interjected. "I mean, here. With you. I don't know why I've come this far."

Suddenly, and without provocation, her stomach surged up into her throat, a stinging sensation that coated her eyes with the beginnings of tears. She looked down to her lap, afraid to see them fall, afraid to cry after so many years, to let it out in front of this man of all people, a surrogate who was handsome and nice enough but was really here for one purpose.

Then again, she was no better. She had one purpose as well—the distant hope that she might in some miniscule, fractional way gain back part of what she had lost. It was all too much.

"Just a sec," Evan said. He stood, walked back across the restaurant toward the exit. He grabbed his coat and fled the building, but came back a minute later, his hands clasped around something Ana couldn't see. When he sat back down, he dropped onto the table a pack of cigarettes.

"You could use one, yes?"

"You can't smoke in here. Anywhere, really."

"Oh, come now," Evan said, raising the pack. "If there's anywhere you *can* smoke, it's here."

Ana hadn't smoked a cigarette since college, but she took one. Evan lit hers and then his own. She found it oddly quieting, the waft of smoke masking the smells around her, the singular focus on the burning end replacing the flood inside her. The nicotine coursed hot through her blood. Before she realized it, she had finished it.

When the food arrived, Evan devoured his with adolescent abandon. Ana never liked eating with strangers—the gaping mouths, the carnal chewing, the strange intimacy—but for some reason, Evan's appetite felt palatable, refreshing even. She wished she felt that hungry. With her fork, she tossed the salad anew more than ate it.

Her phone buzzed on the table: Lonnie, likely wanting to harass her about Evan, about not keeping contact. She ignored it.

"You know," Evan said, his mouth full of French dip sandwich, "in some circles, that would mean you pay for dinner."

"I can't remember a meal that my phone didn't interrupt."

"That's depressing."

Evan had so far divided his attention between his two plates, but he focused now on the left one, chicken fried steak and mashed potatoes. His fork tore off a sizeable triangular chunk he had no trouble fitting in his mouth. He looked around for the waitress, couldn't find her, and so instead simply shouted to the back that they could use more water.

Almost in response, the waitress appeared, untied her apron and smacked it on the cash register. A gravelly voice shouted from the kitchen, but the waitress ignored it as she tromped out the door.

"Well then," Evan said. "Think that means our meal is free?"

Ana waited for him to smile, or shrug, or give some other sign that he was joking, but he was not. His appetite, his constant remarks about money — it all suddenly came clear to Ana.

"You don't have relatives here," Ana said. "This visit is all for me."

"That obvious, huh?" He set his fork down for the first time since their food arrived. "I've gone through worse, unfortunately. This business... it's hardcore." He shifted around his plates, finally satiated, and cleared a path on the table from him to Ana. "They screen us. Test our specimen for purity. Even having these," he said, picking up the cigarette pack, "well, let's just say they have standards higher than your average mother-in-law."

"So why do it? You seem like a smart guy."

"Thanks, I think?" He sat back and gave a pained smile. His eyes moved to the old portrait. "I was going to be a fighter pilot. A-4 Skyhawks. My dad's dream, really. The asshole whispered it into my little five-year-old ear at night."

Ana leaned in as Evan continued, her question touching something deeper, something more tragic than she'd expected. He described years of his father's manic abuse, broken fingers and collarbones, and once his femur with a car tailpipe. He spoke of his mother's compliance, her shameless concealments and justifications. The two had worked an astonishing, daily one-two punch. Exercise was his release, the way young Evan steeled himself against them and the world. He was, he realized now, preparing himself for the day he would fight back, would strike his father with the force of a thousand bench presses and arm curls and pulldowns — a day that never came. He still lifted weights five times a week, that child in him afraid that he wouldn't be ready. His father was over sixty now, arthritic and cantankerous, descriptions he got through his sister, who had her own past with the man but was far more forgiving. Evan hadn't spoken to him in over a decade, and had no plans to ever again, but still, he said with a despondent laugh, the goddamn fear wouldn't leave.

"I'm sorry that happened to you," Ana said. "But you should know the feelings you have are perfectly normal."

"It's just... commitments, you know. Not just to people, either. Jobs. FamilyMatch is the best money I can make, but it's also probably some screwed-up way for me to be a father without actually being a father. Without being *my* father, anyway."

He shrugged before he continued. "But you know, a lot of people have it worse. And my life has had some great moments. I met Elton John once in Leeds, and he sang me happy birthday. I've seen the sunset on four continents. I've had it pretty good, considering."

He lit another cigarette. A man in a discolored green polo — apparently the manager — eyed Evan from the kitchen entrance. He seemed to weigh the cigarette infraction against losing two of his few customers. Ultimately, he grunted and returned to the kitchen. Evan watched the smoke drift as though it would reveal to him some image of his past.

"I had a child," Ana said.

Evan's eyes jumped to hers, but his body didn't move.

"We lost her, and I... I needed to move on. My husband couldn't."

In the years since Paul left, this was the first time she'd said this to anyone.

Though it was only half smoked, Evan dunked out his cigarette in his cup of au jus. "Figured that might be the case," he said. "A lot of people on FamilyMatch, actually."

The manager appeared and slid the black billfold on their table. He apologized for the waitress, hoped that it did not ruin their dining experience, and implored them to consider other, more favorable factors if they chose to fill out the online survey listed at the bottom of their bill.

"Please leave now," Evan said to him, for which Ana found herself immeasurably grateful. The manager shuffled away to other tables. Evan reached out and placed a palm to her hands, and something in that moment — his steadiness, the lingering scent of cigarette smoke, the decrepit restaurant — allowed her to see Evan as more than just a surrogate father, but as a person. A friend even.

"The worst parts," she said, "are things you never consider. The big things — they knock you down, paralyze you. But it's the everyday things that keep you pinned to the ground. She called cereal *ceree*, and it always activated Paul's phone. Now I can't use voice recognition technology without..." She retracted her hands.

From the doorway resounded a ding, followed by a pack of boisterous, giggling twenty-something females dressed in uniform bachelorette party shirts. The bride, a bejeweled sash across her chest and a unicorn horn strapped to her head, took a long pull from a stainless-steel flask.

Ana retreated into herself, but Evan pulled her back by slipping from his side and joining hers. He retook her hand.

"Let me help you, Ana," he said. In his eyes resided a deep desperation, but perhaps not just for money. "You can start your life over. You can have another child." The bridal party shouted in unison as Evan said, "You can be whole again."

Why I'll Never Apologize

By Jeanne Haskins
Originally published in mymodernyoutopianlife.you

MY FAVORITE ENGLISH TEACHER, Mrs. Goffard, taught me never to write while angry. "Put it down on paper," she'd say, "and you can't take it back. It's record. It cannot be denied."

Until recently, I adhered to this mantra for everything: emails and texts and status updates. Wait, I would tell myself. Process your emotions. Gain some clarity. And Mrs. Goffard was right, because nearly all the poisonous vitriol bubbling up inside, threating to spew out like a volcano, would eventually cool to a simmer. Nothing in the darkness of night seemed so bad in the light of another day.

Well, despite the title of this essay, I will begin with an apology: Mrs. Goffard, I'm sorry for breaking your cardinal rule. I sincerely am. All my respect, my love, goes to you, but this time it cannot be helped. The vitriol has boiled over, and over, and over again. I was, am now, and will forever be—until I am blissfully rid of this abysmal world—angry.

Of course, you already know my story—the newspapers, the legal battles, the Supreme Court ruling in my favor. (Which, thanks to the indefatigable legal staff at Youtopia, took less than a year. Thank you thank you thank you, Jim, Harland, Penny, and countless others.) You know who I am, and you've already formed an opinion on what I've done. You feel, likely with some strong emotion, one way or the other about how I handle my son Oscar's life.

But if somehow you don't—if you've managed to live under the proverbial rock, and missed the firestorm that has been my life—or even if you've heard of me but have not given me a second thought, then let me first say this: thank you. You cannot realize how much your indifference means to me. My life has been shattered by the fomenting cesspool of online piranhas and trolls and hashtagivists who have little to do except rankle at people whose lives they know nothing about, less than nothing, absolute zero.

For those blank slates lending me the rare chance of a first impression, I will begin with the most basic information. Though I am an actual person, living and breathing like you, with a home and hobbies and a (now former) job and (now former) husband, all of that has now been filtered down to two simple facts:

1. My son Oscar was diagnosed with childhood AML, a rare form of leukemia.
2. He was one of the original six to enter Youtopia.

Returning to my anger: the reason for it — the reason why I'm writing this now — is because somehow, in the skewed perdition of intolerance and faux-morality we call a world, of the two facts above, the second is the one that caused a public outrage.

Let me phrase this another way. On the one hand, a child dying of cancer is entirely commonplace. On the other, a mother using the available and humane resources to provide her son the best possible life is entirely contentious.

I WANT YOU TO know Oscar Haskins, because you'll never get him from the newspapers. No media outlet — not a single one — saw his personal story as newsworthy, as attention-grabbing clickbait. He is, to the world at large, two things only: his illness and his Immersion.

Not here. Not my Oscar. Here he will be more than a headline, more than a national scandal. By reading this, you are helping bring him back to this life, the life he had. You are recognizing his humanity.

Oscar entered our world under precarious circumstances. In utero, he grew fast, bloating my stomach outward and upward. He moved perpetually. So when my contractions began five weeks before his due date, I shouldn't have been as surprised as I was, or as nonchalant. By the time my husband and I decided to go to the hospital, I was — I would find out later — already dilated the full ten centimeters. The hospital was thirty minutes away. Until then, I had assumed that fast labors were a Hollywood fable. Nobody gave birth in stalled elevators or friends' basements or backs of taxis. Oscar proved me wrong. In a rush to get to this world, he was born in the backseat of our own car on the side of the highway.

From there, he continued to run — on his feet at nine months, on two bicycle wheels at three. He knew how to navigate our tablets better than us. And stories. He loved stories, loved being read to, loved sitting with books and fashioning his own narrative. Near his fifth birthday, he illustrated his first comic book starring Bunnyish, his beloved gray rabbit, and Mr. Noose, a fictional young man of his own creation. He was an artist, a creator. He was amazing, capable of amazing things.

And he loved ferociously. He attached to everyone—my husband and me, his cousins, neighbors—and everyone attached to him. We sometimes feared for his safety because of the immense trust he had in everyone around him. In his young heart, he believed, as I no longer do, in the inherent goodness of people.

IN THE YEAR AFTER the doctors discovered Oscar's condition, I sought every possible alternative treatment—Western and Eastern medicine, chiropractors and therapists and witch doctors, trying anything that might help even in the slightest way. We endured the chemo, months of seeing my poor Oscar's jaundiced skin and his hollow eyes, and his spirit, that ever-loving spirit, sapped by the very thing endeavoring to save him. We prayed for remission, for negative tests. I compartmentalized my hope, tucked it down deep in the recesses of my heart, thinking that the dark melancholia surrounding us wouldn't find it there. But then one day, after more predictable bad news—months, possibly another year of necessary treatment—even I couldn't find my hope. In its place came a voice that wanted to end his suffering, a voice that, selfishly, wanted to end my own. I prayed for guidance, for a sign. For anything.

Two days later, my prayers were answered. I received a phone call from a woman named Sonya Young. She had read about Oscar in the *Murray Ledger & Times*, had seen our brief spot on WFON. The next day she flew me to her budding clinic in North Dakota. I was ready for any suggestion, any glimmer of hope, however faint. I was ready for a savior.

And as Sonya described her treatment, I soon recognized that I had found one. Rather, she had found me. Oscar could live the life he wanted to live—no, deserved to live—in a way previously unimaginable. He would likely even live longer, since he wouldn't be exposed to common disease or infection, and his physical body could divert all its energies to simply surviving. (As of this writing, he has outlived his prognosis by over a year.) But the most important thing: he would be free of his pain, of chemo migraines and anemia and vomiting, of whimpers and tears I tried to but could never console. He could live cancer-free, in the places he longed for, in the moments he cherished, for the remainder of his short life.

I KNOW THE ARGUMENTS against my decision. I've heard them from friends I've since lost, from strangers in grocery stores and parks and libraries. I've read them on countless X-ACT memes fed to my social media. So before I end this anger-induced diatribe, I'd like to remonstrate just how fucking stupid those arguments are, and how fucking stupid you are if you believe them. I'd like to resurrect bridges long since burned. You will read names here, because these people do not deserve to be anonymous. They will not be forgiven.

The Abandonment Argument

This argument is the most pervasive, and also the most asinine. I'm not spending Oscar's remaining time with him. I deserted my child to the care of someone else. According to loud-mouthed, audacious Griselda, I passed on the responsibility of my child so that he, and I quote, "Won't be my problem anymore."

For Griselda and the rest with romantic notions, picture this instead. Step into my shoes for one minute: you are Oscar's mother, and you see your already thin son lose weight, his hair and eyebrows. You hold him as he simultaneously vomits an unnatural green mucus on your shirt and defecates in your lap. You wrap him in every blanket you own and still watch him shiver. Your hours at the hospital disrupt your work schedule, your marriage — everything — but you don't care, because all you want is to comfort him. You hear him say, "Mommy, I hurt so so so much," and have to lie when you whisper everything will be all right.

As much as you want to shut out the rest of the world, you can't, not when medical bills pummel your mailbox daily. You consider selling your cars, but then how would you get to work? So maybe your house, except rent wouldn't be any cheaper than your mortgage. You might work double shifts, fourteen-hour days, but then who would watch Oscar? Who would hold his head in her lap as he groaned in pain?

So no, don't talk to me about abandonment. Anyone who cares to come at me with that argument can box it, tape it, and cram it right up their self-righteous ass.

The Development Argument

This one is so senseless it seems a waste of words to refute it. I'm endangering Oscar by putting him in Youtopia because the system has not yet been tested, because we don't yet know of any long-term effects the body stasis or sedative drugs might have.

This about a six-year-old boy who was given a miniscule chance of reaching the age of ten. Long-term effects? Please.

The Spiritual Argument

I have lost the most friends to this. By placing Oscar in Youtopia, I've condemned his soul. I've robbed him of the chance at eternal life. Patricia, Bill, Hanne, you were the worst. You preached your bullshit positive spin of a God that is loving, caring, nurturing. According to you, He causes suffering in this life so that we will reap infinite reward in the next.

To you, I say: I can only hope you never have a terminally ill child. I hope God never shows you the merciless, the cruel, the completely fucking arbitrary side of His love.

I will not say I have never felt the "touch of God," however, because I have, on one of the large screens in Youtopia's first headquarters. At first, I was frightened. I imagined seeing Oscar prostrate in a hospital bed, the beeps of his heart monitor painfully spaced apart. I imagined him in pain, because that is all I knew of this world's "cures." But then Sonya— our savior, our angel, a saint if there is one—showed me Oscar's Feed. I didn't see a hospital room, tubes and needles and copper rings of iodine on pale skin. What I did see: me walking in an open meadow, a copse in the distance. The scenery approximated my father's land in Montana, as beautiful a place on Earth as there is. I saw Oscar's hands, one holding mine, the other his beloved Bunnyish. We approached a well that, in real life, had long since dried up. I wheeled up a barrel of water, and together we drank as though from the fountain of youth itself.

He once again had gifts to offer me. And I, I recognized the eternal gift I had given him.

CRITICS WILL DENEGRATE YOUTOPIA as a last resort, a desolate refuge for those whose lives have become unbearable. Well, to Griselda and Patricia and all the online gaslighters, and anyone else who cares to condemn me, I say congratulations: you have created a self-fulfilling prophecy. You have indeed made my life unbearable. I have Evolved, and in days will Immerse myself. I will enter my own world, a wondrous place where Oscar can outlive me, a world free from all the hate that has so infected my life—the hate spewed at me, and the hate bred in me in kind. You can all go find another prey for your venom, because I no longer hear you. I am returning to a place free of echoes, where daisies and meadows and birthday parties and sunshine and Oscar, my sweet Oscar, can reign once more.

JOSEPH REIN

Chapter 4

Ana expected the meeting to happen in some immense office high in one of the Towers. Instead, the office assistant Lexi directed Ana to a middle floor in the second Tower, through large glass double-doors and into a high-end fitness center just for Youtopia employees. They devoted three whole floors to free weights, yoga centers, and courts for all sports, an area so complex it needed its own map. Lexi handed Ana off to a sprightly assistant, a mid-twenties man with dreadlocks and braces who held a bag of toiletries and workout clothes of Ana's size. He waited in the hall as she changed. The locker room was pristine, decorated and carpeted to resemble an upscale bedroom: keyed dressers instead of lockers, chic industrial sconces casting dim light up the stucco walls, individual mirrored tables stocked with expensive makeup. When Ana was ready, the assistant led her down a corridor, his dreads bobbing with the surrounding alt-rock music. They passed an expansive, shimmering cardio center with touchscreen pads built into every machine, free protein shakes in coolers, and then a café and dining tables populated with workout-clad employees. The whole thing made other gyms seem ancient, like relics of a time long forgotten.

The assistant led Ana to a string of stark-white racquetball courts. On one court, two middle-aged men circled each other in slow determination; on another, two richly-dressed twenty-somethings shifted between intense play, banter, and shameless groping. They treated the glass wall like the other three, as though no one could see in. But why shouldn't they? Ana remembered similar times with Paul in their on-again, off-again days of college, when they shared a vigorous physical attraction and little else. In those days, both Paul and Ana had omnipresent roommates, and so they found such passions in sequestered public places, at parks, in movie theaters, on the peaks of Ferris wheels — one time, on kayaks in a well-trafficked river. They had kissed and groped, teased really, as these young workers did now, stealing whatever intense pleasures they could.

"Here we are," the assistant said, leading her to the last court. The inside glass squealed under the squeegee of a custodian dressed in all black, like a high-end restaurant server. The custodian finished, walked out the door, and offered them a slight bow as she passed.

"Ms. Young will arrive shortly," the assistant continued. "She doesn't keep exact meeting times because she's on the Polyphasic sleep cycle. You heard of it?"

"I have an idea," Ana replied.

"An hour here, an hour there. I tried, but I was a wreck. Not Ms. Young—she's a machine." He pointed back to the court. "You've played before, yes?" He didn't wait for an answer before thrusting a light racket into Ana's hands, the strings taut as a violin. "Be careful. She's also a beast on the court." He marched away, already swiping on his phone.

Ana looked down the hall, where the sounds of grunts and wall collisions and smacking balls spilled from the rooms, creating an echoing cacophony along the corridor. Twenty minutes passed. She felt like a patient awaiting a doctor. She pulled out her phone and saw Bruce's last message encouraging her to tread lightly with Sonya. She then opened her FamilyMatch account again, where her inbox shimmered with the red circle of Evan's messages.

> I'm dying to meet up again. Perhaps at night this time? At an establishment with adult beverages? We should really take advantage while we're here. When in Rome.

He smattered his emails with links to Racine happy hour specials and "Best of" lists—Thirsty Thursdays and Sunday Fundays aplenty, the pride of Wisconsin. Ana counted to thirty. If Sonya didn't arrive in five minutes, then she would respond to Evan. Five, then ten, then fifteen minutes passed.

She opened a reply, typed and sent a simple message:

> Tomorrow night.

A minute later, Sonya finally arrived, dressed in clothes identical to Ana. She held her racket in one hand and three devices of various size in the other. She delivered Ana a strong, handsome smile. Her face was pale, remarkably smooth. Though fifty-seven years old, she and Ana could certainly have passed for sisters. Sonya seemed inscrutable, put together. She seemed timeless.

"It is wonderful to meet you at last," Sonya said. She moved fluidly, like a swimmer through calm water. Ana reminded herself not to be charmed. "I apologize for taking so long to see you. I have seen countless politicians and lawmakers regarding the Healthcare Bill. It has been..."

Her hand slackened its grip on the racket, and her eyes shone over with an aggrieved gloss. "But listen to me. Mr. Fowler—Charles, poor Charles. That should be foremost on our minds. Seeking justice."

Just as quickly as she adopted it, Sonya's grieving visage faded. She was either acting, or her moods vacillated so simply. Like Terrance, she had lived for years in the spotlight, and had adapted accordingly.

"I have to admit," Ana said, pointing into the clinical white void of their court, "I haven't played in years."

"Since college."

Sonya said this so simply, so matter-of-factly, that Ana was taken aback. Then again, tech giants and their massive databanks had gathered everything about Americans for a decade. If she wanted to, Sonya likely could have known what Ana purchased for breakfast that very morning.

Sonya opened the door. Her voice rang into the hollow echo of the room. "Men hold meetings on golf courses. This is not so strange, in that context." She approached a large sliding cabinet, where she stored her tablet and two phones. Ana followed. "We both have precious little time to spare. Consider this effective multitasking."

The game began. Ana started slowly but, after only a few points, she pushed to match Sonya's intense pace. Sonya's racket was quick, decisive; she placed shot after shot just out of Ana's reach. When Ana served, she found control in the racket's sheer power, its kinetic spring. She could, at times, fire off a serve that tilted Sonya to her heels. But if she didn't capitalize, Sonya recovered with the agility of a jungle animal. Her center of gravity never faltered. Ana delivered some gems that seemed untouchable, only to find Sonya behind her, lurking inexplicably in the perfect spot to return a spinning jewel. At times, Ana caught herself standing still, watching the ways in which Sonya's body contorted and lunged with angular dexterity, as if she were performing some choreographed ballet Ana could never hope to learn.

Sonya handily won the first game. She offered Ana a towel from the cabinet and took one herself, though she barely broke a sweat. She also pulled two vitamin waters Ana hadn't noticed.

"James has shown you Mr. Fowler's Feed," Sonya said, continuing their conversation as though the interlude of the game never happened. "James is a brilliant man. I recruited him when he hacked into one of my earliest servers. Many tech people get their start in such a way. Unfortunately, however, even he has not been able to track this hacker's source."

"We have our best on it," Ana said. "Personally, I wouldn't know up from down with the technology."

"In truth, I often get lost myself," Sonya said, though this Ana doubted.

Sonya returned to the service line. Like the first game, she called out the score before each serve, but this time she added conversation, assuming Ana would now be comfortable talking and playing simultaneously, which she was not. Ana couldn't concentrate on Sonya's words and the game at the same time, and Sonya won without conceding a single point.

Ana caught her breath as Sonya returned to her water. "You mentioned James Peterson," Ana said. "I need to know any other Youtopia employees who might have—"

"That name," Sonya interrupted. "You-topia." Sonya spaced out the two halves of the word as though saying it for the first time. "I must admit it vexes me still. It does not catch the ear—no poetry at all. As we grew, I wanted it changed. We tested over seventy names on focus groups, common ones like Nirvana, Elysium. We tried strange twists like Paradisio and Heavensent. In the end, we stuck with the original. I still feel it inadequate." She looked at Ana. "You disagree."

"I guess I've never considered an alternative. It's like saying the internet should have been named something else."

"Perhaps, but to me, it is akin to naming a child. They either grow into it or they don't. I'm not sure this has." She dropped the bright blue ball and dribbled it, the smacking timbre reverberating through the room. "But I interrupted you. Please continue."

"I was asking about your employees. Though this is an atypical murder, we still follow typical motives. The first likelihood would be professional, people with access to the network, so current and former employees."

"Of course," Sonya said. "My office has presented you with personnel records, yes?"

"I wanted your opinion. You know their intelligence. There must only be a handful capable."

"My chief engineers, perhaps," Sonya said. "Though none anticipated Mr. Fowler's demise, or its methods. Such is the nature of murder—its unpredictability."

From the next court, the young couple giggled in unison, followed by the sound of bodies colliding against the adjacent wall.

"My answer doesn't satisfy you," Sonya continued. "I will provide you with a detailed list." She reached into the cabinet, retrieved her tablet and swiped. Within a few seconds, Ana's phone rang with a notification. "You said the first likelihood was professional. The second would be personal?"

"Yes. Someone with a vendetta against Fowler himself. Or..." Ana stopped herself. Part of her knew she shouldn't say too much, but a larger part wanted to feel Sonya out. "Or against Youtopia itself. A person like Terrance Martin, for example."

Sonya smirked. "Terrance. He and I have, how should I say, *spiritual* differences. But we are otherwise cordial."

"Do you believe he could be involved?"

"Terrance is animated, yes, but harmless. He is a circus act."

"He has a strong motive: discrediting you, proving you are a danger. It would be the first step toward shutting you down."

"Perhaps, but consider from his perspective: what is his church without Youtopia? Where go all of his slathering followers? To be frank, his entire enterprise is meaningless without us."

"That's a fatalistic outlook."

"Realistic." Sonya's tablet gave a mellifluous ring resonant of a bass strum. Then another. Ana expected Sonya to check on whomever was attempting to reach her, but she kept her eyes strictly on Ana. "Of course, anything is possible. That will be between you and him. Surely my speculations can be of little value. Let us instead focus on how I can help."

She reached into the cabinet and pulled out a final surprise, a baton just like Peterson's, and handed it to Ana. Its warmth quickly radiated into her hand. She could feel her own thumb's pulse shudder up her arm. She prodded for soft spots, protrusions, but found none. She turned it over and looked for buttons, for markings, anything denoting its similarity to a remote control, but she saw only a serial number in small chrome lettering.

Sonya raised the tablet to Ana. Ana hesitated, then pointed the baton at its screen.

Sonya let out a laugh in earnest. "I'm sorry. That is a natural reaction." As Ana lowered the baton, Sonya took Ana's other hand and placed it in the center of the screen. It instantly came alive in pulses of red light, handprints tunneling like echoes down its depths. When Ana pulled her hand away, dialogue boxes with her personal information populated the screen.

Sonya nodded to the baton. "Just keep full contact. One more step."

Sonya piloted the tablet with a finger. Ana watched permission boxes and red octagonal signals vanish with Sonya's quick passwords. She felt the cold slithering feeling of being watched, at this very moment, by forces unknown. Finally, the screen went black.

"That belongs to you," Sonya said. "Your entry to the building, to the Feeds. You can access employee documents, everything. Well, I should say, almost everything."

"Almost?"

"You have access to everything I myself have access to. More than James, or any of our techs. We do not, however, have access to the children's Feeds."

"Children's Feeds," Ana repeated without thinking.

"Twenty-nine in total. I should say minors, not children, because some have grown — young Oscar is sixteen already!"

"You mean Oscar Haskins."

"Yes," Sonya said. "Of course, as one of the first, he holds a special place for me. The doctors gave him such a short life expectancy, but here he remains, these ten years on." Sonya looked to her tablet while jumping through assorted files. "We cannot view their Feeds because the government has locked down their access. They evoked COPPA, FERPA, every existing law available. Guardians or Observers can grant you access, or you can apply for a warrant if necessary, but even I have been denied in the past."

Ana could feel the baton's scintillating pulse in her hand, could hear, underneath the smacks of racquetballs around them, the low drone of its technological force. It felt entrancing. She sensed the twin impulse of wanting, immediately, to walk upstairs and submerge herself in the Feeds, to get lost in the world — no, worlds, infinite worlds — to which she now had access, and the equal desire to drop the baton and run, to escape the rabbit hole into which she saw herself falling. She thought, immediately and unfalteringly, of Paul, the way she fell into and out of him the same way.

She reminded herself to breathe. "Thank you for this."

"No gratitude necessary. It is what you need."

Sonya walked to the court's glass door, but then she stopped, and her gaze returned to Ana. It bore down with a weight Sonya could seemingly summon in an instant. "I built Youtopia at a time when it seemed inconceivable to do so. Mr. Fowler's death is, to me, an intensely personal affront. I fear for the rest, especially for children like Oscar. I want to apprehend this monster before he harms a single person more."

They entered the locker room together. At their dressing drawers, Sonya unabashedly removed her tank top and athletic pants, her sports bra and underwear. Ana tried to avert her gaze but found Sonya's poise both intoxicating and nauseating, like too much wine. Ana removed her own clothes, trying to match Sonya's confidence. She tried not to hide her cesarean scar across her lower stomach, the dark downy hairs beneath her belly button. They entered the communal shower. Sonya looked at Ana but never stared, never fixated, her naked body as simple a fact as a stranger speaking across the room, or a car passing on the opposite side of the street.

Each of them cleansed and fully clothed, Sonya escorted Ana back through the gym. As they passed the corridor, Ana watched Sonya's workers react to her. They hesitated, stuttered, lowered their eyes and raised their postures. They treated her with a reverence reserved for the sovereign.

Then, just before the elevator, as they passed the café, a young man locked eyes with Ana and instantly dropped his spoon into his frozen yogurt. He looked away and acted cagey, overly skittish. He had something to hide. Ana catalogued the young man's face, his high cheeks and dimpled chin and heavy brow, before entering the elevator.

Across the ground floor, Sonya's phones and tablet sirened with the pleasant strums of countless people who wanted to contact her. She ignored them as they stepped outside to overcast clouds, to sheets of gray rain westward and advancing. Two Youtopia workers waited there for Sonya, both holding ready umbrellas. In moments, the dreadlocked assistant joined them.

"I'm due in Phoenix," Sonya said. She handed off her devices save one of the cellphones. Into it, she dialed a number that turned out to be Ana's. "This line comes directly to me. Whenever you need."

Sonya took Ana's hand. Across her face the muscles loosened, creating a barely noticeable difference that softened her harsh edges.

"I understand why you think ill of us," she said. "Of me."

"I don't."

"I can see it in your eyes. It's the same look I receive at restaurants, on Capitol Hill, and even at fundraisers where people are generally supportive. You have every right to your biases, circumstances considered."

Ana felt her chest tightening. But then Sonya moved her hand to Ana's arm, and the comforting weight of her grip centered Ana.

"You see, the problem with human attempts at perfect worlds is the *human* part. For all that our illustrious modern society has explored, no one can account for personal ambition, greed, self-seeking behavior. One side tells us that if everyone seeks for themselves, society will somehow thrive. This is, of course, nonsense. The other side asks us not to want for ourselves at all, to be completely altruistic. That is just as nonsensical.

"Contrary to what people believe, I do not think Youtopia is for everyone. I do not believe it can, or should, take over the world. But for so many of us, the world is unspeakably cruel. It is pain and dejection and little else. Is it wrong to provide those people an alternative?" Sonya looked to the sky, to the storm clouds gathering above them. "Is it idealistic to believe in a perfect world for those who deserve one?"

Ana was unsure how to respond, unsure how she felt about this confession. But before she could speak, the moment passed and Sonya made her exit, buried in the convoy of her three workers behind her.

***

Evan suggested they meet at the grounds of a local county festival, a simple celebration of rural America. *Spring is in the Air*, hand-painted signs constantly reminded them as they parked. There were livestock and other animal contests, carnival rides, a large beer garden. A rusted-out car with sledgehammer dents all along the side awaited its next paying assailant. At the gates, Evan offered to pay their admittance, but Ana insisted, and for the remainder of the evening—cheese curds, two rounds of overpriced High Life beers, and then, at Evan's insistence, tickets to the demolition derby, the night's main event—Ana paid.

Evan strutted the grounds like a local, weaving between large families and swaths of high schoolers with earnest waves. He referenced volunteers by the names on their sticky tags and chatted-up elderly couples at nearby tables. He had an undeniable conviviality about him, unassuming and yet forward. Ana imagined him stirring up long conversations with cashiers at gas stations and grocery stores, holding up lines with exasperating good cheer. He shook the attendant's hand at the grandstand gate as they entered.

"Never been to one of these before," he said as they found a cramped space on the bench bleachers, near the center and higher up than the structure seemed from the outside. There were possibly two hundred people in attendance, and more entering with each minute.

"That makes two of us."

Evan raised his beer. "Here's to trying new things."

The derby began with much ceremony: the national anthem, a string of festival announcements, and then the introduction of each of the twelve cars, all with the look of refurbished furniture and driven by men younger than Evan. They skidded along the dampened ground into a mud-filled oval, revving their unrestricted, unmuffled engines all the way. Along the fence, the drivers' girlfriends jibed and hooted at one another. Just beside Evan, a group of men Ana's age made ridiculous wagers.

Evan nudged Ana. "We should get in on the action."

"I don't even know what constitutes winning."

"Simple. Last man standing."

The derby began. Cars drove about timidly at first, staking out their space, circling one another like prizefighters waiting for an opening. Then one rambunctious teenage driver in an old Chevelle slammed on his gas and sideswiped another. The crowd erupted in boisterous cheers as both cars skidded near the fence. The others followed suit. They dinged and dented and crashed. Puddles of rain and muck flew. The teenager sustained enough front damage for his engine to hiss and spit. It smoked, then burst into flames, which drew an even bigger cheer. The teen himself jumped from the car, marched slowly toward the back, and slammed his fists against the trunk. The cars continued on around him as though he didn't exist. His face bled pure disappointment, his shoulders hung low, the spikes on his helmet shaking, as though his whole year — his whole life — led to this moment of defeat. From the loudspeakers issued Steam's "Na Na Hey Hey Kiss Him Goodbye."

Evan absorbed it all with a child-like sense of wonderment. Ana found herself strangely envious. "Hot damn," he said with a smile. "I would've put my money on the little guy. Shows how much I know." He raised his beer. "To better judgment in all things," he said, but then something in him hitched and foam slipped over his cup's edge. "Shit. I didn't mean, you know. With us. I meant in other things. Work and health and et cetera."

"It is your work."

"I suppose so." He licked at his fingers. "How's work going for you?"

Ana looked at him as his eyes roved the sputtering cars. He knew her full name, and had the opportunity to do some research. It seemed unlikely he knew nothing of Fowler and Youtopia, of her profile at the FBI, and yet his expressions gave no sign. He might not have followed current events. He might have used social media sparsely, might be fairly disconnected. Ana found the prospect equal parts refreshing and unnerving.

Then Evan said, "That good, huh?"

Ana's whole body locked. *'That good, huh'* was one of Paul's expressions, down to the sarcastic delivery. She immediately closed her eyes. When she reopened them, she hoped that she wouldn't see her husband in Evan.

But no, there Paul was, in Evan's eyes, his aquiline nose. It was the same with his mannerisms: his quiet confidence, his poise with strangers, his slight nervousness with those he cared about. Paul and Evan, Evan and Paul. In the moment, she couldn't unsee it.

As Evan watched another car's wheels grind into the mud, Ana excused herself to the restroom, which turned out to be a string of faded-blue portables along the grandstand's far side. A row of women in oversized hooded sweatshirts stood waiting. Instead of joining the line, Ana ripped her wristband off, hearkened an Uber, and fled.

***

"I walked out," she told Lonnie that night.

They video chatted; Lonnie wore a red bra and held a curling iron in her hand, looking most the time down at her own picture box. An early '90s romance song played somewhere behind her. She occasionally mouthed a string of lyrics.

"I feel like an asshole."

"I probably would've walked out too. A... what was it called? Roller derby? Sheesh."

"You noticed his resemblance right away. To Paul."

"Jesus H, Ana. It was clear as a church bell on Sunday. Better question is, why didn't you see it?" She blew at her recently painted fingernails. "Paul hurt you. He hurt all of us when he left. But look on the bright side — at least this Evan guy only *looks* like him. You're not one of those freaky chicks who went after one of Paul's brothers, or worse, his father."

"His brothers are... well, you know them. And his father's dead."

"My *point* is, you're looking for love, and it makes all the sense in the world that you'd seek out a Paul clone."

"He's not a clone."

"Right. Doppelganger. Whatever you want to call him," she said with a flair of the hand. "Look, I've thought about it, and I've come to the conclusion there's no harm in it. Might be a bit unhealthy, but at this point, who gives a fuck? Young guys are definitely where we *should* be." From there, Lonnie launched into a detailed, ribald recount of her latest date with her pseudo-boyfriend. Ana felt glad that Lonnie had, as usual, turned the attention to herself. She threw about the words *limber* and *supple* within crasser descriptions. She would make a good romance writer, if she ever had the inclination or resolve. But for now, she talked and talked, and Ana was thankful for the distraction.

***

The concave screen before Ana burst forth in light. The baton fluttered in her hand. She watched her arm rise, watched her fingers tap and rub to some unheard song in her mind. It was like the Ouija board she used to torment her elementary school friends, attempting to summon grandparents and former presidents and Marilyn Monroe. She controlled the baton, telling it what letter to choose, and yet somehow the baton directed her, as though some preternatural force conducted from beyond.

Early that morning, she had delved into all things Terrance Martin: his childhood; his school records, including two suspensions for drugs; his various employments—office clerk and nonprofit organizer and deli worker, none lasting more than a year; his records with Youtopia, the referrals and visits and interviews with technicians. She read the transcripts, which were alarmingly candid. She had hoped for some discrepancy, but found his autobiographical account, written in *Barbed Wire* and any number of ReaLife documents and documentaries, to be accurate. It seemed he was as forthright as he appeared. And so, with no more leads, with Sergio's assurances that nothing would soon come of the digital pursuit—"You're getting farther than me, I promise you" – she had only one place left to look: the Feeds.

The light of the giant screen, the soft swishing sounds as she moved about, all enticed Ana to go further. The baton purred in her hand. Before she entered, Peterson had given her a quick lesson, brandishing his own baton like a sword. Once revealed, Ana found it a relatively simple system of joystick-like movements and soft presses—hyper-intuitive. Ana now thought not of Peterson's descriptions but of his face, of the drug-user euphoria in his eyes. She reminded herself that none of what she would see was real. It was a transcription of something less than a dream, a door to no room, a pool with no water. Headfirst, Ana dove.

She sifted through countless days of Fowler's Youtopia life, crystalline and beautiful and ultimately monotonous, dull. It was akin to standing in an electronics store, watching the scenic views of exotic locations meant to sell the newest, highest-definition TVs. The technology was rapid and unfaltering — no buffering, no abrupt cuts or glitches. She accelerated the rewind through Fowler's pseudo-life as fast as the system would go, allowing her to cover a day's time in about ten tedious minutes, so long as nothing gave her occasion to pause, which little did. His yard was much larger and his wife Carol younger. She still gardened but in-ground, not in segmented wood planters, her tomatoes and daises and hydrangeas bursting with life.

In his solitary moments, his perfect world was that of the outdoorsman: hours sitting atop deer stands, watching overpopulated, indigenous wildlife prance by like a video game, raising his rifle at only the largest bucks; four-wheeler jaunts along cleared paths in the woods; ice fishing in temperatures too warm for ice, always with bountiful catches. He attended Jimmy Buffet-style concerts once a week.

Ana passed through his Youtopia life with a stupefied attentiveness, the stop-motion speed vertiginous. She hoped in vain for the perpetrator to unexpectedly appear in the wrong place, hiding amidst a crowd, lurking in the shadows. She found few hints of why Fowler would want to enter Youtopia, what world he could enact here that he couldn't in real life, except that his world lacked life's daily responsibilities and disappointments, its overdue bills and bruised fruit and the pained, inevitable distance people put between each other. In Youtopia, such discomforts, if they arose at all, simply resolved themselves.

Then, one unexceptional afternoon, the camera hastened. Fowler sprinted to the shed with arms flailing. Something was amiss. Ana stopped, played it back, the audio rushing into the room like the first notes of a concert.

"...what it is you do in there," Carol said.

"It's not," Fowler replied, stumbling over his words, his voice ringing like Ana's own in her ears, "it's not something you need to worry about."

A rustling came from the shed, which had the same repurposed wood, the same *Start Each Day with a Grateful Heart* sign Ana saw at Carol's real house. Ana rewound back a day, and another, until one night she found Fowler leaving the shed. She went back further. The doors closed on a picturesque twilight across their expansive lawn. Fowler backed in, the strange motion jarring Ana, like facing the wrong way in a car. As the dark space revealed itself to her, Ana felt a peculiar déjà vu—she had been in this room before.

When Fowler turned, she recognized when. Bound to the bed, naked and in tears, lay a teenage girl.

Ana's body startled. This was the same shed Peterson stumbled upon that first day. Of course: Fowler was the rapist. Peterson wouldn't be so inept as to pull an entirely different Immerser. Ana immediately thought back to Fowler's criminal record, but it was entirely clean: no felonies or misdemeanors, no disturbances or domestic calls, no traffic violations. Nothing to follow up on, to investigate further. But of course, many perpetrators—particularly sex criminals—had no prior record. They all started somewhere.

She paused the Feed and phoned Bruce. His voice rang enthusiastic, interrupting her before she could even lay out her plan—a warrant for the shed, the house. She must interview everyone in Crivitz again, pressing them on Fowler's relationships with young girls to unearth potentially malicious behavior. And as for the girls themselves, they needed to catalog every former pupil of his, no matter the age or year, and contact them. She recalled Terrance's suggestion of sexual abuse: she needed to see him again, on neutral ground this time.

Bruce's enthusiasm over another lead was tangible; Ana could almost feel it through the phone. His elevated voice came close to praise. "I'll contact your team and loop you in," he said. "Keep at the Feeds. Find everything."

Ana called Sonya's direct line next. She expected Sonya not to answer, busy in some meeting, and prepared to leave a message, but Sonya picked up on the second ring.

"No trouble with the Feeds I hope?" Sonya said.

"No," Ana said. She heard, through the phone, a sound like a dentist's polishing tool revving behind Sonya.

"I thought you would adapt quickly. To tell the truth, I think James has taken a liking to you."

"Why did you conceal Fowler's..." Ana searched for the right word, "deviances from me?"

"The young girls."

Ana turned back to the screen, realizing she had paused on just that image, the blonde girl in bondage. "If you know this type of information, you need to tell me."

"I'm sorry you feel I deceived you in some way, Miss Downer. I gave you access to the Feeds. They are all there to find."

"You could have saved me time."

"Yes, but you must understand an unfortunate truth about Youtopia: Charles Fowler was in no way exceptional. Many people enter Youtopia to enact unsavory desires. Illegal desires. Charles chose Youtopia to satisfy his aberrant nature without hurting others. In one way, it is deplorable. In another, quite admirable."

"Unless he did the same in real life."

"That will be for you to find out. I am no detective. Please remember, though, no matter how real it feels, those girls you see are not. They exist in his mind only."

Ana turned to the screen. It was entirely possible—plausible even—that everyone who entered Youtopia was high on the risk continuum, that each of the near half-million Immersers was a person who sought out their own private paradises for dubious purposes. "I need more stringent cooperation in the future."

"Anything you require." Sonya spoke to a few people out of the phone. "I must go. Please do not hesitate to call." Then she was gone.

Ana turned back to the screen and again delved into Fowler's Feed, moving through the mundane to the progression of his crimes—casing the girls, luring them to the barn, evading curious policemen and Carol. He watched news stories of the missing girls with disturbing pride. Ana found seven girls in his possession through the ten years of his Youtopia life, and ran facial recognition on all of them. She found, as Sonya suggested, that though some resembled his former pupils, none of them truly existed.

Ana moved to other people's Feeds, curious to see if Sonya's depiction of rampant excesses held true. She started with two acquaintances from Fowler's previous life, a former neighbor and a distant niece. The niece was relatively new, only six months in, and inhabited almost exclusively a BDSM fantasy world. The neighbor, a seemingly humdrum man like Fowler, became a serial killer, stabbing woman after woman with the same butcher knife. Police caught him, but he escaped his lackluster imprisonments. Under the twin powers of curiosity and the baton's uncanny intuition, Ana meandered down the paths of others who had lived in northeastern Wisconsin. She allowed some unfelt wind to swirl her in any direction. She found an Evil Knievel-type stuntman who sometimes missed his mark. The man spent weeks at a time in hospital beds and wheelchairs, an addiction to pain and pity in equal measure. He had predictable sex with his nurses. Another woman caged adolescent boys in her cellar, allowing them out only to perform housework in high heels. Every new Feed Ana explored brought groping during work meetings, drug benders at family gatherings, fellatio in airline seats — excitement and pleasure, danger and climax, in a constant cycle.

Sonya had told the truth. With a long view, Youtopia lives were commonplace, a vestige catering to the superego: cash always on hand, favorite movies in local theaters, chronic pains eradicated, French fries fresh from the fryer, pleasant hangovers, pets that outlived their life expectancy and produced clone-like offspring. Within those secure lives, however, sharp peaks and edges spiked, moments where Immersers walked tightropes without ever falling — all supermodels and skydiving and heroism, all revved-up, cocaine-like excesses of the id. Everyone, like Fowler, had some private desire to enact. All fell prey to a deeper lust.

JOSEPH REIN

Chapter 5

Ana lunched in the Youtopia cafeteria in the first Tower. The line was scarce, the tables empty. After, she found a mass of people huddled in a collaboration center, surrounding the largest flatscreen to watch CNN, which displayed the stagnant image of the senate floor with a vote count superimposed across the bottom. The numbers slowly ticked upward on both the YEA and NAY sides. Ana entered the room to a gust of conditioned air and a strange silence. The NAY votes reached 30, then 35, and a collective groan issued from the workers. One young woman shouted "Come on, assholes!" and the group nodded its head in chorus. A minute passed without a vote. Then a string of senators pushed for YEA, surging it up toward the NAY numbers, then past, beyond 40 and rising. The group raised its murmurs. When the number hit 45, they clapped and softly cheered. When it surpassed 50, they erupted.

Ana watched their jubilation fan out and spread. They looped around chairs and tables, high-fiving like members of a high school pep rally. They danced to imagined music. Ana stayed and observed, not because she enjoyed their triumph, but because in the dispersed crowd she spotted the tentative, heavy-browed young man from the day before.

She had pulled his employment record last night: Constantine Peoples, 25, Master's in Information Systems Management from BYU. Hired by Youtopia straight out of college to the team that handled Feed processing and storage. He held a woman about the waist, dipping and spinning her as they paraded around the room.

Ana accosted him only as he exited minutes later. He tensed immediately upon seeing her.

"Constantine," she said, further alarming him at the sound of his own name. "I need a minute of your time."

The woman by his side excused herself, and he watched her go with an infantile concern on his face. Ana almost wanted to tell him it was all right, to reassure him that he wasn't in trouble. At least, not yet.

"Okay," he finally said. "But we're kinda busy today. You saw the vote."

"I did. I'll only take the time I need."

He made for the cafeteria, but Ana stopped him. "Somewhere else."

"Look, I don't know anything about the murder."

"That may be true. Still, we'll speak somewhere more private."

He giggled. "Private doesn't exist here."

"Then we'll find somewhere it does."

On the drive out of Youtopia's lot, Ana remarked on the unfamiliar yet classic nature of his name, on the impressiveness of his ascension through college and into the most coveted company in the industry. She lavished flatteries upon him that did nothing to break down his nervous defenses.

They drove toward a secluded coffee shop south of Racine, but Ana had no intention of entering. She would get what she needed from him on the drive.

He fiddled with his phone, his hands a jumble of nerves.

Ana decided to push. "Look, Constantine, the only way you get into trouble here is if you withhold information."

He stared at his phone as one would a ticking bomb, with the desire to throw it as far away as possible. He shut it down, and then buried it deep into her glove box for good measure. He reached over and turned on the radio to a loud, preening country song from years past.

"I told him we'd get caught," he said, and sighed with the weight of a heavy conscience. "How could we know that one of them would be Fowler's? It was, wasn't it? One of them was Fowler's?"

Constantine turned to Ana now, looking for answers she didn't have. He presumed she already knew his misconduct, an assumption she allowed. She would keep her questions vague, would let his guilt guide them.

"If you knew you'd get caught, why do it?"

"Why does anyone do anything?" he said. "Money money money. *Way* more than Youtopia pays. Pete said *five figures* for each video."

Ana nodded, repeated the name *Pete* to herself. She took an onramp toward Kenosha, ready to ask another question when Constantine continued.

"I never thought someone could get hurt. I mean, the dark web is *way* worse. This was like high-class porn. People get off on all kinds of kinky shit. So what if it's someone's Feed?"

"How many buyers did you have?"

"Just one. We never distributed."

"I need the name."

Constantine looked again to Ana's glove box. He opened it, pulled out his phone, and abruptly tossed it out his window.

"Who do you think is listening?" Ana asked.

"His name is Tramel. Last I heard, his place is on Fourth and Pike in Chicago, under an old consignment shop. But he moves around a lot."

Ana repeated silently to herself: *Tramel, Fourth and Pike.* "Can you give me a description?"

"Squirrely looking guy. Long hair but, you know —" He picked at his own hair as though grooming himself. "Real wispy. Glasses. Squished nose, like a pug."

Ana resisted trying to picture the man herself, and instead focused on Constantine's words: *long, wispy hair. Glasses. Pug nose.*

"We were careful," Constantine continued. "At first anyway. No targeted content. Whatever we could grab. If we were constantly looking up the same Immerser, of course there'd be red flags. But then Tramel started getting *real* specific. Not just Immersers but dates, times. We should've cut that fucker off the second he pushed."

A large RV passed them, rattling the car and setting Constantine on higher edge.

"Are you still stealing Feeds?" Ana asked.

"Hell no. Stopped the second we heard about Fowler. *'We'll be fine, man,'* Pete says. *'It didn't have anything to do with us.'* Fucking Pete."

Constantine fell silent. They neared the Kenosha exits and Ana rode them out until the last one, just before the Illinois border. She turned right, away from Lake Michigan and out to farmlands, half of which were filled with wind turbines that spun in dizzying unison. At a vacant intersection, she paused at a stop sign to allow Constantine's discomfort to sink in.

She waited.

"Sonya knows, doesn't she," he finally said, his head hung with the look of a disobedient child. "Of course she knows. What doesn't she know."

"I can't tell you exactly what your boss does and doesn't know."

"You don't understand. Youtopia isn't just —" He looked at Ana with pleading eyes. "My parents are ReaLifers. My whole goddamn family is a cult. So you can imagine their reaction when I took the job. If I get fired..." He shook his head. "I've got nowhere else to go."

You should have thought of that before you stole Feeds, the motherly side of Ana thought but did not say. Instead, she flipped on her blinker, U-turned in the intersection, and headed back to Youtopia Towers.

***

Ana conference-called her team immediately and looped in Bruce. She sent Jade to Crivitz: as the most personable member of her team, Jade was the strongest choice to coax Fowler's indiscretions out of his former acquaintances. That meant the job of looking into Constantine and Pete—Peter Alistair, also young and newer to Youtopia—and their video theft fell to Michael. Michael's voice boomed confidence: he was on it, was already looking into them. Ana would have something within hours.

Bruce cut in to say they needed more people. The urgency of the Healthcare Bill passing both chambers hung thick in his voice. He told Michael to bring on two people of his choosing, offered Jade two of her own, and then assigned two from Chicago to follow up on the Tramel lead.

"I'm taking Tramel," Ana said.

"No," Bruce said in a deep tone. "Let the local agents handle it."

"Bruce, those kids might tip him off. We need to move before he does."

A silence fell over the line. Ana was used to these clashes with Bruce, with any superior at the Bureau, but they rarely happened in front of her team. The sound of his bouncing ball started in through the line, and the noise immediately grated on Ana.

"You're the only one on the Feeds," Bruce said. "Find everything you can there. If nothing materializes, then you can join your new team members."

The ball stopped. Bruce had offered her an unsatisfying truce. But before Ana could object, he cut the line. In the new silence, Ana heard the ticking of laptop keys.

"Got one of the videos already," Michael said. "Not Fowler. I'll log it anyway."

"Great catch, Ana," Jade said. "Bruce didn't say it, but it was great."

"Yes," Michael agreed. "Finally feels like we're crawling out of the hole."

"I'm hitting Tramel," Ana said. "I'll let you know after."

Jade began, "But Bruce said to—"

"I know what Bruce said. It's my goddamn lead. The Feeds aren't going anywhere." She wanted to add, '*And they aren't even real,*' but held back.

Silence. Jade and Michael clearly had little experience with superiors butting heads.

"Jade, take your two people to Crivitz. And Michael, use yours if you can."

"Got it," Jade said.

Michael's fingers stopped clicking as he said, "Go kick some ass."

***

Chicago welcomed Ana like a disapproving parent. The inner city felt unnaturally dark. From the sky fell a rain so cold it bordered on hail. Cars drove with aggression, cutting her off and spattering her windshield with more rain.

It was past dinnertime when she reached Fourth and Pike. Tramel's place was underground, fusty. Its entrance at the base of a stairwell had the feel of a speakeasy, no signage or sound, heavy wooden door with an ocular peephole. Ana stood before it in jeans and a sweatshirt with the hood sticking to her hair. She knocked, shivered, watched the hole until the light behind flickered.

"Closed," a voice said.

"I hear you've got Youtopia Feeds."

The door swung open with slow reluctance. The man behind — who must've been Tramel — was older than Ana expected, his wispy gray hair in shocks above his head. He appeared as though she'd just woken him from deep sleep.

"Wanna announce it to the whole city, sweetheart?" His eyes skittered up the stairwell. "One, I got no clue what you're talking about. Two, like I said, we're closed. Not taking new clients."

Ana looked behind Tramel to a dark hallway littered in graffiti. From her pocket, she pulled a thousand dollars in lumped hundred-dollar bills.

Tramel's stare tunneled on the cash. He fought an internal struggle not to take it, but as Ana knew, like any good dealer, he would eventually accept. He slid aside, making way for Ana to enter.

The inside was even dingier, smelling of damp drywall and hidden pockets of mold. Unmarked doors dotted the hallway like entrances to lonely apartments. From behind one, a man issued a soft groan of pain or pleasure — Ana couldn't tell. If there were any lucrative aspects of the business, she found no signs of them.

"Who told you about us?" Tramel asked.

"Alistair," Ana replied. She looked for Tramel's reaction, but his face gave nothing.

He marched her all the way to the end of the row. The door creaked from wear. Inside sat a small dilapidated couch, a bulky virtual reality headset wired to a small black box, and nothing else.

"Your grand gets you an hour," Tramel said. "Two-fifty more for every ten minutes you go over. You think that's too steep, you can piss off and find someone else crazy enough to supply right now."

"Money's not a problem," Ana said. "I'm looking for something specific."

"Everybody is sweetheart." He picked up the VR headset, a clunky, black band with fingerprints smudged on the front plastic. With a rag that looked no cleaner, he wiped at it. "Menu will take you through. Time travel, crime, daredevil stuff. Sex and drugs and rock n' roll."

"Even more specific."

"Like?"

"I need to find a particular Immerser."

Tramel leaned toward Ana, squinting. His eyes lit in recognition. "Oh fuck. You're Downer."

He dropped the VR headset to the couch. Ana chided herself for moving too quickly, before she could peruse his setup, but she was also relieved to drop the façade. His confidence shed like a snake's skin, his body cowering. He was no longer in control. He'd allowed her in, and she would get something from him before he could force her back out.

"This is entrapment."

"I'm not here to bust you. I need to know about Charles Fowler."

"I didn't kill the guy."

"I never said you did."

A door opened down the hall. Tramel quickly excused himself to intercept his other customer. They whispered; Ana heard Tramel say "FBI." The customer scurried out.

Ana picked up the headset and peered in. The backdrop was a cloudy sky, similar to Youtopia's label and in stark contrast with the menu in front of it, holding categories like *Gangbang* and *Dismemberment*.

"I'd put that down, sweetheart," Tramel said as he returned, his back straighter, some of his confidence regained. "Paying customers only."

"Do all your clients come here? Or do you distribute too?"

"Take a guess."

She stepped to Tramel. "I know where you got your Feeds. I need to know your buyers."

"Want me to sandbag my whole client list?"

"Someone asked for early Feeds, for the original Immersers. Who was it?"

Tramel smiled, displaying dark stains on his front teeth. "I know what you're thinking. I'm a lowlife. A cockroach. A maggot."

"I'm not thinking anything except—"

"Well let me tell you, sweetheart, I provide something these people *need*. And it don't ruin their lives like smack or crystal. I'm the safest dealer in the whole damn country."

"Until someone gets murdered."

Tramel waved a dismissive hand. "Yeah, well, like I said, I don't know jack shit about that."

"Unless this person you sold to is the killer." Ana softened, attempted to get to his level, tried to reach his morality, if he had any. "You had no idea at the time, but now you do. You can make it right, help keep this man from killing again."

This seemed to land. Tramel contemplated for a moment. But only a moment.

"When some guy shoots up a school," he said, "you don't blame the gun shop owner."

"Some would."

"Is it the cliff's fault," he continued as though he hadn't heard, "when some asshole jumps off? Didn't think so." He locked eyes with Ana. "Time to scram."

"I need to know who wanted the Feeds."

"And I need a warrant." He held out a greasy hand. "No? Didn't think so."

"You know I can get one."

"We'll talk then, sweetheart."

Before she left, Ana turned back to Tramel. "You should stay put. It will be trouble for you if you don't."

He flashed his smile a final time. "I promise," he said, with the thick, dark intention of never keeping it.

***

Twenty-four hours for the subpoena, Bruce barked between admonitions. She was given specific orders. She likely spooked Tramel into running. She needlessly risked her own life.

"I needed to see his operations. Trust me, Bruce, this is way over his head. He'll cave."

"You're willing to bet the whole lead on that."

"I wouldn't have done it if I wasn't."

Bruce went silent.

Ana still felt assured, though, that she'd done the right thing, that this branch of the investigation would provide more fruit than any other they'd picked so far. Still, as a consolation to Bruce, she agreed to let the two from Chicago take on Tramel from here on out. She agreed as well to scour the ends of the Youtopia Feed world. She would caffeinate, she would drudge and crawl, and if there was anything like Fowler's rape fantasies to unearth there, she pledged to find it.

"You're on thin ice," Bruce said. "Don't disobey me again."

***

She entered Central Control early. Most employees had yet to arrive. And although Ana felt a deep lethargy, a weariness like some deficiency in her blood, she primed herself for the fast-forward monotony of the Youtopia Feeds. Of lakeshores and ornate kitchens and concert halls, of bean bag toss and kayaking and sex, of lazy white-sand beaches and easy bank robberies. Hour after hour of fantasy worlds. She accepted snacks from the brunette at the front desk; she thrice refilled her coffee. She watched Fowler eat and sleep and shit and fish and attend concerts in a stop-motion frenzy, in scenes that were both frantic and also hypnotizingly sluggish. She watched him fondle his wife and young girls. She discovered nothing.

She moved on to everyone who might have ever known him, trying to uncover a meaningful connection. All these Youtopias were individual, and yet, insipidly similar echoes of these Immersers' lives appeared. They drew on a distinct past and imagined a distinct future, and yet within their flashing moments, Ana found a sad, primal portrait of the human mind.

She slowed the Feed as it darkened — this Immerser taking one of his many catnaps — and her eyes blurred. She shook her head, felt the depths of hunger in her lower stomach. No telling how long since she last had a decent meal, or how many hours she'd inhabited these pseudo-lives. Like someone binging on television, she lost any corporeal sense. Around her, nothing changed, the dim lights the same. Her phone said 5:17, and she had to believe it when it said PM and not AM. Her phone buzzed continually, though not with news from Bruce or her team, but instead with messages from Evan. She regretted giving him her cell number. He called, texted, tried instant messaging through WhatsApp and FamilyMatch. He apologized for actions he didn't do, for reasons he didn't understand. Ana needed to message him, to cut off the contact now. She needed to let him go.

She wanted to let go of the Feeds too, where she found nothing, nothing at all. It felt as though she studied surveillance footage of a glossy underworld, the same loop over and over, full of vice and vicious desires, pleasures and pains and the sordid fantasies one never truly lived. There was nothing for her investigation here. She should've been out in the field, helping Jade gather information on Fowler's potential unpunished crimes. She should've been shaking down Tramel and his buyer, whoever he was.

But the baton, fiery in her hand from so much connection, made a sudden decision. A new path. She looked to its smooth black surface. It accepted her touch like a lover. Together, they reached an understanding as to where this new search would lead.

The idea, of course, had surfaced from her unconscious and floated on the shores of her mind many times before this moment. 'You have access to everything I myself have access to,' Sonya had said. In those words, Ana now heard the echoing toll of her own downfall. They all contained sordid fantasies, so why would his be any different? Youtopia held the secrets he harbored, ones he could never tell Ana. His most private desires. She shouldn't, and yet she knew she would, that she had to. She'd expected that she could do her job, could examine the Feeds without faltering to her own weakness, but as the baton retrieved the Feed— Immerser S217720, Paul Downer—she realized how foolish she'd been to believe in her own strength.

Paul's Feed opened in immediate, startling clarity, to their bedroom years ago. The details were strikingly accurate: their wedding photos arranged across their bureau, each picture in its correct frame; the nail holes spattered about the windows, curtain rod failures all; the bedposts scratched by their former cat Cinders; the lavender-vanilla candle they lit only during sex. Paul was apparently far more observant than she'd given him credit for.

Here, the candle burned: she'd landed straight on an intimate moment. Rumbling came from the bathroom as the thin sliver of light below the door flicked off. Ana herself emerged. But immediately it felt skewed: it wasn't exactly her, but Paul's Youtopian version of her. In nude-colored lingerie, breasts heavy, legs elongated, ass wider and yet tighter. No cesarean scar, no beginnings of cellulite. Youtopia Ana

JOSEPH REIN

laughed, sashayed with latent confidence. Her hair shone dark in the room's light, held tight by a ponytail she unfurled with a flick. There was something of an anime artist in Paul's rendition of her, the femme fatale she'd never been. She sauntered about him in sultry steps, her movements in time with one of Paul's favorite country songs, a yearning for a simple woman in bluejeans and American pride and older times. Ana wanted to close her eyes; she bit at her lip. Laid bare before her, as though she was an expert psychologist, were her husband's furtive desires, his wishes for her betterment. Comparatively tame, she knew, against the rape fantasies of Fowler. And yet all the same, it weakened her.

Suddenly, into his fantasy erupted a high beeping sound, an errant smoke detector, and Ana recognized the moment—an approximation of a memory. A funfetti birthday cake, forgotten in the oven, had burned to thin black marble. In real life Ana hadn't been performing this elaborate dance—they were having sex, her mostly on top, his fingers grasping and slapping in pleasure. Ana felt the blood rush to her cheeks. Her pulse quickened. She wished this were simply the memory. But then, this was a surprise too. Instead of enacting baser, fleshier desires upon this anime version of herself, Paul's mind softened the moment, had given it a made-for-TV whitewash. Youtopia Ana laughed, even as Paul sprung off the bed.

His gaze approached the door, and Ana, the real Ana, dropped the baton. The reason for his mind's deception revealed herself in a slow push on the door, in Paul scrambling to cover his erect nakedness with a white tee.

"Mommy?"

Ana expelled a hollow, dry moan. Pressure immediately smacked her temples. A fog blurred her vision, blurred her mind, as though she'd been thrust into the middle of a deep migraine, with no fuzzy spots or slight nausea, no warning signs. She wasn't ready for this. She rubbed her thumb to pause, to rewind, to cut the Feed, but the baton lay somewhere on the ground. She couldn't move to reach it.

"It's okay, sweetie," Paul said, looping his legs into the wrong holes of his boxer briefs. "Mommy and Daddy are here."

The door opened, and with it the cavern in Ana's heart. The brown curls, matted to her head. The freckle below her left eye. Her face, rounded with the baby weight she would never lose. She was unaltered, down to the hazel eyes alight in worry over the alarm engulfing them. Paul swooped her, their daughter, her Charlotte, into his arms and shushed softly into her ear.

The cavern pulled Ana down, and she did not fight against it. Her head dizzied and her eyes tunneled in starlit blurs. It wrapped around her, encapsulated and then swallowed her whole.

***

Another alarm rose, grating and resonant. Ana's mind floated about the sound. At first it registered as the smoke detector—but no, this was different, its pitch lower and pressing, like a foghorn with endless air, a police siren perhaps. She worried that someone could be in trouble, and then, that the someone could be her. Her eyes opened to the screen, to Paul's world, now brightened with slats of sun and taupe walls—his painting room. His focus jumped from a nearly bare canvas to his subject, Ana herself, or the buxom version of her. She sat perched atop a wooden stool, a grape-colored sheet draped about her shoulders, her hair in a vine-like braid. Youtopia Ana posed for a portrait, as Ana herself never had in real life. As she would have, if only Paul had asked. His left hand swooped across the canvas but barely left a mark. He was unsure, afraid of mistakes. Even in his perfect world, he aimed to impress her.

The alarm continued its high bleat into the room. It had nothing to do with her, with Paul's Feed. Ana looked to the ground, saw her baton in the corner of the room. She scrambled to it just as the door opened.

Peterson entered. He found Ana in front of the screen projecting her bastardized self, on her knees as though in prayer.

"There's been a situation," he said. He waited for Ana to rise, to retake the baton and close the imbroglio before them.

Ana considered offering an explanation, but could conjure nothing better than an admission of her own weakness, so she said, with a tone harsher than she intended, "Yes? What kind of situation?"

Peterson let go of the door. It closed with vacuum-sealed suction behind him. His face slackened as he adjusted his glasses. In his white coat, he seemed an unprepared doctor about to deliver fatal news.

And then he did: "There's been another murder."

Youtopia Incident Report

Incident #: TW31914
Incident Type: Autonomous Cataclysmic Disruption
Immerser #: S000007
Date/Time of Incident: 2/17/2024; 17:07:14 PM ET
Report Filed By: Seamus Brown, Employee ID 25749

Incident Description:
On the date and time listed above, the Immerser stepped out from a high-profile appointment at a huge government building — think Pentagon on steroids — in Washington, D.C. There was a light rain nobody seemed to feel. Car volume was ample but fluid, speeding past in the way of city traffic. The Immerser shook hands with applauding constituents in your typical Immerser popularity fantasy, his adoring fans running the gamut — men and women and children, black and white and everywhere between. Even dogs perked up when he passed.

Then, suddenly, his view jutted forward. He fell into the busy street. Whether he simply slipped or was nudged is impossible to judge. With such busy and fast traffic, the Immerser was struck immediately by a flashy, pretty decked-out 1969 Chevy Impala.

His Feed sent a distress signal back to his Nest instantaneously. As per regulation, it Reset exactly two minutes later, at 17:09:14 PM ET.

Necessary Background Information:
Caveat: none of what follows is exactly *necessary* to understand the Incident itself, which is a pretty straightforward ACD, an injection of mental certainty, his mind's test to make sure there are still boundaries, that the unreal world around him is still real. The rest of this report is only necessary to explain where things thereafter went a bit, how shall I say, *weird.*

As is also regulation, I continued watching his Feed after Reset. In the first day, the Immerser's healing process was a smoothly sailing ship. He perceived his two Reset minutes as one day, give or take. He awoke in a hospital bed, surrounded by family and friends and all those loving constituents. I mean, a *lot* of admirers crammed into that room. Handsome doctors and shapely nurses served him. All pretty run-of-the-mill.

The first hint that caught my attention though: when the doctor explained the Immerser's injuries, the list went on and on. And on. You know, generally speaking, when Immersers hurt themselves, it's scrapes and concussions and bruised bones, injuries that heal within days and leave no scars. Some minds do worse, but they're the pain junkies, which didn't seem to fit this guy's MO. So here he is, slammed with a laundry list of things that *would* happen if you got hit by speeding traffic: whiplash, herniated disc, internal bleeding, broken ribs.

So, at this point I'm thinking, maybe not pain junkie, but victim complex: i.e., the Immerser's about to revel in the lavish, deferential attention of a long road back. Heroism by recovery. I followed up the next day, expecting hand-delivered meals and extravagant bouquets and sponge baths. I expected his wife to read to him. I expected, eventually, for him to have sex with one or more of the nurses.

Instead, get this: one day later and his ribs have *already healed*! Internal bleeding stopped. This guy went from broken to almost full recovery in what he perceived as *one day*. The man was Wolverine.

So I'm geeking out a bit here. Thinking I stumbled on an Immerser who actually created a comic book out of his world. I mean, superpowers man! I'm expecting tights and flying and hyperbolic villains and daring-do. I had to see more.

But lo and behold, I find that's not it, not it at all. It turns out, in his world, he's no superhero, it's just that *everybody* recovers from this type of thing rapidly. He's not Wolverine; *everyone* is.

I found multiple references in his past—dating back *seven* years!— that planted the seeds of technological advances to accelerate healing. New infrared body baths, mysterious healing herbs discovered in Malaysia. Some real voodoo shit. All there so that, when he gets hit by this car, his mind accepts lightning-speed recovery.

But wait, there's more! I dug deep into this guy—too deep, I'll admit—but boy, did I find gold. To wit: Immersers love bacon. *Love* it. Breakfast and brunch and lunch and linner and dinner, atop burgers, crumbled on ice cream. Everyone can eat unhealthy amounts with no adverse effects, no obesity, no heart disease, no high blood pressure. They get the good without the bad. After all, isn't that what Youtopia is for?

But this Immerser, get this: he has developed an entire *science* around the study of bacon. It's called — no surprises here! — Baconology. And as you've guessed by now, four out of five doctors agree that bacon is the new health food craze, salubrious as celery, cornerstone of a perfect diet. I mean, all Immersers' realities are BS in some way, but I got to hand it to this guy: his logistical gymnastics are impressive.

Another example, in his profession. Lots of people dream of being President, right? It's a common power-trip fantasy. Most Youtopia users never get that far though, because it's too much a stretch from the life they'd led up to that point. No political experience is a big one, but also lack of patience to campaign, to participate in debates, to withstand a nationwide election, et cetera et cetera. In other words, they want to *be* president, but don't want to *become* president.

From what I understand, Immerser S000007 was a Senator, and a fairly prominent one, before entering Youtopia. And so, unlike the common person, his path to the presidency wasn't far-fetched at all. Becoming president would slide into his previous reality like a cold hand into a warm glove. But instead of doing that — instead of fulfilling dreams within the paradigm of a slightly bendable but established reality — this guy went and *bent the paradigm* itself.

To explain: after about a year of Immersion, this guy went from a Senator to the head of the Environmental Protection Agency. The EPA! Not exactly lucrative or preeminent stuff here. I mean, I can't name you a single one in history. The two normal explanations didn't hold: first would be the live-the-good-life mentality, the desire to step out of the limelight. Keep the money, lose the job. But nope, this guy is as narcissistic as ever. He'd sooner get hit by another car than lose his legion of followers. Second is an altruistic-do-gooderism, as in, save the environment and save the world. Again, we've seen where his Youtopia eventually leads, and it ain't there.

So I followed him throughout his career, only to find that, through the years, the head of the EPA slowly but surely *becomes* the preeminent figure in our country. A President in the shadows. The garrulous man behind the men. He has everybody's ear, and they kowtow to him like he's Caesar, but when scandals hit, he is masterfully shielded from scrutiny.

In short, instead of simply becoming POTUS without the common problems of presidency, this Immerser has constructed an entire world of puppet men, with him as ardent puppetmaster.

He is an Original—or the next one after, I guess, lucky number 000007—and so it's possible that the longevity of his stay in Youtopia has caused a drastic inversion of—or tangents from—his original reality. But hey, I'm not a scientist. I'll leave that to the long-term case studies, if they ever happen.

All in all, pretty fascinating stuff. Fascinating to me, anyway. The actual incident is pretty cut-and-dried. It's likely you haven't read this far. Probably no one ever will. I'm just a lowly clerk, filling out what is—despite all the insane stuff I've just mentioned—a pretty humdrum report. File me away on some cloud with the rest, never to be seen again.

Probability of Incident Recidivism:
Slim to zilch.

Recommendation for Further Action:
Monitor Immerser account for two weeks; follow up with Analytics & Logistics if any anomalies. (Which won't happen, but if it does: halloo Stacey! Hope you and baby George are rocking it!)

Chapter 6

"Officially, it's an Autonomous Cataclysmic Disruption," Peterson said. "We usually call them Resets."

Peterson explained this on the drive from Austin-Bergstrom to downtown. Traffic was thick with mid-afternoon commuters. The group rode in a three-tiered SUV, with Sonya's personal guard behind the wheel and Peterson next to him, his eyes squinting through his glasses, his hands often steadying himself on the dash. In the second row, Sonya sat silent, her eyes transfixed on the stream of red taillights before them. In the third row sat Ana, directly behind Sonya and next to Sergio, whom she had not seen in person since their first meeting in her hotel. He ticked away at a miniscule laptop, his screen open to code only he could decipher.

At the terminal, Ana had hoped to speak to Sergio alone, but the three were already together, standing in a stoic semicircle near baggage claim. Ana could only steal a moment as Peterson and Sonya walked ahead, asking Sergio if the Senator's murder could get him any closer to pinpointing the identity of the hacker. Even alone, Sergio seemed distant, his eyes fidgety. "Everything okay?" Ana had asked, to which Sergio nodded. He gave her nothing else, walking ahead until they had reached the rental car.

"This Reset," Ana said. "What is its purpose?"

"It's fundamental to the entire program," Peterson said. They crossed a metro rail track as he explained how death was a necessary part of life, even in a perfect world. Immersers themselves would die eventually, after all. Take S444106 for example, he said. A free solo climber. Part of her perfect world was exactly that thrill, close calls, adrenaline rushes, living on the edge. From time to time the climber needed to err, to slip on slick rock. When she did, smack, down she went on the rocks.

Peterson hit a stride now. He clearly loved describing these things and rarely got the opportunity. The climber perceived a blackout, he continued, and although she remained unharmed overall, her Immersion would be temporarily disrupted. A Youtopia blackout, so to speak. The system sent a distress signal back to the body—to the Nest—where it Reset. In the Immerser's perception of time, this translated to anything from a few minutes to a few weeks, depending on the perceived severity. In real time, exactly two minutes. From there the Immersion continued, like waking from sleep. And, he said with a proud finality, reality remained in check.

"The Immerser wakes up," Ana said, "battered and bruised but alive. Danger still exists, and the world is still plausible."

"That's it," Peterson said.

"But that didn't happen this time."

Peterson didn't respond. He looked to Sonya, whose gaze was adrift in Austin high-rises. He waited a long moment before answering. "It did. It's just that... we didn't know the cause of the Reset was malicious. There were no audio or visual cues. It seemed like an everyday accident. We had no idea the murderer was behind him. We had no idea there *was* a murderer, let alone one lurking in our system, so we couldn't know he'd follow the signal back to the Nest."

"When did the Reset happen?"

"Forty-six days ago."

They entered the Medical District, turning past the capital building and the impressively pillared Governor's mansion. The driver pulled them into the parking garage of the Contemporary Austin, a squat three-story art gallery cornered by taller buildings, its windowless white wall stippled with random blocks of green. Bold letters angled the building with the words WITH LIBERTY AND JUSTICE FOR ALL.

Ana had again been told not to expect the usual crime scene—this time, no slew of squad cars or taped-off areas, with as limited visibility as possible to protect the location—but as they pulled into the parking structure, she saw nothing that would indicate a holding cell of fifty-thousand bodies, let alone the scene of a murder.

She shifted, attempting to get into Sonya's view. "You knew him, before Youtopia."

"They grew up in the same town," Peterson said as the driver put the car in park.

Ana thought to stop Peterson and his toady answering for Sonya, to force Sonya from her implacable silence. She wanted to hear it from Sonya herself.

"He was a great help to us," he continued. "Hard to overstate how important his support was."

Sonya made a quick exit. The driver killed the engine. Sergio shut his laptop. They all followed Sonya to a glass elevator where, once inside, neither Sonya nor Peterson pushed a button to rise. Ana verged on asking why they were here, in a downtown art gallery in Texas and not the Nest itself, not the scene of the crime, when Sonya removed from her jacket pocket a miniscule key the shape and size of a fingernail. She inserted it into a barely visible lock just below the emergency button. A down arrow alighted, even though they were on the ground floor.

Ana looked out into the busied streets of Austin and realized: of course. The Nest was underground.

***

The night before, after Peterson's revelation about the murder, when Ana had returned to her hotel room from Youtopia Towers, it was past ten p.m. The earliest flights were not until mid-morning. She'd received a message from Michael, which she'd listened to with the offhand hope that his work on the stolen Feeds would intersect with both Fowler and the Senator, a triangulation that would seed their arrest. Surprisingly, Michael had uncovered not too little, but too much: he had pinpointed every stolen Feed—his efficiency remarkable—and a large number of them, thousands, were of Fowler and the Senator and the other original Immersers. With the exception of Oscar Haskins, it seemed the original Immersers were prized commodities on the black market. Michael was working with the new members of the team on narrowing down the buyers, and Tramel was proving—as Ana had guessed—a cowering, cooperative perpetrator. But there were so many dead ends, Michael said. It would take time. Time, Bruce was sure to remind them, they didn't have, especially since another was now dead, and in an entirely different manner.

Restless, shaken by the Senator's death and the specter of Paul's Feed, Ana drank one glass of cabernet that quickly became two as she scrolled the internet on her phone. She Googled recipes and sports headlines and tabloid columns, anything mindless to occupy her sleepless time as she awaited her flight. But in the banner of almost every page, popping up like so many spring flowers, were ads for cribs, for pacifiers and unisex blankets and jungle-themed bouncers. Somewhere, her algorithm noticed the increased frequency of her visits to her FamilyMatch account. It quantified her desires. At first, she was upset that the creators of such algorithms didn't care about the emotionally manipulative consequences of their actions, but then onto her screen flashed one for preemie diapers and her hands sunk to her lap. Charlotte had been premature, just over five pounds and — though she avoided the NICU — still barely big enough for the smallest diapers. They had to fold the tops under her healing umbilical cord. Most parents complained about diapers, the cost and smell and pervasiveness of them, but Ana enjoyed how quickly Charlotte went up a number, how, like a height chart, the simple size of her waist indicated something extraordinarily natural. She closed her internet browser and immediately called Evan.

He answered after the first ring, a jumble of music and broken voices behind his. He excused himself for a long minute, long enough for Ana to consider hanging up, but then he returned. Faucets and hand driers thrummed behind his voice.

"This isn't much better," he said. "I'll text you."

Immediately, he sent a photo of himself in the men's room of an Irish bar. *Look at this guy!* he captioned, referencing a muscular man in a revealing shirt behind him. *Not sure if he wants to punch me or kiss me.* He followed with a string of absurd emojis. He was at O'Malley's, just a few blocks from Ana's hotel. It was karaoke night.

Ana changed, threw mascara over her swollen eyes, and headed out.

At the door of O'Malley's, Evan hugged her with the familiarity of old friends. He didn't mention the county festival, her desertion of him, which was more generous than she deserved.

She ordered another cabernet as Evan took the stage and performed a middling but comical '80s one-hit wonder. After, she told him about her pending trip to Austin.

"You get to go everywhere!" he said. "Your job is rad. And I say that with full knowledge of how un-rad the word rad is."

"It's not that great," she said, shouting over a screeching Lady Gaga number. "We're in and out in a flash. In California, I didn't get a single minute on a beach."

"Oh, I've got the one," he said, and then, when the song ended, pulled Ana on stage and thrust a mic into her hand. As the opening notes of The Mamas & The Papas flooded the bar, Ana thought again to flee, but then, wasn't this why she had called him? His infectious amiability? His chummy California dreams? And so she sang.

They ordered another drink. Evan ate free popcorn with the hunger of a teenager. The bill came; Evan ignored it, and so Ana took it up. As the rest of the patrons filtered out, Evan turned to Ana and placed a hand on hers.

"I don't want to read too much into things, but..." He dragged out the word, wanting it to say the rest. Ana looked away. "Are we doing this?"

Ana felt a sweet taste in her mouth. She would need to sleep, and wake, in a matter of hours, would need her sharpest eye, her most focused lens, for the Senator's crime scene. She started in with the normal excuses: the day had been too much; it was too late for such weighty decisions; she needed a clear head, not to be swayed by simple emotions; it needed to be right.

"Bah," Evan said. "Doesn't *everyone* choose this by feel? Babies wail and whine. They smell. They're expensive. God, they're expensive."

"You're not doing a great job of persuading me."

"All I'm saying is, if we went by logic, nobody would ever have a child. Ever."

The bartender walked near them, hovered in an obvious attempt to shuffle them toward the door. Evan still held Ana's hand. But what could she tell him? How could she explain that her feel, her emotion, slid so sneakily on a scale from yes to no, from everything to nothing, without reason? She didn't know. She might never know, and yet had little time to decide. She was stringing him along, yes, and that was entirely unfair to him. He had a right to keep asking. But she also recognized that giving him an answer, even if it was yes, would extricate Evan from her life. Though she found it hard to believe, she wasn't ready to let him go.

As she said goodbye, he offered a weak smile, the fun-loving look in his eyes replaced by something else — not quite anger, but its kin. For the first time, he walked away without asking to meet again.

At the airport, awaiting her plane and needing sleep that wouldn't come, Ana turned to the news cycles, all of which caught wind of the Senator's death far too quickly — obituaries, X trends, editorials across the spectrum of hagiography and hatred. Conspiracy theories from X-ACT, some of which seemed increasingly plausible. She checked the ReaLife website and social media feeds but found nothing, a strange silence from the same Terrance Martin who commented on American events as they happened, who live-tweeted television shows and tennis matches in a celebration of life and creativity. In the past, he had even condemned the Senator by name, had called him Charon escorting people by the thousands across the River Styx.

Curious, too, was Washington's mild reaction. Ana had expected, with an assault on one of their own — no matter the possible animosity caused by his departure — that the President would immediately veto the Healthcare Bill, would reconsider handing millions of Americans the keys to a house in which a murderer lurked, soundless and omniscient. But inside sources said that no, it wouldn't happen. The train was chugging ahead on course, and this murderer wouldn't be the conductor. The United States, after all, never negotiated with terrorists, never played by their terms. If anything, more media focus had turned to Ana herself, to the lack of progress in the FBI's investigation. Youtopia was the technological marvel of the country, if not the world. Their systems, patented and hidden behind impregnable walls, had now proven susceptible to an insidious hacker not once but twice. And the FBI had done... what? If anyone should have had better knowledge than a private company, it was the United States government. Morning news anchors across the political spectrum questioned whether the Bureau was the correct answer, or whether the investigation might be better outsourced to more knowledgeable private firms. They wondered if Anabel Downer was the answer. And Ana, sitting in the airport, then the plane, then Peterson's rental car, then the elevator descending them into an underground murder scene, wondered if they might be right.

***

The elevator doors opened to a room with six men—two Youtopia guards, two local PDs, and two Kevlar-suited, AR-15-donning Feds—standing beside a small table and undersized door. Into a small tray, as though going through airline security, Peterson cleared his pockets and removed his belt. Sonya placed her satchel beneath the table. Sergio and Ana followed, removing all metal, standing arms akimbo in front of the Feds' squealing wands. One guard handed Peterson a tablet donned in thick patterned rubber, like an SUV tire. The door behind them had no handle, only a coin-sized keypad, which Peterson called one of the most secure lock mechanisms in the world.

"These men arrived this morning," he said. "We have guards, but they're down in the Nest. Or they were." The weight of the deceased dragged him down, but he recovered quickly and motioned to the door. "The murderer used a Worm to get through, which should be impossible."

"A Worm?"

"An untraceable encryption key," Sergio said. "A bypass of sorts. Think of it this way: you reach the door, but can't pick the lock, so you use a Worm, which overrides the old lock and makes a new one. Once you get through, both lock and key erase themselves from the door's memory."

"Which is why no alarms sounded," Peterson said. On the tablet, he opened bird's-eye surveillance footage of the room in which they stood. The room was, as he'd said, unoccupied. Ana watched as the elevator doors opened and the muscular body of the assailant strode into the room with aplomb. He was dressed in all black, pants seamlessly connecting to pliant shoes, sleeves underlapping gloves. Tinted glasses, tight cloth about the nose and mouth. Hardly a trace of skin showed, save the small slivers of his forehead. He looked shorter than Terrance Martin, but the view was imprecise at best. She tried to compare him to the height of the elevator door, the keyhole, and even then, she couldn't account for the camera angle, the fish-eye effect that obscured depth. She would need the right machines back in DC, and time. Meanwhile, the assailant marched on, all clandestine confidence, pulling what must have been the Worm from an unseen pocket at his waist. The door opened, the light from the hallway bathing in on him, as he made his murderous way forward.

Peterson escorted them through as well. A succession of widening hallways followed, all high-performance concrete and steel doors and halogen overheads that hummed like summer cicadas. Guards stood along the way, armed men who were not, Peterson reminded them, stationed there yesterday. At each impasse, Sergio watched over Peterson's shoulder, but all the pad showed was similar footage of the assailant marching his way through. Every few seconds, tepid air puffed through slatted vents in the wall. It felt, as underground spaces often did, claustrophobic and cavernous. Finally, they reached another elevator, where Sonya swiped her card—Peterson again showing them the assailant doing the same with his Worm—and pressed the lone button, the circle flashing red. They descended again.

"Who would have a Worm capable of this?" Ana asked.

"Worms sell on the dark web for a pretty penny," Peterson said. "But none this sophisticated. None that could override our system."

"But this one did."

"This murderer, whoever he is—he's a step ahead," Peterson said, drawing a noticeable cringe from Sonya. "Likely, he coded the Worm himself."

Down deeper now—three, four stories—how deep was impossible to tell. Finally the elevator settled with a disorienting shake. The doors opened.

The crowded room opened itself to Ana, narrow but deep, very deep and ominous, dimly lit but for the spotlights of the evidence crews. It felt like the interior aisle of a densely packed auditorium. She counted twelve, fifteen, twenty authorities from Youtopia, Austin, and the Fed alike, all huddled in bunches around the three corpses on the floor. The local field agent in charge was a shaved-bald man who introduced himself as Darren, but Ana hardly heard him speak, mesmerized by what lay beyond them, by the hallowed glow of the Nest itself.

Ana stepped forward. Peterson and Darren spoke, but she only saw the floor-to-ceiling, wall-to-wall glass containing some viscous liquid that floated and pulsated with small fissures, almost like mini bursts of lightning, everywhere and at random. The liquid was cloudy, like curdled milk spilled into water, and seemed endless. It swayed in perpetual motion. It was as though Ana could see through a window into the ocean's twilight zone.

She continued forward until she stood just feet from the glass. The air around her felt saturated with humidity. She reached out, partly expecting her touch to generate some sort of static electricity, to fuse at her fingertips like a plasma globe. But then she saw something deeper. Its color and shape peeked through, then disappeared just as quickly. She fixated on the point, lost it entirely, believed she might not have seen it at all, only for it to appear again. It pressed forth for a second, no longer, but long enough to register: the distinct, bean-shaped curve of a human foot.

"Miss Downer," Peterson said. He placed a hand on her arm.

"How many are in there?" she asked.

"Fifty thousand. Well, minus one."

"And they all share this," Ana said, waving a hand at what she could only describe as an elaborate aquarium.

"Yes. I know the popular conceptions of the Nests: a catacomb, or a prison." Into Peterson's eyes came a reverence, almost a longing. "But their physical stasis actually works better when together."

"There's an irony in that."

"Yes. Yes, I suppose there is."

"Perhaps," Sonya interjected, calling out from behind, her voice an echoing shock into the room, "first you would like to see how the Nest works."

At the behest of Sonya, her own guards parted from an unremarkable patch of wall. She pressed her palm and it immediately enlivened in a peach-red glow, a handprint echo reverberating out, until a small command platform rose from the ground. It contained unlabeled buttons and rotating hemisphere controls and a keyboard into which Sonya typed, even though no screen revealed the output.

"Another system the intruder hacked," Peterson said over Ana's shoulder. "Different recognitions, but they share unfortunate weaknesses."

Over his voice came an echoing hone, almost like the underwater wail of some deep ocean creature. Sonya finished typing and turned to the Nest, where, from the depths of the clouds, materialized a sudden and shocking horde of human feet. There were hundreds, one atop the other and separated by something unseen, their legs visible only to the calf. The toes were curled like arthritic hands, but the skin was smooth, unworn. Ana recalled Fowler on the autopsy table. On each heel, tattooed in miniscule print, was their Youtopia Immerser number.

"The Retrieval Pod is right there," Peterson said, pointing to a spot on the glass just beside the Senator's body. "We designed this feature as a safety precaution. To pacify the government, mostly."

"There is your true irony," Sonya said, looking directly to Ana. "An unnecessary feature, meant to appease needless worries, and it has caused a man's death."

Ana looked at the feet, at the strange disembodiment of the legs, wondering if any of them would seem familiar — the crook in the second toe, the high arch, S217720, Paul's identification number — but it was all a blur.

Sonya typed in another command, and the feet withdrew back into the clouds.

Ana turned her attention to the dead bodies on the floor, starting with the Senator's. Like Fowler's, his body was pallid and ashen, covered in grayish-white hair, though his was far patchier, bald in inexplicable places, like some sickly animal. His face, under the halogen glow of the spotlight, was almost unrecognizable. And yet it was the Senator.

Around her she heard only footsteps and shuttering cameras. She asked into the silence, "Who was first on the scene?"

A local officer stepped forward. Mustachioed, middle-aged, he appeared dumbstruck by her, by everything.

"Was the body just as it is now?"

"Didn't touch a thing," he said, nodding to his men, who did the same. He looked to the Senator, then up at the Nest itself, not with wonder or natural curiosity but with fear. Ana wondered if he had ever had contact with Youtopia before this. She knew the high concentration of ReaLifers in the South, in law enforcement, and she wondered if he, if his men, felt a particular way about the Senator, about everything around them.

She approached Darren, who had his team scattered about the room searching for hairs or fingerprints, trying to fill the gaps in the surveillance, if there were any. The look on the agent's smooth face told Ana they'd found nothing.

"Get the locals out of here," Ana said. "The guards too. Anyone who's not collecting evidence."

Darren nodded toward Sonya and Peterson. "What about them?"

"I'll send them up in a minute."

She rounded up Sergio, walked to Peterson, and pointed to his tablet. "Show us the rest."

Peterson cued up the video. Where they stood now, Ana saw the two guards perched against the wall, chatting in unsuspecting wait. One flipped a coin in the air, caught it, and then slapped it with an audible clap on his hand. He shook his head, and the other guard thrusted up an enthusiastic fist. Ana felt a sudden sympathy for these men, who knew nothing of their imminent fate.

Abruptly, the elevator doors opened. The guards lifted their heads but slowly, expecting a superior, one of the very few people with access to the Nests, perhaps Sonya herself. The assailant moved swiftly in surprise. The first guard looked to the coin as though searching for a spot to place it, a ridiculous concern in hindsight. The other reached for his rifle, and Ana expected the assailant to retrieve some blunt, untraceable weapon, or to turn the rifles against them, but he attacked with only his limbs, knocking the guard unconscious with a single kick. The rifle clacked down with his limp body. This all in less than two seconds. Then the assailant turned to the first guard, who drew his weapon but not quickly enough—the assailant maneuvered in deft, feline-like pounces across the room, and before the guard could fire a single shot, the assailant swept his feet from under him. The guard fell. In the assailant's movements Ana recognized the method: Silat, one of the world's deadliest martial arts. She would check the backgrounds of Terrance Martin, Fowler and his wife, Jeanne Haskins, Peterson and Sonya themselves — anyone and everyone, no matter how implausible — for history of such training.

Both guards lay on the ground, unmoving. The assailant kicked at the guard's rifle, sending it up into his hands. He approached the incapacitated men and unceremoniously loosed bullets into their chests.

Ana looked to Sonya, whose eyes were pinched shut. Peterson said, "We've sent a team to their families. Funeral coverage, college expenses for their children... it's important to make this right." When Sonya opened her eyes, tears slipped from the corners.

Ana returned to the video and focused on the assailant, who discarded the rifle and stood now at the glass, placing his hand on it, same as Ana had, in a kind of wonder. Then he tapped, first with a finger, as though trying to attract the Immersers' unconscious attention. He ran his hand all along the glass to the wall, searching for and ultimately finding the control panel censor. Ana briefly looked over at Sergio, who was no longer watching the surveillance, but stood instead before the control panel, probing it with professional scrutiny.

As the feet emerged, the assailant crossed the room. Slowly, a corner of the glass stretched out into the room in a coffin-like rectangular shape. "The Retrieval Pod," Peterson said. Inside it rested the pale, hairless body of the Senator.

Ana wanted to stop the tape there, to ask Peterson to show her the Retrieval Pod now, wanting to recall some Immerser at random just so she could get a better sense of it, so she could see that, beyond the haze, the feet and legs were connected to real, alive people.

But then, on the video, the assailant reached into the pod, submerging his arms and torso into the treacly liquid. Within seconds, he tore the Senator's supine, sedentary body from its sedation. It broke free swiftly, leaving behind any number of thin, clear, tentacle-like tubes in its wake. It shed what seemed to be a layer of skin. The only snag happened at the throat, the Senator's mouth gaping open and expunging a thick tracheal tube. The assailant was strong, handled the body with ease, but then, the Senator's body was almost entirely devoid of muscle, pale and infantile. It looked, Ana couldn't help but think, dead already. Ana waited for the assailant to retrieve the gun, to do what he came to do. Instead, he simply dropped the body and walked back to the elevator.

"Cardiac arrest," Peterson said. "Reintegration into our world is purely hypothetical, of course, but this... this won't do."

"Show me his death."

With hesitation, Peterson sped up the video, fast-forwarding through nearly thirty minutes of footage until the Senator's body jerked in stiff, spastic motions. He slowed it down to live speed, but the feral, shaking body looked no less grotesque as it writhed and writhed until, anymore, it didn't.

Ana returned to the Nest wall, to the floating mass of bodies contained within. Darren arrived at her side, and together they shared a long moment of staring uncertainty.

"We could order in the scuba team?" Darren said at last. "We've used them down on the coast. And this is a hell of a lot smaller than an ocean."

Ana considered this, considered the time it would take to get inside—if it was even safe for their team or the Immersers to do so—and begin extracting whatever they might find. And what might that be? A hair? A flake of skin? Even if they did find something, they would need to run it against the fifty thousand other bodies in that same tank for which the match would be more likely. Such a process would take far more time than they had.

She turned to Sonya. "How does this stay clean? Some sort of filter?"

"You mean like a swimming pool," Peterson said. "It's a bit more sophisticated than that, but yes, there is a cleansing process."

"We'll scan those." She turned to Darren. "Send anything that has come through there in the past twenty-four hours to Washington. It's a longshot, but it's the best we can do right now."

"Work with our team," Sonya said. "We need to proceed cautiously, for the safety of those still inside."

Ana turned to Sonya with an elevated feeling in her chest. Sonya's silence, her guards demurring to her simple stares, grated at Ana. She realized for a brief moment that she'd often felt this way with Charlotte—a simple yet intense frustration—and felt now a similar inability to stop herself from acting upon it. "And what about the safety of the other Nests? I assume you've added security to each one."

"Now we have, yes," Peterson answered.

Ana bristled at the sound of Peterson's voice. "She can speak for herself." She stepped toward Sonya's face, too close. "I need all Nest locations sent to the DOJ. We need Marshals, Secret Service even. If you had put these measures in place beforehand, this man would still be alive. A single person monitoring your Immersers' drug levels could have saved Charles Fowler. These two deaths didn't need to happen."

Sonya's face was imperturbable; she seemed not to breathe. "Miss Downer, you have locks on your front door, yes? On the handle, and perhaps a deadbolt. The outside door to your building likewise has a lock. This you consider sufficient. Do you also lock your bedroom door when you sleep? Have you installed motion sensors in your living areas? Would you employ armed guards to keep watch at your door?"

"My apartment and a place that stores thousands of susceptible people are hardly comparable."

"That is correct. We do receive death threats. Hundreds a day, from extremists on all sides. We ward off more cyberattacks in a day than the United States government. I have considered all angles of security, even extra when it is warranted."

"You didn't feel Fowler's death warranted it?"

Sonya inhaled a long breath. "The murderer infiltrated our system. We believed we had flushed him out. We also believed he was never there in the first place. So if he is still there, he will certainly see any order for increased security, Federal Marshals and Secret Service all going to the same place. Would we not hand him the very thing we mean to protect?"

Sonya's eyes returned to the Nest, to the Senator's body. "You asked about him before. Yes, we shared a brief past. He came to me with every skepticism, and I showed him — " Her voice caught. "I showed him what was possible. He, in turn, showed me that anybody can believe. That I must believe in *myself.*

"One does not employ twenty guards when, for ten years, two have sufficed. One does not hire countless workers to monitor, second by second, the Feeds of half a million Immersers. I don't think, Miss Downer, you realize the gravity of the criminal with whom we are dealing.

"We have increased our measures to ensure these travesties do not happen again — more locks and walls and barriers — but these implementations are all defensive.

"We at Youtopia do not track down murderers. We are not the Federal Bureau of Investigation. That is you."

***

The ride back to Austin-Bergstrom was somber. Peterson linked his phone to the console, and they proceeded silently to a strange soundtrack of samba, acapella classics, and grunge. Sonya answered an endless string of emails on her tablet. After a few, Ana began counting: Sonya averaged three per minute. Sergio also swiped away on his phone. Ana expected work, but when she peeked, she saw messages between him and his wife. He told her, in three separate messages, that he loved her.

They reached I-35, and the car became flecked intermittently with streetlights and billboard reflections. For Ana, the implications of the Senator's death rested discomfiting, like a suffocating blanket. She found

Sonya's and Sergio's focus on menial tasks impossible. Fowler's death was detailed, thorough, but ultimately unrepeatable. They simply monitored the Immersers' levels more closely, and installed further failsafes to prevent overdose. But these Resets — virtual near-deaths that reroute an Immerser's signal — were, they assured her, vital for the Youtopia Immersion process. They couldn't be stopped. But even if they could, the Senator's had occurred nearly two months before his murder.

Ana waited for a break in Sonya's furious correspondence, but there was none, the stream of people to whom she must answer apparently endless, the conversations stitching into one another with no seam. They would arrive at the airport in minutes. Ana reached forward and placed a hand on Sonya's shoulder. Sonya's body absorbed the hand without flinching.

"We need all the Resets," Ana said, "starting with the most recent."

Sonya remained silent. She slashed about on her tablet and then handed it back to Ana. Across the screen appeared a spreadsheet of Youtopia Incident Reports of Autonomous Cataclysmic Disruptions, all the way back to the beginning — a comprehensive and immense list. In the past year alone, over four hundred had occurred. Ana scanned for any notable names, anyone who might be the next target: an aging actress, a handful of former religious leaders, a musician from Ohio. She looked for the original Immersers. She tilted the screen to Sergio, interrupting his own flurry of messages. "We'll cross-reference all of these names," she said. "First thing when we return."

Sergio finished typing before he looked over, offering only a curt nod.

One of Peterson's symphonious songs ended and the brazen chords of a '90s metal song screeched into the car. He apologized as he muted it, and shuffled through his phone for something lighter. Ana returned Sonya's tablet. As the low mum of an acoustic song filled the car, she imagined the forceful body of the assailant hefting the Senator's body like a knapsack, like nothing at all. She saw the legs and arms of the ghost-like body flail downward, dripping and drab, the octopus tubes retracting as though alive.

But as the body rested, as the head turned to view, she saw not the Senator's face, but Paul's.

∗∗∗

Inside the terminal, Sergio parted toward his gate. Ana watched him shuffle away, head in his phone, nearly bumping into businessmen and families dressed for vacation. She couldn't just let him go. She weaved around a line for coffee, a band leaning on guitar cases. When she grabbed Sergio's arm, he jolted, blinked. His eyes struggled in adjusting to her sudden reemergence.

"We need to talk," she said.

He looked about, as though for an emergency. Seeing none, he lowered his phone and focused back on her. "This isn't the best place."

"It'll have to do." Ana placed a hand on Sergio's shoulder. He appeared aged, even since the car ride to the Nest just hours ago. "Is everything all right? You're not acting like yourself."

He shook his head. "It's not me you should be worried about right now."

"That's what we need to discuss."

She led him to the wall, near an unmanned station selling overpriced headphones. And though she shouldn't have, she whispered out things he might have already considered: that, by tracing other Resets, the assailant likely knew the location of the other Nests. That he was unlikely to try another murder like this one. That, in fact, the single act itself was probably a message, a display of power. That his real aim was likely a larger-scale attack. That he could, if he wanted —

"Yes," Sergio interrupted. "He could kill every single person in Youtopia."

JOSEPH REIN

Chapter 7

Ana spent two hours watching the security footage in Central Control, over and over again, beginning to end, pausing and rewinding, until it appeared: not a clue, but the rainbow blur of a migraine, hovering just over the killer's covered face on the screen.

Not now. She reached for her purse. *Not now.*

Her visit to the Nest, the Senator's death, the importunate danger that the murderer now presented to Paul, to all in Youtopia: all of this needed to steel Ana's resolve. She had leads. She had a possible catastrophic event — no, even more: a mass genocide. She needed to be invigorated, infused with caffeine-like jolts of focus. In previous cases, she had reached such a point, and none of those had possessed nearly the scope, the scale of consequences, she now faced. She needed to hum.

She started by sending field agents back into the Nest to scan for DNA. Taking Darren's suggestion, and against Sonya's wishes, she called for the scuba team. It was the longest shot of all, but a shot nonetheless, and cases had been solved with less. They might match a non-Immerser skin flake with a sample lifted from a Coke can given to some suspect during questioning. Almost all perpetrators of this magnitude committed petty crimes earlier in life. But then, this was no common perpetrator. He possessed prowess both technical and physical, could hack the digital and the material. This combination of online sophistication and the sheer force, savvy, and calm during an actual murder, was something Ana had never before witnessed. Unlikely he'd left a trace in the Nest, but she needed to try.

Michael's people were focused on the traffic cameras in downtown Austin, scanning every license plate, running facial rec on anyone with a clear shot. Because of the urgency of the case, they'd subpoenaed local cellphone footage as well, lifting any video or pictures taken within a half-mile radius. They got subpoenas too to access location data for Terrance Martin and his associates, which would arrive any minute. Ana hoped that Michael moved with his regular speed, that he would have something by the end of the day. She checked her phone to see if she missed anything from him, but she had nothing.

Some things she needed to do herself, to put her expertise to work. It began with the profile. With this new murder — and unless they found a connection between the Senator and Fowler — the likelihood of a personal motive had diminished. This had become anti-Youtopia. A clear message. The entire team needed to focus on people with personal, moral, or financial incentive to see Youtopia fall. The newspaper clippings on Terrance Martin's door returned to her mind, crisp and prescient. They needed to question him again.

But most of all, she needed something from the surveillance video. This killer — who had the know-how to infiltrate Fowler's Youtopia and murder him in the only possible fashion — had not bothered to dismantle the security cameras that oversaw the Nest. He wanted them to see. For Ana to see. He left her with the type of evidence normally reserved for the supercilious or the careless. The video evidence had allowed her to analyze angles and comparative heights of other marks, to identify his height and body type — six-foot-two, roughly 190 pounds — and handedness — right. She pinpointed a particular posture he returned to, chest out and shoulders back, elbows bent, more feminine than masculine. Exactly this type of evidence had launched her career in the Villalobos case, where the killer, a 39-year-old man named Jerry Slate, sent taunting and ultimately incriminating videos to the family's close relatives — his performance pieces. The relatives didn't watch them in full; even some of her colleagues shied away from their grotesquery. But Ana watched again and again, each time assessing a different peculiarity, the slanted crown molding, the carpet stains, the morbid, juvenile artwork Slate hung on his walls. After two days, her eyes scorched from digital burn and her head in the throes of a migraine, Ana had finally found it — a window. Or rather, a reflection when the sun hit it just so. In a split second where he believed himself off camera, as he marched from the room, Slate peeled off his macabre mask and revealed just a sliver of his face, enough to show the distinguishing melasma on his left cheek. They captured him the next day. It was too late for the Villalobos girls, but not too late for his next victims, whom he'd already scouted and had planned to abduct that afternoon.

The Youtopia murderer left this video there for her to watch, over and over again — ten minutes on a continuous loop. She watched it anew each time, burning the commonplace into her memory so that any aberration might spring forth, might take her by surprise. She needed another Jerry Slate moment, another strike of her particular brand of lightning.

But as the migraine blur coated her vision, as she tried to ride it out, she felt weary, heavy in her limbs. The pain meds made her thick with lethargy. She closed her eyes and nearly fell asleep. Peterson's voice echoed in her mind: *a step ahead*. Her body sunk under the weight of the days both behind and ahead of her. She felt shaken, shook up. And now the migraine attacked; she knew she could only stave off its worst effects for so long. The mental demands of her job weighed down on the physical limitations of her body, bullying her into inaction.

She needed to change tactics, leave the surveillance footage, if only for an hour. She also had a new victim, a full ten years of Youtopian life to examine, and though she might not find anything—this murderer was too calculated to show himself unnecessarily, to slip up in the worlds over which he hovered like a pressing, prescient hand—she needed to shake off her doubt. The murder victims couldn't be chosen at random, no matter how widespread the killer's motive. It was this man, in this moment, for a reason—a reason she alone might discover.

She started from the Reset and worked backward. The Senator's memory of D.C. was impeccable, immense: the screen filled with familiar buildings, the Capitol, the Smithsonian, the Eisenhower, the vast swaths of unmarked white stones at Arlington, but also gyro and taco street vendors, one-way streets, serviceable newspaper stands. He attended meetings, during which he mostly spoke. Fawning interns showered him with lavish praise. His wife cooked him dinner every night. He visited whores, both male and female. He attended a version of some Christian church that castigated all the illicit behavior in which he later engaged. Ana found his Feed a curious mix of hyperbolic solipsism and seething ignominy—a strange perfection of opposites.

Noon passed, and she had found nothing. She traced all the way back to his Feed's commencement, to the disconcerting moment when it went live, the nascent eyelids opening like waking from sleep. Like a second birth. She wondered what the Immersion process itself felt like, if it was perhaps the opposite—if, upon closing their eyes, Immersers felt a sort of death. Or perhaps it felt like any other night's rest, leading to a following day both familiar but utterly different.

Paul hadn't asked Ana to be his Observer, but he did ask her to be present during his Immersion, to hold his hand as he said goodbye. Immediately her mind had flashed to a time with Charlotte in the hospital, a minor surgery for an umbilical hernia. Charlotte had inhaled bubble-gum-scented anesthetic and gripped tight to Ana's finger and had been brave, braver than a three-year-old ought to be, braver than Ana herself. The doctor had removed Charlotte's mask while a nurse escorted Ana out, Charlotte's eyelids open just a slit, as often happened while she slept, her hair draped behind her like a pillow. When Ana left the room, her legs seized. She had to brace herself against the nurse.

"She'll be okay," he'd said, and Ana nodded, but she was still struck with the paralyzing fear that Charlotte would never wake up, that the temporary goodbye would become permanent. And even though Charlotte did wake—just an hour later, eyes lolling and tongue pasty in her mouth—Ana couldn't remove from her mind the image of Charlotte disappearing from her view, or its engrossing fear, when Paul had asked her to be there. She couldn't watch him fade away into permanent anesthesia. She couldn't feel that paralysis again, couldn't risk inviting it in. She was afraid it might never leave.

With the Senator's Youtopia yielding nothing, Ana turned to his records of admittance and the myriad signatures on his legal forms. She searched for the name of anyone in the room while he was Immersed, his wife perhaps. Ana went to her laptop and scanned newspaper archives for articles related to his Immersion, remembering something of the shock, the surprise that this man, a highly decorated and impeccable Washington persona, would even consider something that, at the time, was quite radical. His opinion had changed so many others. She hoped to see Terrance Martin's name peek out, like a rabbit from a magician's hat, but his encounters with Youtopia were still years away. She found articles detailing the Senator's decision, accounts of its grandiosity. It was dubbed *The Day Youtopia Became Possible* and *The GOAT Immersion* and, through the lens of X-ACT, *Judgment Day*. Each report was second-hand, reports on reports of watching the broadcast on CNN, a broadcast Ana herself had never seen. Pictures of the event showed the Senator only, pixelated with the filter of screens capturing screens. She pulled up CNN's archives but received an error message: *Footage cannot be found.* She followed up with Youtube and Vimeo, trying to uncover a video that inexplicably didn't exist.

As she reached for her phone, the sudden weight of liquid rushed into her bladder like a dam's release. She needed to use the bathroom, to eat something of substance. She needed caffeine. She wanted to call Sergio but saw numerous voicemails and texts from Bruce. She scrolled through his controlled hectoring: the gist was that Terrance Martin had finally posted something inflammatory on social media. By the time Ana searched it, it had already been taken down, apparently deleted after only a few minutes. Online bloggers caught screenshots of the X thread, which

Ana immediately cross-checked against each other for accuracy. Much of it was dogmatic garble, but around the seventh tweet in, she hit what must have caught Bruce's attention:

> *This person infiltrating Youtopia enacts the will of the Higher Power! what Hell on earth hasn't invited Their scorn! and who are we but to follow Their will???*

Bruce's subsequent texts warned of copycats, of Terrance inciting others to break the law. He feared the pandemonium Terrance might unleash.

Ana called Bruce and looped in her team. She planned to assign one of Jade's people to LA, but before she could speak, Bruce jumped in.

"Just spoke to the President. She's sitting on the Healthcare Bill, asking *us* what to do. Is it more dangerous to sign it or punt it? What's going to prevent more murders?"

Ana considered this, but Bruce cut off her thoughts.

"We're on the defensive. Already talking like this asshole has won. Makes me sick." He spoke briefly to someone off the line, then shot a loud breath through the phone. "Shit. All right. I'm on damage control, but I could use some good news." And then he was gone.

Into the silence, Ana said, "We have anything for him? Jade?"

"Nothing," Jade said, the disappointment thick in her voice. She was driving around Crivitz, the voice of a talk radio host distant in the background. "I got someone from nearly every graduating class. Other than an occasional lingering stare, Fowler never did anything unseemly." Then she added, "I'm sorry, Ana."

"Leads have dead-ends. Never apologize for things that aren't your fault." Ana thought for a moment, then said, "Go to LA. Take both your team members. Shake Terrance Martin up a bit."

"Can do."

"I have something," Michael said. "Maybe something. It took a lot of hoop-jumping, but I was able to identify some of Tramel's buyers. We got some big ones. Whales."

"Like?"

"Like three of our top-ten, including VikkarAll from X-ACT."

"Shit," Jade said.

"He fits the profile," Michael continued. "The technical skill. Plus, he has a hacker's motive to take down Youtopia."

"Can we bring him in for questioning?" Ana asked.

"We'd have to find him first. Hackers that high don't exactly give away their Clark Kent. We have a list, but honestly, none of them seem the right guy, at least to me."

"Go to them anyway."

"You got it, boss."

Ana hung up, and immediately called Sergio. He answered, characteristically, on the first ring.

"I'm trying to find the CNN footage of the Senator's decision to Immerse. For some reason, it's eluding me."

She heard Sergio's fingers click away. Even through the phone it was rhythmic, soothing. A minute passed, and Ana became aware again of her hunger, the primal needs she neglected. The clicking stopped.

"Huh," Sergio said. "I'll look into it. Possible his family had it removed for privacy purposes. That happened sometimes, before video became prolific."

"Michael pins VikkarAll as a suspect. Any chance he has something to do with its disappearance?"

"Maybe. Probably not. Hackers tend to spread information, not delete it."

Silence again, but no tapping. Sergio seemed to believe the conversation over. "So," she asked, "what are our options if it's not online?"

"Hope CNN has it buried somewhere in their analog," Sergio said. Then he laughed. "Or find some relative with an old VHS collection."

"Seriously?"

"No. I can send someone to Atlanta to check the stacks. Give me two hours."

Two hours. She looked at the massive black screen before her, and it all suddenly seemed too much. She needed to leave, to go to LA herself to take on Martin. She needed to eat. She alighted the Feeds, but even a minute more of the Senator's obsequious footage made her queasy with growing, gnawing disdain. These were meant to be perfect worlds of the Immersers' fascinations, but more and more they seemed like vulnerable hotspots, open to the subtle machinations of a murderer. They seemed like easy killing grounds.

She scanned and scanned, her arm heavy and vision blurred, until her hand moved of its own accord. She left the Senator behind and traveled elsewhere. Her subconscious and the wand had reached their tacit agreement, and she moved ultimately, inevitably, where she likely intended to go from the start. Of course, she wasn't going to LA. She wasn't going to eat. She was always going to return here. To return to Paul.

She knew she shouldn't do it—enter into the black hole, the abyss, the gaping maw from which she was unlikely to return. Bruce shouldn't have put her on the case; she should have immediately refused. She should have asked for restrictions on her Feed access. And yet how easy it proved, to simply rub the baton as though testing the ripeness of a fruit. The metallic feel of its veneer, the whistling hum of its brain at work. She was no longer in Youtopia Towers, trying to uncover an ethereal murderer. She was not on the plane, not in the underground Nest in Austin. She was back in that room, seeing the brown freckle-like flakes in Charlotte's worried eyes, her timid steps, her frightened face. "It's okay sweetie," Paul mollified. "Mommy and Daddy are here." Charlotte eased, trusting the stability of his grasp to protect her. She was with Charlotte. She was with Charlotte.

In this way, she discovered the small but crucial incongruencies that made Paul's lie, his Youtopia life, possible. Charlotte's accident was a close call that left her bedridden for weeks but ultimately unharmed. Ana and Paul had referenced it often as a reminder to more closely monitor her near open water. There followed, of course, no funeral, no immediate rift between them. Ana did not submerge herself in the vast oceans of national FBI work, taking the longest assignments possible at the farthest distance from Chicago. She didn't eschew home, and Paul, with the devotion of sorrow. Not drunk on bourbon, Paul never admitted that he had seen a Youtopia specialist, and the ensuing argument didn't push him further toward it. He never shouted, "Give me a good reason to stay!" He didn't shatter a full bottle of Buffalo Trace on their kitchen floor. He never said, "You drove me to this," and this Ana, his Youtopian version, never agreed.

Instead, his Ana took on part-time consultation work. She received intermittent, necessary phone calls but returned quickly. She wore tight, revealing clothing. She smiled often. Paul had likewise landed his own steady job, adjuncting in Art History at Northwestern, a vocation that stimulated him mentally but afforded him more time than he'd had as an unpaid artist. She watched his productivity blossom; he painted Rockwell-style representationalism, still too nostalgic for Ana but not for his mind's version of the downtown Chicago art scene. He landed his first show at Gallery 400 and received all the recognition he needed in compliments and minor sales. Girard Vengale, a Chicago Impressionist whom Paul, and perhaps only Paul, admired, attended and offered muted praise. It was cheap, Ana knew, for one's loftiest dreams to be realized only in Youtopia. All the same, she almost felt, with each handshake, the collective heart-shock of Paul's pride. She almost felt pride herself.

But then she discovered it. She didn't know why she thought it might never materialize, why Paul, of all Immersers, could have been the exception. It happened on an otherwise unremarkable day, with Charlotte reading as Paul painted beside the bay window. Ana watched herself enter from the bedroom, dressed in her full pantsuit, a suitcase by her side. She had been called on assignment out east, for how long she didn't know. It was a scene that had played out in their real lives time and again, with Paul offering an understanding sigh as they mutually made childcare and other arrangements. He'd always kissed her goodbye. He was as supportive as he could be, while also saddened, which felt natural, healthy even. He'd neither begged her to stay nor pushed her out the door.

This Paul, though, stood and walked swiftly toward his Ana.

"Leaving me again."

His voice dripped disdain. His Ana cowered. He took hold of the nearest object to him — a television remote — and coldly smashed it down atop her head. Again, then again. He thrashed her until she bled. He shouted, punishing her for abandoning her daughter, her husband, for leaving all the real work to him while she selfishly built her career. In a mirror, she caught glimpse of his face, bloated and alive with vehemence.

The sight of it startled Ana into pausing the Feed. At his feet, she saw the image of herself with a battered face. On the couch, across the room, Charlotte read her book, unphased by the abuse before her.

Ana fast-forwarded through her recovery, which was swift. She never went on the assignment. Paul apologized. They had aggressive, reconciliatory sex. The cycle repeated every few months. Ana found herself less surprised by the violence of it than by his underlying animosity. In real life he'd never said a word, never let on. But then, Charlotte had been very young when she died, and perhaps the seedlings of Paul's nascent violence just hadn't yet had time to grow. Perhaps it was coming. Or perhaps Youtopia simply provided the mind, as Sonya had suggested, an easy route toward the extreme. Perhaps it catered to and nurtured what might otherwise have been fleeting feelings. Perhaps it brought out the worst.

But Ana moved past Paul's worst, because she hadn't returned for him. She fast-forwarded to moments with her daughter, with Charlotte, spending minutes, hours perhaps, lingering. She had so much time to watch her, and yet so little. Her stomach sang out to her in sudden, sharp refrain as years passed in Paul's world. With them Charlotte grew, gangly and knobby, all sharp angles. Tall, like Paul always wanted. For some reason, she went without a haircut, her chestnut-brown waves reaching beyond her waist. Her face lost its roundness, but was otherwise an extension of itself, like a computer-generated age-progression. Like Ana's falsified body, this perfected face couldn't account for the strange places in which freckles bloom, or how certain features outgrow one another, the lips too thin for the face, the thick eyebrows. She never became ill, lost no teeth. Paul's version of her couldn't account for the spurts and stops of childhood, instead progressing Charlotte—as nobody did—in a steady, rhythmic march to maturity.

Same, too, with her emotional development. This Charlotte was wonderfully articulate, using words few grade schoolers would, yet still she needed help cutting meats, still called Paul *Daddiest*. She still sang the lullaby tune of Paul's mother: *Night will fall too soon, choo-chooing under the moon.* In these moments, Paul's emotional distress became imminently clear: Charlotte was the child he wanted her to be, or needed her to be, her independence floundering in the quicksand of his desires. In these moments, Ana could barely watch more.

But then there were moments—often when Paul was otherwise preoccupied, Charlotte in the periphery or offscreen altogether, only her soft voice resonating from somewhere beyond—that Ana sensed a truer Charlotte. Like the one she arrived at now: Paul watched a World Cup match, two European countries he'd visited when studying abroad in college, his sympathies vying for the one in which he got laid. Ana was off somewhere, at work perhaps. Charlotte sat on the couch adjacent. She read from some old book with no jacket, the television noise and *gooooooooooooooooooal* calls never reaching her. Her eyes scanned in unbreakable attention, and Ana saw in her the vestiges of Ana's own broken memory, a moment she had lost until now.

The lights were low, the house silent. "Char," Ana called out to no reply. "Char. Charlotte." A minute passed, maybe less, but it was enough for the knot in Ana's chest to cinch. She turned into Charlotte's room, where her bedsheet spilled over the edge. A flashlight underneath casted the ghost-like haunt of her shadow. Ana sighed as the knot released. She lifted the sheet just enough to see her two-year-old lying on her stomach, flashlight illuminating the pictureless pages of a book full of words she could never read—Arundhati Roy's *The God of Small Things*, as tragic a love novel as could be—that she'd swiped from Ana's own bedstand.

Charlotte gave the book's incomprehensible words that wonderful, eternal gift of her devout attention.

It was this moment in which the real Charlotte resided; not on the screen, but in the dissipating memory of Ana's own subconscious—a moment that Ana had forgot, that she was forgetting. The moment would be forever gone, if not for the triggering effects of Paul's Youtopia. It was for this moment that she watched. For the real Charlotte. For her own memories.

***

She emerged from Youtopia Towers to find that night had fallen. Immediately, the need to cleanse herself overpowered her. Or not cleanse, perhaps, but punish, for she had wallowed in her own sorrow, indulged iniquitous behavior with no worldly reward, like a drug addict seeking her high. So she grinded out an hour jogging on the dark, desolate sidewalks of Racine, circling around the paths with the most light, gripping her pepper spray like a lifeline. She sweated even in the cool night air. Her phone buzzed at her hip and she instinctively answered, expecting Sergio. It had been long past his two-hour promise. But instead it was Evan.

"A-ha! So you *do* answer your phone."

Ana resisted the impulse to hang up. She waited.

"Just wanted you to know that a friend's coming to pick me up tomorrow morning. Think I've had enough Wisconsin for now. No, check that: forever."

"Oh." She felt incapable of adding more. She thought back to the first time she saw his profile, her finger hovering hesitantly over her touchpad. How she could have just closed her browser and forgotten it all. Or how she could have just said yes, paid the money for his sample. How they could have proceeded with a business-like transaction, sight unseen. How, as unlikely as it would be, she could've been at this moment pregnant again.

"Anyway, I'm staying at Pier 22, one more night, obviously. They've got this sculpture out on the lake. It's... well, it's something to see. You could swing by."

He was offering her an olive branch, one last chance. But she answered, "I'm waiting on some information."

"Right. Well, I guess this is adios then." He waited for Ana to say something, but when she didn't, he added, "To better judgment in all things, Anabel Downer." Then he hung up.

She stared at her phone for a long moment. In truth, she had legitimate reasons to accept this fallout with Evan, to let his existence in her life slide, like so many former friends, into the annals of memory. It was a fever dream decision, one that might have ended with an impulsive text and a hasty e-signature on consent forms and an immediate funneling of a down payment into her FamilyMatch account. One that would ignore the myriad challenges and near-impossibilities. Ana was eight years older now, the age where complications became commonplace — gestational diabetes and preeclampsia and potential miscarriage. Her body would not recover so crisply as before. With Charlotte, a varicose vein had flared up behind her right knee, pulsing and painful, and she imagined it only worsening with another pregnancy. And once the baby arrived, there would be the issue of sleep, which might come natural for some children but no, Charlotte had to be taught, at every step, how to do it on her own, making for a nightly, ritualistic torment of crying and comforting, snatches of stolen sleep until more crying, more comforting, a tortuous, dithering rhythm of expectation and despair. Ana spent months in stupefied sleeplessness. This led her to be brusque, abrupt with Charlotte and Paul, prone to anger. Charlotte was so little, and yet Ana demanded so much. She required her three-year-old to process intense emotions with adult poise. She yelled more times than she liked to remember, and in hindsight regretted raising her voice, regretted the unnecessary reprimands, which were all of them. She became that irascible, incendiary person before, and even with the tragedy, it was possible — probable — she would become the same for a new child. This all before taking into account her job. How could she go on any assignment, much less one of this caliber? Her career would indelibly suffer, as so many mothers' had. She advanced on the heels of her grief, her aloneness. To be a single, working mother at her age would inevitably stunt that advancement. It seemed rash and foolish. It seemed impossible.

And still.

***

Ana slowed. The car behind her blared its horn and bolted into the next lane. She parked along the curb next to Pier 22 Lakeside, one of the higher-end hotels in Racine with lake views. Walking through the front parking lot, along the hotel's window-pocked side, she arrived at the shoreline.

A string of hotels dotted the coast, modest in size and yet competing in humble elegance. Each had a fat dock with benches and in-house rental pontoons on lifts. The black water reflected the docks' dim solar-powered lanterns and the higher, starker lights from lampposts along the shore. It was a beautiful sight, belied only by a pungent, sulfuric scent, years upon years of pollutants saturating and telling the true tale of the dark depths beneath.

And on a bench near a large stone fountain, Evan sat with his thumbs racing along his phone. His leg bounced beneath him; he was in sweats, disheveled. He was beautiful. With sudden clarity, she intuited that the child would have been a boy, a similarly beautiful boy. She saw this son, sixteen years later, a young version of Evan waking her from a vivid dream, smiling at nothing and everything, at the profundity of his mother and his vast, possible world.

"I didn't know you were staying here," Ana said as she approached.

He looked up, a genuine smile on his face. "You never asked." He stood to offer her a seat beside him. "My sister's mother-in-law. She manages, what, maybe twenty hotels in this chain? Anyway, they give me a bed while I'm on prospective visits, for a short while at least. Kind of wearing out my welcome with this one."

They sat beside one another as other hotel guests paced the boardwalk, couples hand-in-hand all. A middle-aged woman on the dock leaned her head into another's shoulder. Two teens shared earbuds attached to a tablet. She and Evan must've looked like one of them, like a couple soon to retire to their room.

Ana turned her attention to the sculpture before them, which was really a ten-foot high, non-functional fountain: two lithe, genderless bodies entwined, all legs and arms and curvatures, in what was likely meant as a sort of dance. It came off, however, as entirely lewd. Ana imagined bemused adolescents with uncomfortable parents steering them away, tittering teenagers taking selfies before it. It was meant to be a symbol of beauty, of unity, and in a way it was, though not in the way the hotel intended.

"Crazy, isn't it?" Evan said. "Like those optical illusions — the countess or the old lady."

Ana reached out, giving in to the impulse to touch it. The stone felt icy in the night air. She didn't know why she'd expected it to be warm.

Evan joined her, placing both hands around what appeared to be one of the figure's waists. "Where do you think the water's supposed to come out?"

Ana removed her hand and her vision blurred in remnants of her migraine. She felt faint again; her knees involuntarily bent. Her last meal had been a bag of chips, though she couldn't say when. Evan turned back to the lake, and Ana sat at the lip of the fountain's empty pool, her hands and arms locking her in place. She needed sustenance. She needed to investigate the Senator and Terrance Martin and all potential Immerser victims and everyone at Youtopia. She needed to not have another child. She needed to not want to have another child.

She lifted her head and said, "I wish this were easier."

"Nothing's easy. Certainly not this."

"I know I haven't been fair. You staying around here like this. Waiting on me."

His head bobbed in large nods. He clasped his hands on his lap. "You see, that gets me."

A shrill, unbridled laugh boomed from one of the women on the dock. The sound caught, amplified across the water.

"What gets you?"

"The whole *I know what I'm doing is wrong* bit. I'm sorry, but..." He paused. He looked to the water, to the sculpture, everywhere but Ana. He stopped on two teenagers at the shore who tossed landscape stones for sport, not seeming to care that others noticed. "Like those two. Walk up to them and they'll say, *'Oh, aren't we just awful for tossing these expensive rocks!'* Like that excuses them because they recognize they're shitheads. It's like... no, just stop being shitheads."

"So I'm a shithead then."

"No, that's not what..." He raised his hands, but then didn't know what to do with them, and so let them drop. Ana waited for a moment, but he said nothing. She stood.

He quickly stood beside her. His upper lip contorted into a face he had never before shown. His voice carried echoes of Paul when he said, "Big surprise. You're bailing again."

"I think you're being unreasonable—"

Suddenly, Evan grabbed at Ana's wrist. She instinctively twisted, snapped his hand away, hard. The encounter made a loud smack that turned the attention of the others around the lake to them. Ana felt the heat of their eyes on them, on what came next: her words would be weighed not only by Evan but by these onlookers, eight witnesses if the situation escalated.

Evan looked at his hand, stunned. He hadn't meant aggression, hadn't meant to restrain her in any way. In his eyes Ana saw, caught deep in the recesses of his blue irises, a sorrow. A betrayal. A good intention turned awry. They were Evan's eyes, heavy with disappointment that she strung him this far only to slap him away, but they were also Paul's eyes, staring down at her with the controlled anger of a latent domestic abuser, heavy with virulence about her centering her life on something other than him. Anymore, she couldn't distinguish the two.

Without a word, Evan slipped past the bench and up the hotel stairs. She watched him go with the dejected suspicion that she would never see him again.

***

Her motel room sang with the inner workings of an old building. When she closed her eyes, she could hear it all. Hot and cold air warred in the overhead HVAC pipes; water hummed through drains as though with independent purpose. The television in the next room spilled audience laughter through her wall. Still clad in her pantsuit, onto the bed Ana fell.

Ten minutes passed. An hour. She hadn't heard from Sergio about the tape, or from Michael or Jade or Bruce. Her phone had gone eerily silent. She watched the clock like a forlorn lover, hoping its ever-shifting numbers would somehow change the last few days, change her. A gap in the curtains shot slivers of light onto the floor, across the dead television, onto her feet still in heels. In a surge of energy, she stood to close the gap, to grab a spare pillow to place atop her head, to erase the lights and noise and ascending minutes and to just leave it, leave it, for now. She wanted oblivion. Instead, she heard a faint thrum from her briefcase, soft and somnambulant. The Youtopia baton. She answered its call.

It came alive in her hand, searching for its absent screen. She wondered whether she could access the Feeds remotely, wondered why she hadn't asked earlier, even if Sonya had refused. She wondered if Sergio could've hacked it, if he was awake, lying in his bed next to his wife, or at CNN headquarters hunting down the mysterious missing tape. She wondered where Paul's mind was now, in his dreamworld, whether he was asleep or awake, whether he played with his daughter or thrashed his complacent wife. She wondered whether any of it was real, or mattered.

She placed the baton back into her briefcase with care, as though returning some precious scepter to its proper casing. Tomorrow she would return, because that was what mattered. She would see her daughter again. She sensed it in the baton's reverberations, its strange precognitions. Back in bed, she pulled the thin comforter over her head, smothering herself in stale shadow. *Tomorrow*, she thought. *Tomorrow.* The chant repeated like a meditation mantra: *tomorrow, tomorrow.* And then Charlotte was there too: *tomorrow and Charlotte. Charlotte and tomorrow, and tomorrow and Charlotte and Charlotte and tomorrow and*

JOSEPH REIN

Daily Caller Exclusive: Breaking News

DOWNER AND OUT: LEAD FBI AGENT OUSTED IN YOUTOPIA
MURDER CASES
Artemis Tran, The Daily Caller
May 3, 2024

Downer is out for the count.

The most recent Youtopia murder shook the once-impenetrable company to its core. Now it has shaken the FBI as well, so much so that they're shaking up the investigative team.

Anabel Downer, lead Special Agent on the case, has been ousted. The Daily Caller has learned from an exclusive anonymous tip that Downer may now face her own investigation into potentially incriminating behavior.

While on the case, Downer committed multiple errant or even felonious behaviors. Our anonymous source also cited Downer's slipshod professionalism. During the investigation, she allegedly refused communication with members of her own team and actively deflected promising leads.

Downer is also suspected of abusing her access privileges to the Youtopia Immerser Feeds. A source from Youtopia has confirmed that Downer spent hours watching the Feed of her former husband and Youtopia client, Paul Downer, in an obvious breach of ethics, if not the law.

Indeed, Downer's unsuitability for the case should have been apparent from the start. A separate anonymous source reported that, on her first day at Youtopia Towers, Downer searched the web for anti-Youtopia propaganda.

The FBI has so far deflected these suitability accusations. Bruce Klose, head of the FBI Violent Crimes Division, cited only a lack of progress as grounds for Downer's dismissal. In a terse official statement, Klose stated that, "Such changes in primary investigators—especially in high-profile cases—are commonplace." When asked about putting

Downer on administrative leave, a seemingly punitive measure, Klose offered no comment.

Downer, 41, has worked at the Bureau for fourteen years. Before this incident, she received near-perfect marks on evaluations and solved most cases in a timely fashion, including the infamous murders of the Villalobos children by Jerry Slate.

Downer herself has declined to comment. The Daily Caller will update the situation as it progresses.

Chapter 8

"Do you think I did anything wrong?"

At the outset, the well-dressed man across from her had been gregarious and laid-back, all smiles. Now he entirely soured. Ana awaited an answer that never came. He looked at his silver watch; he forced a dejected cough; he turned to the prospect in the next seat, a woman two-thirds Ana's age, full of eyeliner and pep and cleavage. When the tinny bell finally tolled for them, he fled to her as though seeking asylum.

Her next man, hardly a man at all, college-aged at best, with a white baseball cap and tight-fitting collared shirt, noticed his predecessor's hasty flight. He set his glass of pinkish wine down with hesitation. He introduced himself as Steve, not terribly close to the name Evan, but close enough, the ending of Steve blending into Evan's beginning with ease in her mind. And so, as she'd done with the other six men she met tonight, she began with their story.

***

The news of her removal from the case had ransacked Ana without warning. She'd been lying on her hotel bed in a self-loathing stupor that morning, and first received a text from Bruce to call him immediately — nothing out of the ordinary. No amount of wine could erase Evan's eyes — Paul's eyes — from her mind, the way they had smarted. She had cut him to the quick, had reached a depth to which she hadn't known she had access. She would give herself an hour, would eat something and read headlines, before returning Bruce's call and diving back into the murders.

But the hour was apparently too long. The *Daily Caller* had no intention of sitting on its scoop. So, instead of from Bruce, where Ana ought to have heard it, she got a message from Lonnie.

What the fuck is going on with you?

And so the dominoes fell.

When she finally called Bruce, he was snippy, huffy. He threw out the terms petulant and disreputable and unethical. But eventually, he ran out of steam and his voice softened. He wouldn't reprimand her, other than requiring leave to let the smoke clear, for her to regain herself. In officially releasing her from the case, it seemed he finally discovered a soft spot for her. He wished only that his initial instinct was correct, that Ana could have resisted Paul's Feed.

She tried to take it gracefully. "Who's taking over?"

"Hatch."

"Hatch? He hasn't been on it at all. And he's such—"

"I know," Bruce said. "But maybe he's the kind of person we need right now."

She called Sergio next, who answered only after multiple attempts. He sounded nonplussed. "Really sorry, Ana." Ana could hear his fingers clacking their rhythmic dance across a keyboard, and she felt a sudden fear that she might never see him again. "What a shit this Tran is. Worse than tabloids."

"Nothing that isn't true," she said, to which Sergio had no reply. He remained silent, apparently reading, or thinking, or doing whatever he did in his moments of silence. After half a minute, she finally said, "You knew. In Austin."

The ticking stopped. "Sonya told us. We were hoping it was a one-off. I mean, everyone makes mistakes, right? And with the new murder..." Sergio let the idea hang between them: what could have been, had Ana been stronger. "But then you went back."

"I don't know what came over me."

"I do," Sergio said. "Are you kidding? The chance to see what your ex-husband dreams about, to see your..." He stopped himself just short of saying *daughter*. "Between you and me, Bruce threw you to the dogs on this one. Should be his head too."

Ana was about to thank Sergio, but in the background his wife's voice called out.

"What a crazy fucking world!" he said. "Take care of yourself, Ana." Then he was gone.

***

Two nights later, back in Chicago with little to do besides wallow in the shallow pool of her self-pity, Ana called Lonnie and invited her for a drink at Gilmore's, their favorite bar. A familiar face in a familiar place would do her good.

But even Lonnie seemed not to know how to handle Ana. She arrived late and agitated. She ordered tequila shots and took hers before the bartender could even offer a lime slice.

They sat silently as Lonnie gave devout attention to a list of local tap beers. Ana ordered and finished a cosmopolitan. Lonnie ordered a dark beer that, once served, she ignored in lieu of her phone.

Ana finally placed a hand on Lonnie's arm. "Anything interesting going on in the world?"

Lonnie forced a smile. "Funny."

Ana took back her hand.

"Look," Lonnie said. "Fuck. I'm sorry. This must totally suck for you."

"It does."

A cadre of young men stepped beside Lonnie, IDs in hand. They hovered over their barstools.

"Did you... do what the article claims?" Lonnie asked. "I mean, the Caller is trash. No argument there. But how much of it is BS?"

Ana watched the men size up the crowd, eyes appraising both her and Lonnie before moving on. "I don't know what came over me," she admitted. "I made a huge mistake."

Lonnie let out a low whistle. "Shit. You can say that again." Lonnie leaned back, and Ana sensed one of her friend's caustic quips coming. She hoped Lonnie would swallow it, would recognize Ana's vulnerability and just, this one time, keep it to herself. Lonnie took a deep draw from her beer and decided not to. "You know," she said, "you might've shown Paul that kind of attention when he was still here."

Ana sucked in a breath. She closed her eyes. The sounds of poppy country and inane chatter surrounded her. She counted to sixty, and imagined, upon opening her eyes, that Lonnie would either already be gone, or would wear a contrite look, would be ready to, if not make Ana feel better, at least not make her feel worse.

When she opened them, Lonnie still sat there, her face back in her phone, ready to ignore Ana again. So instead it was Ana standing, tromping past the young men, knocking one in the shoulder on the way without apology. Lonnie didn't try to stop her. She may never have looked past her phone or her bitter beer or her callow morality. As Ana drove away, she felt a strange mixture of relief and a deep, unassailable sadness.

***

Steve, like those before him, slipped lower in his booth as Ana prattled on about Evan. He finished his wine. There were no established rules for such divulgences, but Ana clearly broke an unspoken one by going on about Evan. These men were here to move forward, to begin anew, or at least to get laid, but Ana forced him into the position of surrogate friend, of unsuspecting counselor, listening as she poured out her and Evan's strange relationship. Steve's smiles were anxious but still there; he was too new at this to be outwardly rude. When Ana finished, Steve nodded. In the silence, Ana heard the hushed twitters of the pair beside them. Steve looked to the back of his hands, as though searching them for some path that would absolve him of this woman some fifteen years his senior.

"I don't know," he started. Ana felt like standing, running away, giving this young man the release he wanted and deserved. Then he added, "It's all pretty over my head. Having kids and whatnot. I've always been told *not* to get a girl pregnant."

Ana laughed, and Steve did too. He shuffled upward and leaned onto the table for the first time. Ana's shoulders relaxed.

"But just based on what you've told me, it seems —"

The bell cut into Steve's voice. Leather groaned as men began the shift. Steve looked to his left, where a balding man migrated toward them.

"Seems?" Ana asked. She touched his hand, and Steve's eyes returned to hers.

"Seems like you might've given this Evan guy a raw deal."

Steve slid out of his chair, his hand slipping from under Ana's. He made it nearly to the next table before abruptly looking back. "But what the hell do I know? He could've been some sort of predator. Maybe we all get what we deserve."

The balding man looked at Ana with darting eyes, his mind full of questions Ana no longer had the desire or the energy to answer. It was time to leave.

***

Her apartment felt vacated, as though she was already halfway gone. The refrigerator was bare, the surfaces blanketed with a hazy layer of dust. She turned on her radio and even the music, a hard rock station, felt anthropomorphic, from another life. Soon she would need to properly move, likely from Chicago altogether. She might need a drastic reinvention of herself, an entirely new Anabel Downer, if she was to survive.

"It's probably better this way," Peterson had said, the last time she visited Youtopia Towers. "I mean, I liked you. I thought you were good at your job." He offered his hand for her to shake. "Not that my validation matters, but there you have it."

In the moment, part of her was glad that she would never again enter Central Control, would never be tempted by the hallucinogenic, visceral space of Paul's Feed. Ana had never tried drugs stronger than marijuana but imagined their effects to be similarly hypnotic and encompassing. Impossible to ignore. Better to separate herself from its gravitational pull, to stand as far away as possible.

She waited for Peterson to ask for her baton. In her mind, she would place it onto the table with some ceremony, like a dishonored detective in a B-film handing over her badge. It sat like stone in the bottom of her work satchel, buried beneath her files and uneaten granola bars. But Peterson never mentioned it, and that other part of her — the larger part, the part that clearly could not be trusted — said nothing.

Sonya herself was busy, in D.C. visiting with the President. "Sonya has her ear," Peterson said with elation. "I'm not a betting man, but if I was, I'd never bet against Sonya Young."

Ana left Peterson to his adorations, exiting the Towers one last time to an overcast but temperate spring morning. She bypassed the shuttle and walked the half-mile to her car. She expected some sense of disappointment, of remorse, for failing so completely on such a high-profile case, for losing an assured promotion, a minor amount of celebrity. But all she had felt was a deep emptiness, like a vacuum bag sucked of its air. Like nothing.

She found a half-empty bottle of red behind some expired perishables in her pantry. It was overly bitter, past its time, but still she poured a full glass while opening a text message to Evan.

Please reply.

It was all she could think to say, but there above rested the same message three times over, all from the past few days. He had replied to none, so instead she opened her FamilyMatch profile — no messages from Evan, just three more potential matches she immediately dismissed. She attempted to pull Evan's profile but found that he had blocked her correspondence — a feature she didn't know existed. They likely meant it to keep donors from harassing potential new parents, or for the very situation Ana had created.

All the same, Ana opened the user discussion forum page and scrolled through various topics — success stories, metrics vs. feel, questions to ask in the interview — until she recognized an overly-active user, a Debbie from Ohio, who chatted more than any of the others combined. Her posts were full of dread and desperation. Ana sent her a message, fabricating a story about faulty web browsers and botched account settings. She asked if Debbie would be willing to contact Evan on her behalf. She expected an immediate response, but ten minutes, then twenty, then more passed, as she waited on this haphazard intermediary to deliver her to Evan.

***

A buzz came at her door. She'd fallen asleep at her computer, waiting for a response that never came. It was nearly midnight. She walked to the kitchen, to the video monitor flashing red with the call from below. In her building entryway stood three men, two in all black flanking a trench coat-donning Terrance Martin.

She let them in. At her door, Terrance shed his men like an animal shaking dry, with a shiver of relief. He sauntered in, surveyed her scant apartment with a quizzical eye. "You're either very minimalist," he said, dropping his coat on one of the stools overlooking Ana's kitchen island, "or never home."

"A bit of both."

She offered him tea, then wine, and finally water, all of which he waved away. "Chicago sucks ass," he said. "All wind and mud."

"It has its charms," Ana said. "You should know. Your franchise is booming here."

"Sometimes roses grow best in piles of shit." Terrance's phone vibrated. He silenced it, then worried a piece of thread loose on his sweater's shoulder, needing to pull it free. "All right. Give me the goddamn wine."

Ana poured the red. She waited for his face to sour, for him to reprove her, but he sipped it without comment. He took the remainder of the bottle to her door and offered it to his accompaniments. "Always keep the help happy," he said when he returned, pacing about the open living space of Ana's apartment. He ran a finger along her leather couch, eyed the empty end tables, the coffee table holding Ana's laptop, its bluish glow casting angled shadows onto the carpet. "The muscle is mostly for show. Can you believe I've never had a serious threat on my life? My most grandiose accomplishment. Even you probably can't say that."

Ana took up her glass but felt, while looking at the dim light refracted in its curves, a sudden queasiness in her stomach. She inhaled. "Is that why you're here? To gloat?"

"The opposite. I was sorry to hear about your, how shall we say, *situation*. You had a sense for the truth. Fired because you were getting too close, I suspect."

"Not close enough."

Terrance let out a huff. "You knew I wasn't the killer from the start."

"Maybe that was my mistake."

"If you believed that, would you have let me in?"

Ana thought for a moment, unsure of her answer. "Did you know the Senator?"

"Asking as an FBI agent or a friend?"

"We're not friends."

Terrance gave one of his devilish smiles, the one that ensnared ReaLife patrons across America, the one that men and women alike, the old and the young, swooned over. He kept pacing. Ana wanted to tell him to stop. She felt the sweet tinge of bile rise into her mouth and she sucked it back down. Nodding, pacing, ever-moving he was, but behind his eyes she could see a difference even from weeks ago, the capillaries swollen, the lids drooping. Though she looked worse as well, both of them aged by the shared devastation of the Youtopia murders.

"You rub elbows with the bigwigs, no? And yet no pictures of you and Obama. Not even Michelle. Maybe you're the Bush type."

"I tucked all those photos away in the closet."

"Next to the ones of your family." Terrance stopped, pausing to let his wound fester. He had gone back to pure performance, a man not so much inhabiting his own body as watching it from above, a spectator of his own life, one who fully enjoyed what he saw. "No," he said. "I never met the good Senator. But you know all about his record by now. Suppressed urban votes. Pro-fetus and anti-woman. No, I didn't know him. All the same, I lost no sleep over his passing."

"He was one of the first, like Fowler. Maybe your father knew him too."

"You are fully off the case. So why still pry like an agent?" Terrance took a final sip and then set his wine down. "Anyway, you wanted to know why I'm here. Simple: to offer you a job."

"You're joking."

"I don't joke about business. I'm an opportunist, and I know timing is everything." He took his cell, punched at it for a few seconds, and held it before her. On the screen read the CNN headline: *President to sign Healthcare Bill, changing landscape of American life.* "This is our time. Our Berlin Wall. Our fucking Normandy. This begins our revolution."

"*Our* revolution?" Ana said. "Why would you need me?"

"You've stared the Devil in its very eye! And here you've emerged, battered and broken and yet, still *living*. For that, I offer six figures for the first three months. A stop at each of our larger chapels, live streams on every platform, a huge virtual presence. Imagine it," he said, his arms gesticulating, his hair flipping. "You sweep on stage, renounce the Devil for what it is. You place us all on a higher moral plane. With the way they ousted you, and that part about your husband... you can just see them, Anabel." He approached her side, holding his hands out and peeling them back as though they were the curtain to his envisioned world. "My gay Lord in heaven, you can see them. They cry over you. Start an offering in your name. They *feel* your suffering. It's like you were made for this. For me."

A ring came from Ana's laptop. She walked over to it, checked her new FamilyMatch inbox, waiting to see a message from Debbie, or even Evan himself, but it was only some other donor match, a Jaxson from New York. Her face flushed with the heat of nausea. Terrance waited for her to finish her business, but she wanted him to leave, and *now*, so she opened a reply, began typing nonsensical sentences.

He retrieved his coat. "No need to answer tonight. But just so you know: here in good ol' America, we're already larger than Judaism and Islam *combined*. We've outpaced a lot of the Protestant tracks. People are finally waking up, realizing that humanitarianism — that *life*, the here and fucking now — is what matters. Imagine what we can do together, Anabel. Imagine the world we can create."

He saw himself out. At the foot of the door, his guards abandoned Ana's wine bottle. They whistled an unfamiliar tune as Ana deadbolted her door. She returned to her laptop to delete the spurious message. There, in stark black against her humming screen, the words she typed came into focus, as though emerging from a mist.

Night will fall too soon. Choo-chooing under the moon.

She ran to the bathroom. Her knees buckled. She barely reached the toilet in time for the rancorous rumbling in her stomach to spew forth.

***

Ana woke the next morning to a dull headache and the news, scrolling across every ticker and appearing in various notifications on her phone: the President had signed the Healthcare Bill. The event happened with some pomp, camera bulbs flashing, the VP and Senate Majority Leader and House Speaker all standing with hands folded behind her. She punctuated her signature with a quick, blotting dot of her pen. She smiled as she held the Bill in the air like a prize catch. But behind her smile, Ana saw the hesitation that no one in the news media seemed to share — the fear. The *New York Post* was among the first to suggest that, with the Bill signed, the murder case might all but close itself. With healthcare backing, Youtopia had evolved from a steam locomotive to a high-speed railer, slick and silver and unstoppable. It shot like a bullet into America and the murderer's hopes of stopping it alike. Ana could tell, by the fear in the President's eye, that they both knew better.

Ana ate a light breakfast she could barely stomach. The incessant hum in her temples, the scratch deep in her throat, felt as though they had been there for days, or longer — since she took the case, since Paul's Immersion. Since Charlotte's death. Buzzfeed proclaimed the day *The Dawning of Our New World*, and she could only think of the tornado storm of her past, the muck and mess she'd left in her wake. She tried to see forward into the world, into the time she had left, to her new world.

Then it jumped to her, unbidden, an answer almost too obvious for her to see: Youtopia. Yes. Ana should enter Youtopia herself.

She had the money, but even if she didn't, a psychiatrist could certainly attest to her instability, to her erratic behavior at work, as a sign for its necessity. She had few who would miss her. She had little, if anything, holding her back. She knew not where her mind would take her — whether she could similarly recreate an alive Charlotte as Paul did, or more simply create a new life with a new husband and child; whether her mind's versions of Lonnie and Evan would always bid her well. She didn't know, but in any case, it would be preferable to what she had now, to her crumbling reality.

A shower. Cold, unremitting. She wanted the icy shock on her scalp to drive away these thoughts, to help her un-think them, but even after twenty minutes, after drying and dressing for the day, the possibility of living out a perfect world lingered.

She considered her other options instead, beginning with, and immediately dismissing, Terrance's proposition. The thought of monetizing her suffering stuck like the residual taste of her vomit, sour and sordid. She also considered returning to Bruce, contrite, to ask for immediate reassignment. For years, she nose-dived into cases and subsumed her days with work. It helped, but, she wondered now, to what end? To be here, alone and still suffering? She might have reconciled with Evan by finally saying yes, by signing the forms and depositing the down payment to his account. She could've given herself over to their child. No, to her child. She could've built her life around someone who depended wholly on her, someone who would never know all that had come before them, someone to make Ana new.

She turned to X, where Youtopia dominated all the trending hashtags. The first four were positive, but then came the fifth, #stillatlarge, in reference to the murderer. Ana followed the various threads. Most came from doomsday theorists or trolls or grammatically-challenged bots, but a few not-as-crazy ones echoed exactly what Ana had been thinking since she lost the case: things wouldn't get better; they would only get worse. The murderer would soon strike his biggest blow. A user named Justice4Nones voiced something so close to Ana's mind that she felt eerie reading it:

> Why would the killer stop now? Prez just unlocked the door and invited millions in for the explosion.

In the end, she couldn't let go. Not yet. The urge inside was too great, to call Michael, to find out if any of the men they interrogated were indeed VikkarAll, to hear Jade's admiring, chirpy voice inspire hope. She wanted Bruce's admonishments to drive her forward. She was Special Agent Downer, first and foremost. This was her case, the case she was, perhaps, born to solve—one that merged her personal and professional lives with Youtopia as the bridge. The fact that the murderer still held the advantage sung like Charlotte's lullaby in her head, and she needed both gone. Let her walk the bridge until she couldn't anymore. Either that, or let her throw one final, resounding wrecking ball into it, leaving her to fall somewhere, anywhere but here, at the pit of failure. At rock bottom.

***

The flight to Tallahassee was overcrowded with northern travelers, many of whom spoke too loudly to one another in their vacation delight. It was not the nearest airport to Sergio in Gainesville; Ana hoped that, if Bruce or others were monitoring her, they would think her trip a vacation as well. She took the long cab ride southeast, fruitlessly searching the web for anything related to the Senator's entrance into Youtopia the entire way. She found op-eds, roundtable panels, a profile on *60 Minutes*. His wife Barbara, who passed shortly thereafter, was interviewed only once. Her hair was dyed so black it was nearly blue. She waved her fingers in outward hostility at a nonplussed Katie Couric. "As far as I'm concerned, he's dead," she said as a conclusion.

Ana continued to search for something she knew wasn't there, something she wouldn't just stumble upon. After all, as Sergio explained to her numerous times, a common Google search got you one percent of the internet at best. She needed the dark web, and she needed Sergio to navigate it.

On I-75 they hit commuting traffic, spasmodic bursts of speed-limit coasting abruptly cut by sluggish lurches. She rolled down her window, heard the familiar beat of Latin music. A man in a Lexus smiled at her with intention across two lanes. And some seven and a half hours after she had left Chicago, she arrived at Sergio's house.

His home was smaller than she'd imagined, a one-story Mission-style with no garage or driveway. She carried a briefcase containing only a toothbrush and notebook. The sun bled a fiery red into the horizon as she finally reached his door and knocked.

His wife Sarah answered. Young, beautiful, and nearly full-term pregnant, she wore an untied pineapple-patterned apron around her neck, soiled with flour and streaks of something red. "Sergio," she called out before Ana could ask for him. Of course she knew who Ana was. She spoke to Sergio about his coworkers. She watched the news.

Sarah left and Sergio soon appeared, wearing sweatpants and a clear look of surprise. "You shouldn't be here," he said, even though his words belied his tone, the lift of his eyebrow, which said he was happy to see her. He stepped aside and extended his door. "You could use coffee."

In the kitchen, Sarah baked a cherry pie. She was congenial to Ana, earnestly hospitable. She either entirely trusted Sergio, or was used to his job bringing in people with whom she needed to convivially interact. She handed Ana a snowflake-covered mug of coffee and apologized for not having decaf.

"Haven't been sleeping anyway," Ana said. The steam of her cup dissipated between them. "This is great."

Sergio retreated to his office, where he took a long time shuffling away. Sarah jumped between offering Ana small talk and scrolling on her phone. After a while, she twisted the phone in her hand and rolled her eyes. "I know I should turn the notifications off, but there's just..." She approached and offered Ana the phone. Her screen displayed nurseries, elaborately decorated and high style, drapery matching bedding, crib wood matching crown molding. "Pinterest will be the death of me."

"No, no," Ana said, handing back the phone. "Every mother deserves these moments."

Sarah looked down to her phone, then back up. She would ask, as Ana knew from many conversations past, if Ana herself had any children. Or perhaps she already knew. Perhaps the world of past pains, of grief and loss, no longer belonged to the grieving.

Before she could speak, Sergio thankfully interrupted. "Ready," he said. "Or presentable, at least."

Even after it all, his office was unkempt. Underneath an antique desk lay tomes on UK governance, farming practices, Florida law. He had framed pictures of Sarah and Jorge Luis Borges. In lieu of a desk chair, he had a bright red exercise ball. "Doctor's orders," he said. He offered Ana a foldout chair and another apology for the way her dismissal was handled. "They grilled me, of course. I never thought they'd come down like *that*." He, consequently, was reassigned as well, though not entirely off the case. He was now an equal member in a four-person team reporting directly to Bruce. When Ana told him that she harbored no ill will toward Bruce, or the Bureau, or anyone, Sergio expressed gratitude.

"I was wondering," Ana said, finally getting to her purpose, "if you ever found the CNN tape."

"Hmm. Thinking I shouldn't talk to you about the case." He smiled. "But... no. Nada. Zip. One of those strange aberrations. Rare now, but not as much back then."

"You ever look on the dark web?"

"If Big Brother asks me to."

"What if I ask?"

He tapped at his desk. Then he performed his cigarette ritual, slowly crumbling out the tobacco and licking the papers with affection, until it rippled from his lips as he spoke. "I shouldn't. Ana, you know I shouldn't."

In the pause, Ana recognized the opportunity to let Sergio off the hook, to not jeopardize his position as well, to not bring him down with her. But she also saw, in his eyes, the challenge of finding this video, and the desire to help her out. If she pressed, or just remained silent, he would agree. So she held for a minute, and then one more, and he did.

He hunched over his keyboard, the laptop's glow exaggerating the features of his face, casting a shadow under his mustache. He opened up several pages in TOR browsers, using the Senator's name and the date of the CNN video as his guide. In several instances, he closed out, redirected, moved across screens with a zipping fluidity. "If it's here, a peer-to-peer site will be the place to find it. Like Napster — remember Napster? Shit, my kid will never get that reference. Pirate Bay is the biggest now — maybe too big." From what she could glean, Sergio's search on the peer sharing sites pulled up nearly infinite media in all forms, news transcripts and wayward Youtube clips and podcasts and even music videos, none of which were on the right track.

Sergio mumbled something, a slur about bitcoin purchasers. "Of course, the vile stuff on here is worse — genocide videos, human trafficking — all done with a disgusting amount of pride. And don't get me started with this AI bullshit. You want to get depressed about the world, just visit the dark side." He chuckled to himself, but then stopped. "But when you just want to find something basic, it's the idiots that make it so onerous."

Ana watched him sort the video files related to the Senator, many of them recordings of Senate meetings and filibusters, infinitely vast and boring. He unearthed campaign videos, some repurposed with regularity during election cycles, others mildly misogynist and never aired. Beyond the public, Sergio found a copy of a home video recording, a nephew's birthday party. The Senator himself made only a brief appearance in the background, a whiskey tumbler in his hand and cigar in his mouth. They unearthed a video related to an alleged affair, and this one small seed blossomed infinite copies of assorted length and quality — hand-holding, clandestine kisses. Even deeper they found a bland public video Ana recognized but couldn't place — a lunch meeting on the outdoor patio of an illustrious café. The video was shot from a shifty first-person, and yet it was glossy, beyond high definition. It had that familiar luster.

"Stolen Youtopia footage," Ana said.

"Yep."

"From Constantine?"

"Maybe, though he's not the only looter." Sergio gnawed at the cigarette. "Heard Sonya canned him and his buddy."

"How do you know they're not deepfakes?" Ana asked.

"Pretty easy, actually. Every real video has a timestamp, a digital fingerprint of sorts. The deepfakers can't replicate that."

He pulled a digital notepad up on his screen and recorded information on the Senator's luncheon video. He followed the video's source as far as it would take him, but then abruptly closed it and opened others. Sites with names like Arpanet and OnionShare and anything that allowed for anonymous giving and taking. Each offered its own fare, some the same and some different, but never what they were looking for.

"The dark web," Sergio said, "is five hundred times its counterpart. Have I told you that before?" Ana nodded. "I could have Sarah make up a bed."

"I don't want to impose." She looked at her phone — 7:47. She'd already imposed, was imposing. "Can you give me until nine? If nothing materializes, I'll be on my way."

"Sure." Sergio retrieved a Zippo from his desk drawer and lit the cigarette.

Ana watched him and wished, though it was impossible now, that she had brought Sergio to the Youtopia Feeds with her, if even once. What a striking sight it would have been, watching this man so masterful with technology stand before the concave behemoth screen and orchestrate the Immerser Feeds with his deft, artistic hands. Hands that typed for just half a minute more, until they stopped. They hovered with a soft quiver over the keys. He sat back and reached over to a thin stack of tobacco papers.

She had seen this before — in his keenest concentration, he stopped to roll more cigarettes. The smoke lingered in fine wisps in the air. Ana felt the pulse of her thumb around her mug handle, the coffee inside gone cold. Underneath Sergio's rolling fingers, she registered for the first time the serpentine hiss of his computer, the outsized tick of a grandfather clock in the corner. Outside the door, Sarah's footsteps stomped along the hallway.

She could wait no longer. "Anything?"

Sergio licked his fingertips, twisted the paper true in one swift motion, then lit the second cigarette off the dying embers of the first. "Got someone claiming to be VikkarAll."

Ana's body heated in a sudden jolt of adrenaline. "Holy shit."

"Don't get too excited. All sorts of minnows claim to be whales."

"But it's promising."

"We'll see."

Sergio and VikkarAll jabbed back and forth, the fluid lines of text rolling like a native language and she, the foreigner, attempting in vain to translate. Eventually, Sergio stopped as a price flashed onto his screen: $100K US.

Sergio whistled through his front teeth. "Fucking steep."

"But the Bureau would pay. You're still on the case."

"Maybe." He entered in a lowball counteroffer.

"What are you doing?"

"Think of this like a Mexican marketplace. If you don't haggle, you stick out. I pay right up and he'll suss us out. As you can imagine, the black market doesn't play nice with Johnny Q Law."

Sergio and VikkarAll bantered for a minute more, Ana watching with the distinct feeling that this man — or woman, or whomever was on the other end of the exchange—did indeed possess the video, and that by bartering in small quibbles Sergio might lose it. Sergio chuckled at something he himself wrote; Sarah entered and refreshed Ana's coffee. Ana almost pleaded with Sergio to stop, to just accept the offer, to take any small remainder from her personally when he said, "Shit." He exited the screen and opened multiple others, repeating the pseudonym of the hacker, the Senator, CNN, typing frenetically into a chasm that Ana hoped against but recognized as desperation, as the precursor to failure.

"He's gone, isn't he," Ana said.

Sergio didn't answer.

"Can we trace him?"

Sergio ignored her, his breaths so labored that he inhaled and exhaled puffs of his cigarette without trying. Then his fingers stopped. He raised his hands, rubbed at the base of his forehead. He bit at the nub in his mouth before stubbing it out.

"Skittish bastard," he said. "But I tell you, that's a surefire sign he's not the real VikkarAll. Just some punk trying to tap me."

Ana masked her own disappointment with her coffee mug. Though when she spoke, her words came out languid, lethargic, thick with the weight of her travels and Bruce's voice and Evan and the *Daily Caller* and all of her mistakes. "It's all right," she said, feeling that nothing was, and that it might never be again.

Sarah offered Ana a blow-up mattress in the still-unoccupied nursery for the night. Ana thanked her but no, she couldn't impose. She was grateful for all the hospitality they'd shown her so far. She exited hastily, almost leaving her briefcase. The thought of sleeping next to a mattress-less crib, beside a rocker and changing table in the center of what would soon be their baby's nursery, sent her rushing out, made her long for some begrimed bed in a strip motel into which she could escape and never return.

***

The next morning, Ana flew directly back to Chicago, to her home, the bustling place that once offered comfort but now felt increasingly alien. Like some record repeating the same song, the weather was murky. A mist turned to rain turned back to mist, leaving everything soppy, sodden. She ordered Chinese takeout from a restaurant ten blocks away, trying to find comfort in the damp, brisk walk, to feel the solace of the city. But the rain drove everyone inside, and she felt only a sad emptiness, a lack of any purpose. Lonnie, Evan, Sergio, Terrance: she didn't know to whom she could reach out, or what it would accomplish. With a wet brown bag of cooling food in her hand, she reached her block, feeling as lost as she ever had.

A homeless man stood at the entrance to her building, hood over his head. Ana planned to hand him the Chinese, to drown herself in wine and mindless TV, but then the man looked up to her. He tipped back his hood.

It was Tramel.

"Ditch your phone," he said.

"I don't have it with me."

He made her prove this by opening her purse and food bag, by showing him her pocketless pants. Then he nodded, his eyes dim in the shadow of his hood. He led her across the street to the front of a closed bakery, ducking beneath the darkened awning. Ana set the food down at her feet, staying in the light.

Tramel reached into his hoodie pocket. Ana braced her hands, ready to slap away any weapon Tramel might retrieve, but the sleek black object he pulled looked more like futuristic, designer sunglasses. He offered them up to Ana.

"This goes dead after you watch," he said.

Ana turned the object, a slim VR headset, in her hand. It was much sleeker, better than any Tramel had in his shop.

He looked to an oversized watch on his wrist. "You've got less than an hour."

For Tramel, this seemed to complete the transaction. He retreated farther into the shadows.

"Wait," Ana said. "Why are you doing this?"

He offered her his dark smile a final time. "He wants you to see."

***

Sitting on her couch, Ana tensely held the headset before her, as though it may at any moment disappear, or explode. Her legs bounced beneath her. She wondered if she should call Bruce, should offer up the headset to the investigation of which she was no longer part. If she should—in this moment and unlike all the others that led her here—fall in line. She wondered if she was dreaming, if she had been dreaming. If she could still dream at all.

No, the headset was real, its weight as light as real sunglasses, its plasticine gloss shimmering. "He wants *you* to see," Tramel had said. Not Bruce, not Sergio. This was made for her, its contents disappearing in short time, evaporating like mist. If she gave the headset up, it might force VikkarAll back into hiding. The lead would go cold, the killer running farther free. More death.

She breathed deep. Then she flipped open the temples, placed the bridge atop her nose. She prepared to see.

Nothing immediately happened. The lenses were full black. She could hardly see through them, couldn't catch anything in her peripherals — only opaque darkness. She waited a minute. Then another. She touched along the frame, flipped the hinges, searched for a button that didn't exist. As another minute passed, she wondered if she had been duped, if these glasses were a simple tracking device, or something more malicious. Perhaps VikkarAll and Tramel had access now to things in her apartment. Perhaps she had further jeopardized the case. She needed to call Bruce, needed to let him know right away. He would be livid, as always, but at least her honesty might save her.

But then, into Ana's vision flashed a brilliant, blinding white. The murmur of a crowd rushed to her ears. The VR headset encompassed her entirely as the video opened.

And there, at the bottom of her screen, appearing as if by some stroke of marvelous magic, scrolled the CNN news ticker of a decade past.

A crowd waited in giddy anticipation. Within seconds, onto the platform outside of the original Youtopia headquarters in North Dakota, the Senator emerged.

The crowd's cheers were overly enthusiastic for a message they hadn't yet heard. The Senator walked with arms raised, his smile ebullient, his hair pristine white, his face euphoric. He donned the podium with a career politician's elegance. "Thank you, thank you. I am as happy to see every one of your faces as you are to see mine."

As the Senator droned on about his life accomplishments, she kept her eyes on the fringes, watching for Sonya, for Peterson, for any recognizable face. For the black-donned body of the assailant, as though he was there from the start. As though his presence would somehow tell her what she needed to know.

The Senator held in dramatic pause. A minute of the video remained. Then thirty seconds. The Senator finally reached his crescendo, the reveal of his Immersion that boomed the audience into applause. The cheers continued as, without warning, the video cut.

Ana's head swooned, but before she could even begin to make sense of it, the white flashed again and the video looped from the start. She watched again, and again. On the third viewing, as the audience showered the Senator with approbation, as spectators in the first two rows turned to one another and revealed half of their faces, Ana finally saw what was giving her that strange, slightly unreal feeling, that left-of-center shimmer. She finally saw.

Slowly, she removed the headset. She placed it down on her coffee table with a strange feeling that, without it on, the video would instantly vanish. She listened to the video's end, fearing that it would not loop back again.

But it did, and so Ana rushed to her phone and pulled up a search engine. In a search for *first Youtopia employees* she could make two people in the front row, both of whom had since died. Nobody else notable stood around them. Sonya was curiously absent, but a brunette near the stage looked eerily like her — so much so that Ana, on impulse, typed in *Sonya Young's sister* and hit search. Nothing. She was an only child, daughter of two immigrant parents. Ana clicked on the profile of her mother, Veronica Young, and then to public photos. Her screen filled with Veronica from middle-age all the way up to her death in 2007.

Ana put back on the headset, eyeing the brunette near the stage. The woman cheered with animated hands. When she turned, Ana saw.

The brunette was, undeniably, Veronica Young — deceased in 2007, and yet somehow alive for the biggest day of her daughter's life in 2014.

Once Ana followed this line, the offerings cropped up similar hits: Sonya's aunt, who mentored Sonya in her younger years; a former high school teacher named Agatha Hunt; her two grandmothers, who stood with hands raised together in pride.

Ana replayed the video again, and immediately it showed. Of course. The glossy filter, the dream-like mistiness of it. It was exactly like all the other Youtopia footage she had watched, like Paul's dreams of Charlotte. The CNN footage was not real.

It was Sonya Young's Youtopia.

Just then, like a strange omen, Ana's phone vibrated. She saw the number, one entered into her phone not long ago but now forgotten, a number from which she had never before received a call: Sonya Young's private line.

Chapter 9

Midnight. Flights from Chicago to Jamestown to Devils Lake Regional Airport. Coffee and middling food at the airport kiosk, fruitless requests to three separate cab companies to take her to her obscure destination. Finally, she caught a shuttle to the rental car station, with a driver thriving on Coca-Cola and his own voice. There was something evanescent, something flitting about Ana's sleep-deprived mind as she veered off the main highway and began driving down ambling roads blanketed in flora and heavy darkness. The farther in she went, the less she felt any connection to her body, to the world itself. Her hands seemed miniscule on the slick steering wheel. Radio stations played the same religious talk show hosts. Her phone lost and regained signal with remarkable consistency. Each fork in the country road seemed the one she should take. But somehow, amidst the burgeoning spring of North Dakota around her, she found her way forward.

"You must see for yourself," Sonya had said on the phone, before Ana could even speak. Her voice had been quiet, whisper-like, softer than Ana had ever heard it. "You must come to me." Ana bumbled for a moment before realizing that Sonya had meant immediately, right at that moment. Sonya was lax on details but high on urgency. She'd nearly pleaded.

Ana had driven straight to O'Hare, arriving in the bustling morning hours of the day. While awaiting her flight, the guilt of not calling Bruce weighed on her. She pulled up his number a dozen times, more, but knew that if she told him of her discovery, he would make her stop, make her return home. He would send a team for Sonya, and *her* case, her discovery, would become theirs. He would force her out again, and in doing so, likely force Sonya out of whatever confession she wanted to give. Despite the hour, Ana nearly dialed Sergio as well, just to tell him that she'd found the video, and that once he saw it he would understand. But with that information, Sergio's allegiance to her might end, leading to the same outcome. Anyone in the Bureau could take this from her. Nobody she worked with could know.

But someone needed to know. So she opened emails and composed two, the first to Lonnie.

I'm sorry about the last time we spoke, but I need you to know
what I'm doing, in case something happens to me.

As she continued, detailing her flights and plan, it all seemed surreal, as though it was happening to someone else. She hit send before she could rethink it all, and opened another message, this one in FamilyMatch to Debbie in Ohio.

Please forward this to Evan...

Writing the message to an unseen intermediary proved even more difficult. She'd started, deleted, started again. In her long layover in Jamestown, she had finally sent the same description that she sent to Lonnie, with the subject line: *For Evan Lancaster: I'm sorry.*

The road pattered under Ana's passenger-side tires as she veered onto the shoulder; she had to correct back. She took to the immediate center of the road, assured by its emptiness that no other cars would come opposite. But then, like springing apparitions from the cavernous darkness, she spotted two, three, a whole family of deer as they leaped out and froze in a row. They blocked the entire road. Her headlights refracted in the vacuous blackness of the smallest fawn's eyes, and she instinctively steered toward them, to the tail end of the line. She mashed her brakes as hard as she could. The doe bound forward and the fawns followed. Ana's whole body clenched as the thin brown of the smallest fawn's hind legs curled upward and streaked sprite-like just beyond her windshield.

Ana slowed to a stop. Behind her, the family vanished into the darkness, into the cover of night woods. She had almost hit the youngest, almost crashed her only mode of transportation in the middle of the night on an abandoned road. Or she didn't. They were gone, and anymore, she couldn't even be sure they were ever there.

***

At one-thirty, dead of night, she arrived on the dirt-patch parking lot of the original Youtopia headquarters. The place was unimpressive, less than unimpressive, especially when compared to the architectural wonder that was Youtopia Towers. This derelict, abandoned warehouse had one elongated end that stretched into infinite darkness. It seemed more of a haunted house than mansion, more mausoleum than museum. If this was once the mighty ship, now all that remained was a dilapidated hull. Spatters of leaves from last fall painted the ground. Half the surrounding bur oak trees were dead, and those alive were pocked with woodpecker holes. A susurrus of wind cut through them, hitting Ana's neck and exposed wrists. She took crunched steps toward the one apparent entrance, a wooden door dappled with moss. It seemed impossible that, only ten years ago, this had been the hub of what eventually became one of the most powerful companies in America.

Impossible too that Ana should feel, as she stepped to the door, the cold stone of the small stoop through her shoes, but there it was, seeping into her calves like rising water. The door had no knob or handle, no knocker or window or peephole. There was only, waist-high along the right-hand side, a small black box that must've been an entry panel. Ana knocked softly, then with force, again and again. She took her cell from her pocket and waved it absurdly in the air until it regained reception. Her third attempt finally garnered a ringtone, but still Sonya didn't answer. Ana stepped back, looked along the broad side of the building that masqueraded itself in the woods, along the shorter side held up along a steep drop-off, neither of which she could risk. She banged on the door for another minute, until her palms smarted. Then she considered gathering the small rocks scattered among the leaves and peppering them along the building. She considered driving back to the airport and never again answering Sonya's calls. Or she could've driven straight into the door itself, transformed her rental car into a battering ram, to see how sturdy Youtopia really was. She imagined herself thrown like a crash test dummy through the windshield and headfirst into the warehouse before her. She felt the beginning stages of what could be a massive, debilitating migraine. She needed sleep.

Then a soft vibration came from her purse. Ana's whole body started, her jittery hands fumbling for her phone. Sonya was calling, the line finally connecting, but her phone showed only black — a phantom ring, a wistful mirage.

But she still heard the buzz. She couldn't be hallucinating it. She could feel it too, like the thrum of a pulse, faint but alive. She dug more, under lip balm and corporate credit cards and mascara until she saw it, sleek and black, alive and humming: her Youtopia baton. She looked up at the black box on the wall, now dotted with two glowing aquamarine lights. They were communicating.

Baton in hand, Ana faced the box to no effect. She jiggled, swung, swiped it across like a magician over a hat, waving and stupidly waving until the lights popped red and the door, with the deep-sounding thud of released metal, snapped open.

All inside was dark. From what Ana could see, the inside of the building had fared worse than outside. When she stepped forward, a solitary overhead motion light burst to life, then another, but only one at a time, on down a line, the one before shutting off instantly after the next turned on. She proceeded under these tracking lights, her feet clicking on linoleum tile as the building revealed itself to her.

To her left, a darkened hallway stretched endlessly like the wall outside, and to her right a sliding glass door led to an outdoor amphitheater. *The* amphitheater, or at least its moldering remnants. It retained none of its immaculate newness from the video in which the Senator gave—or purported to give—his Immersion address. As Ana stood at the window, she had the sensation of being spotlighted on the eerie stage herself, as if she would now deliver some grand proclamation to those ghosts of Sonya's life, to all the Youtopia mind projections like the Senator's slavish assistants and Fowler's rape victims and Paul's Charlotte, people who never were and never would be. Except, Ana couldn't picture them now. She only saw, reflected in the glass, a hollowed-out version of herself, too close to be in the audience, staring with a vague look of sorrow.

"I am glad you came."

Sonya entered the reflection dressed in all white. Somehow, she hadn't set off any lights herself. To her side stood a tall, black Great Dane. The dog stood utterly still, its head up and chest out in valiant poise.

"This is Sita," she said of the dog. "Even more beautiful and patient than her mother."

Ana turned to Sonya, who looked harsh in the scarce light, the shadows of her nose and chin draping down about her.

"You must be wondering," Sonya continued, "which came first. The video or the amphitheater."

"Don't presume to know what I'm wondering," Ana replied.

"One must always test one's own creations," Sonya said, disregarding Ana's response. "I knew entering Youtopia for only a brief time was dangerous, potentially perilous. But it turned out to be the exact opposite. At the time, I was unsure of how to bring Youtopia to the world, how to begin the slow but inevitable road to public acceptance. Then I stepped inside myself, and like that—" She removed a hand from the dog's back and burst her fingers open like fireworks. "My unconscious mind provided the answer."

Sonya flickered the baton in her other hand, and beams of stadium lights poured onto the amphitheater. It appeared even gloomier in full light, like a disgraced beauty queen. Ana remembered she was still holding her baton, though it had stopped humming, had gone dead in her hand.

"You doctored the video," Ana said. "Sent it to CNN as though it was reality."

Sonya began her answer with a low, guttural keen. But no, it was the dog, the sound deep and primal, as though from its very center, or from nowhere at all.

"You admit you never had the Senator's consent," Ana continued. "You forced him into Youtopia."

"By now, you will have realized the same holds true for Mr. Fowler."

"So you admit your whole company was founded on criminal behavior."

Ana let the thought sit, but Sonya was unmoving, an impossibly indomitable pillar. Ana returned her attention to the dog, whose eyes had taken to flitting back and forth, though its body remained still as the sound issued again from its belly. Ana was so concentrated on the dog that she missed the entrance of another person, a woman dressed entirely in black, muscular and tall, completely covered up to the neck. Ana stepped backward into the glass.

It was the assailant, the Senator's murderer. It was a woman born out of Charles Fowler's Youtopia, here in the flesh. It was Nikita.

Ana looked to her hands, to the baton clenched like a lifeline in her fist. She wanted to shout, to sprint away, to shatter glass. To be able to recognize again what was real.

Nikita stalked to Ana with the same determined steps of the murderer, with the same powerful confidence. She outstretched her arm for Ana to shake, but the hand went higher — not a handshake. She held something — a small tube. A syringe.

Ana ducked and slid, shifted along the plate glass, her academy training taking over. Disarm, don't try to overpower. Let her aggression lead to a mistake. When Nikita lunged, Ana grabbed her hand and twisted it into a wristlock, but Nikita's other arm countered quickly — too quickly. She moved so fast. Nikita's fingers jabbed up to Ana's jaw, right on the pressure point, sending shocks of pain up through her scalp and behind her eyes. The world alighted in dazzling shades of yellow. Her brain pressed against her skull as though trying to escape. Stupid, stupid, she should have seen this coming. Her mouth gasped out stifled cries. Nikita freed her other hand from Ana's weakened grasp and plunged the syringe into her upper arm.

Sonya stepped forward, her face still placid. "Miss Downer."

"Why are you," Ana managed, but then she felt saliva leak from her mouth. Her shoulder blades seized. Her chest constricted. A high-pitched ring bandied about her ears. Her legs felt distant, disembodied, just before she collapsed to the ground.

"Miss Downer," Sonya repeated, her voice fighting against the din awash in Ana's ears. She removed a handkerchief and wiped at Ana's mouth. Ana felt nothing. "I have no intention of harming you. Please believe that. I have nothing but admiration for you.

"I simply need to show you something. You need to see, as I have seen. After, everything will be perfectly clear."

Feed Link: 000001: 1.29.24

Our screen alights to...

<u>AN OPEN PRAIRIE</u>
...and we stand on wide swaths of tall, lush grass. The sun looms, a force in the sky. Flowers blossom in copious display, dancing in cheerful unison with the wind.

In the distance, a small but ominous Forest lurks.

The first friend we see is BUNNYISH, our lovable rabbit, with ears braided like hair and a perpetual pep in his hop. He wears a casual collared shirt and shorts. He buries his face in the flowers, pleasantly consuming them with loud MUNCHING sounds.

Next is poor MR. NOOSE, a small, dwarf-like man in a business suit. His face wears a pleasant beard. At present, he appears a bit bored.

MR. NOOSE: What wonders will today bring?

BUNNYISH (*through SMACKS*): We could go to the Wishing Well.

MR. NOOSE: The Well is always your answer.

Into our scene booms OSCAR'S VOICE, coming from behind and above, from nowhere and everywhere at once.

OSCAR: You should want to go, Mr. Noose. The Well always surprises.

BUNNYISH: Exactly!

Enter our final friend, CANDY, a teenaged girl dressed in vibrant patterns, with hair of every color. She flicks the heads off dandelion-like flowers with her thumb.

Upon landing, the decapitated blossoms cling to the ground. They root and grow, sprouting miniature offspring.

CANDY: Huh. Cool-i-o.

Candy stands. Turns to the gang.

CANDY: So... we going or not? Tell you what, I'll race ya.

She darts off. Bunnyish and Mr. Noose follow to the...

WISHING WELL

...which is waist-high, made of murky brown brick, its depths unknown, its air tingling with the scent of *magic*.

Bunnyish leads the race handily. He reaches the Well and WHOOPS in victory. Candy follows, and finally poor Mr. Noose.

BUNNYISH: Bunnyish for the win!

MR. NOOSE: Not all of us... have been blessed... with those hind legs.

OSCAR: Well, Mr. Noose, here's your chance.

Oscar flips Mr. Noose a gold, nondescript coin.

Mr. Noose hugs it to himself. He knows what to do. He kisses it before flipping.

CANDY: Fly, you miracle maker, fly!

The coin falls for an impossibly long time. They TITTER in anticipation.

Finally, it lands with an ECHOING PLOP.

And poor Mr. Noose... his legs begin to grow. Up, up, his squat body goes heavenward on legs that lengthen and fatten like tree trunks.

CANDY: That's what I'm talking about!

BUNNYISH: Great, now I gotta waste a wish on shrinking 'em back down.

OSCAR: Wait—

Oscar's gaze moves to the Forest beyond, where branches of trees gnarl and extend like tendrils.

A spate of black clouds billow. Lightning CRASHES.

BUNNYISH: Man, not again!

CANDY: I thought you got rid of this dude for good, Oscar.

Oscar crouches. His legs press off the ground with a WHOOSH. From His view, Bunnyish and Candy grow smaller and smaller. He goes higher than even Mr. Noose, whose legs have finally stopped growing.

Oscar hovers high up in the air. *He's flying.*

OSCAR: Back to the fortress. I'll handle him.

BUNNYISH: No argument here!

MR. NOOSE: How am I supposed to run on these?

OSCAR: Carefully.

The three friends turn away from the Forest. Bunnyish jumps ahead, followed by Candy. Mr. Noose hobbles behind, Oscar hovering high above, as they move to the...

FORTRESS

...though, indeed, it is just a common house.

And poor Mr. Noose, he figures out his legs. Like a giraffe in flight, he uses their length to his advantage. He arrives at the door first.

Candy rides on Bunnyish's back. She dismounts and points at Mr. Noose's new legs.

CANDY: Great. Now *I* need a pair of those.

But poor Mr. Noose struggles to enter the front door. He bends, he contorts.

Oscar snickers at his struggle, a thick BELLOW that drowns out the thunder.

OSCAR: Poor Mr. Noose. Come. You will be safe.

Mr. Noose trundles to the backyard, where Oscar looms, His arms extended in flight.

He is the house's guardian. Its protector.

Forging at them, the dark Forest multiplies in size, consuming the horizon. Inky black clouds cast ominous shadows.

Oscar tilts His palms upward. He focuses His energy. And up from the ground, sprouting like flowers themselves, come rows of particolored bricks. They stack and interlock in front of the house with impressive speed.

OSCAR: Let's see how you —

Thunder BOOMS in response, cutting Him off. Lightning bolts shriek down from the clouds, shattering the heart of Oscar's wall.

OSCAR: Learned some new tricks, I see.

Oscar's hands turn and clasp, bracketing around the Fortress.

OSCAR: Luckily, I did too.

The Fortress shakes. A living thing itself, it too multiplies. It grows upward, outward, stacks upon itself at unlikely angles. It twists and bends, forks and funnels. Impossible to know where one place ends and another begins in this beautiful labyrinth.

Candy sticks her head out of a high curved window.

CANDY: Cool-i-o!

Mr. Noose rushes to a door now big enough for his massive legs. He enters.

OSCAR: Catch us if you can.

The Forest tendrils snake through Oscar's broken wall and approach the Fortress. Windows spatter glass as they crash through.

Bunnyish's muffled voice comes from behind a wall.

BUNNYISH: Get out. This is my spot!

Suddenly, stunning Oscar and His friends alike, from the house issues a large EXPLOSION.

The world goes eerily silent.

The tendrils shoot outward from a large window. They hold something, soft and small...

It's *Bunnyish's arm*. The tendrils fling it to the ground.

OSCAR: No. Not today.

Next out fly Bunnyish's two legs. Piece by piece, Oscar's best friend falls to the ground.

Candy's head peeks out again.

CANDY: Oh boy. Now he's done it.

Oscar's feet land on the ground as the clouds gather and grow. He picks up Bunnyish's head, eyes now glossed black. His mouth is a stitched-on smile. Oscar's best friend, gone.

BOOM BOOM.

Thunder. But not Forest thunder. No. From above, parting the clouds, shines a sliver of hope. This sliver is an oval, a face with long blonde hair and a deep smile. It is MOTHER.

Her voice is a mere WHISPER. And yet, stronger than Oscar's.

MOTHER: Oscar. My sweet Oscar.

Oscar drops Bunnyish's head. He flies again.

Our vision tunnels. Blurred edges move inward, consuming first the sky and ground, then the Fortress. The sliver reflects what is behind Oscar and what is in front, what has come and what will be.

In this mirror, Oscar sees Himself: long black hair over one eye, t-shirt and tattered jeans—a lean, lengthy teenager.

Behind the reflection, the house and clouds and His friends and Bunnyish's parts all lift. They tumble and cyclone in a massive hurricane.

CANDY: Hang on!

MR. NOOSE: I hate this part!

Everything swirls, swirls. Life converges.

MOTHER: Now.

Oscar slaps His hands together in a vicious, vivacious CLAP.

All *cuts to white*.

THE WISHING WELL

...is where we return, ever faithful, ever Wishing.

Oscar stands with hands on the Well. The Forest beyond has regained its true, original, intended form.

Candy saunters to the Well.

CANDY: I told you wimps there was nothing to be afraid of.

Mr. Noose stumbles in on his stilted legs. He wishes with absolute concentration. Then he flips another coin.

PLOP.

His legs shorten. He's back, and content.

Candy turns a concerned eye to Oscar.

CANDY: How long we plan on leaving Bunnyish?

OSCAR: It's been long enough, I suppose.

Oscar takes His own coin, kisses it, flips it down. The PLOP echoes as they turn again to the...

FORTRESS

...which has retained its labyrinthine form. Oscar HUMS while looking at it: unwieldy. Crazy. Beautiful.

Candy KNOCKS loudly on the front door.

CANDY: You can come out, you know!

The door opens. A *fully formed* Bunnyish emerges.

He lumbers over to Oscar and throws a light punch at Him.

BUNNYISH: One of these times: please, please stop him before he tears me to pieces.

OSCAR: What would be the fun in that?

BUNNYISH: Oh, so you're telling me you had it under control, huh? Yeah right.

MR. NOOSE: I'm with Bunnyish.

Oscar looks to Candy, who shrugs in reply. Oscar turns to the front yard of the Fortress.

OSCAR: Oh, all right.

He lifts a Godly arm. From the ground, an impregnable army of clay soldiers emerge, bearing massive shields and swords. Some stand at immediate attention. Others look themselves over, impressed by their own creation.

OSCAR: You'll guard this Fortress. Always.

The Clay Soldiers turn their heads in unison.

CLAY SOLDIERS: Yes sir!

OSCAR: Happy now?

BUNNYISH: Over the moon, my friend.

Chapter 10

"It is so... so...

"I apologize, Miss Downer. I've wanted to share this with you since our first meeting. This conversation has played out in my mind. And yet, I watch young Oscar's Feed beside you and words fail me. I feel only the true... beauty of it.

"No, that is not the right word. And yet, is there another? It rings like a bell, ticks like a metronome of truth in my mind. I feel its beauty. Its sheer beauty.

"Please, Miss Downer, you must not try to move from your chair. You must relax. The effects will subside within the hour, I promise you. Sensation returns slowly, like blood seeping to sleeping limbs. You may experience it already in your fingertips, in the crown of your forehead. As you can guess, we have perfected the dosage. Your mind is still sharply intact, even if your body is not—harmless in the long term, and effective.

"You wonder why. Why would I devise the demise of my own company? I can see it in your eyes, your intensely auburn, never faltering, Federal Bureau eyes. I so admired you, that first day we met. I wanted to reveal it all to you. I knew then that you would understand.

"For what you must come to realize is this: my work these past weeks has been the culmination of many years—years of indecision, of reservation, of trusting and doubting my instincts. When the world whispered, then talked, then shouted this outrageous Healthcare Bill, I knew I could no longer waver. This is irony, Miss Downer. You have been hunting Terrance Martin and this VikkarAll person, but in the end, we all want the same thing: for Youtopia to fall. The difference is that their plans would also take me down with them. For obvious reasons, that cannot happen.

"I know that, on the surface, this is difficult to comprehend. I have shown nothing but unwavering devotion to Youtopia's rise. But let me impress upon you how strange a thing it is, marrying oneself so completely to a brainchild whose flaws present themselves only as it ages. That brainchild, perfect in intent, was utterly imperfect in execution.

"My doubts began as our initial Immersers matured, as their minds devolved. Perhaps I should have had more foresight. Perhaps I trusted too blindly in an inherent goodness in humankind. I foolishly believed that underneath everyone's deepest desires lied amity, altruism, compassion—that above all, people loved.

"Instead, I saw reality—the entirety of my creation succumbed to the darkest desires. The more I watched, the deeper I sank into the crass, blackened soul of an adult raised by this world. It was grotesque. The older they were, the worse it was. The Feeds repelled me. I could spend not a minute in Central Control, could not risk glimpsing a single person in Evolution awaiting their disgrace. I despised them. I grew contemptuous of the hungers Youtopia sated for them. These reprobates... they do not deserve my creation. They do not deserve Youtopia.

"But then Oscar. My sweet angel Oscar. He saved me from the hollows. When Jeanne Haskins Immersed, she left Oscar no primary Observer. He was afloat. I had no intention of ever watching his Feed, but then something—kismet, a forethought, Terrance's *Higher Power*—drew me to Central Control. Immediate, *immediate,* was the difference. It was otherworldly. I fell into the screen, ran beside him in his fields, dropped coins down his well. With his hands I brought plants and animals and the Earth itself to new forms of life. Even when I left the room, his world followed me to the racquetball courts, to meetings with dignitaries. I dreamt of it in my brief moments of sleep. I saw it on every blank television and tablet and phone screen I encountered. I am sure you know how this feels.

"Oscar, my dear Oscar, only six when we sought him out, destined to a diminutive life of air tubes and IV carts and torture, physical torture. And now, ten years later, he lives. Not only lives—he *creates*. His mind is unconstrained by logic, by modern science, by oppressive, external psychological phenomena. He has developed far beyond the existential shamble of emotional repression and anxiety and blight that is the adult human. His joys are primal. His fears are straightforward and easily defeated. He is pure, substantial. He is *divine*.

"I believed at the outset that Youtopia was for everyone. That, eventually, the entire world might exist there. That perfection was possible in every person's mind. I realize now that it is possible, but only for the young. For Oscar. The system cannot continue as it is, Miss Downer. I must issue a reckoning, a pandemic, a Great Flood. I must wash my hands of this first iteration so that, when I start again, I can realize its true purpose.

"I recognize your objections. Your muted scowl represents for me years of contemplation, of thinking and rethinking, but I have considered it all, and find no objection of value. To begin with Oscar himself: Youtopia has in no way physically altered Oscar's brain. His growth and development are consistent with any common teenager. He has only made synaptic connections never before thought possible. His mind has accessed areas heretofore considered dormant. The creativity inherent in building his own world has advanced him beyond our inferior imaginations. In our world, he would be beyond genius.

"But aside from Oscar, you might believe my new plan will be difficult, impossible even, for the world to accept. That we are too protective of our children. But remember, Youtopia would have been unthinkable even fifteen years ago. I found a way then, and will do so again.

"A metaphor may help guide us. Imagine, if you will, that you purchase for a child the perfect video game, only to discover the gaming system itself hasn't yet been invented. You have a key to unlock the world, but humanity doesn't yet recognize the room in which it is imprisoned. There will be fear, but that fear can quickly become awe — awe and wonder.

"Imagine it. Infinite children with infinite capacities to build infinite worlds. Never in the world long enough to be tainted, stained, by the scourge of society. No more predatory Fowlers or Senators. Just pure, unadulterated ingenuity. That, Miss Downer, is the perfect world.

"You disagree. Your eyes so often give you away! You wish to regain your body and flee, to arrest me, to reveal to the Bruce Kloses of the world all I am revealing now. Your parental instinct gnaws at you. I see it. You think that you will save the children by exposing me.

"But you must see, you *must* see, that it is the exact opposite! See Oscar, who can envision friends wholly supportive and genuine, who can eradicate all evils, who can *create life* at will. See too the real world, which defiles and corrupts and assaults children like Oscar. It *kills* them, every chance it gets. So no, I do not enslave them. The world enslaves them. Youtopia is their liberator.

"I recognize this is a lot to accept. It took me years, years, to do so. It is possible you may never agree. But you must by now realize that my plan will go forward in either case. It culminates tonight. And, agree or not, you will assist me in its execution.

"Because what is truth if not a story? A version of reality created by one subject's vantage at a particular moment? Youtopia's failures have shown me that all our truths are fungible, and that, without sheer persistence of will, darkness will overtake light. We are the light, Miss Downer. We can make the world possible.

"To wit: this facility is not just a leftover vestige of our humble beginnings, not some monument or historical site. It is also our most isolated and undisclosed Nest. Below us are two hundred of our most private Immersers. In Albany, there lies a similar Nest with similar Immersers. In twenty minutes — right around the time your legs will begin to respond — one of these groups will die.

"The reactions will be predictable and necessary. The murderer has accessed Youtopia's most secretive facilities. He has wiped out an entire small Nest. He has access to the larger Nests. He could kill every remaining Immerser. In the face of this mass murder, the Healthcare Bill is moot. In order to ensure the safety of the remaining Immersers, Youtopia must be shut down altogether. These Immersers must Reintegrate into society. It is the only assured option, the option with which I, as a responsible caretaker and citizen, must reluctantly agree.

"Nearly half a million people will come back. Each one will need unflagging assistance in returning to life, in overcoming, in healing. To renege on the promise of Immersion is nearly impossible. Of this, I know intimately. Imagine what it will be for them. For him.

"Yes, Paul. He holds to your daughter with a ferocity most admirable. And all over again, she will be thrust from...

"I do not mean to induce tears. It is not my intention to hurt you. Only to help you see. Your husband will need you. His mind cannot overcome on its own. You will need to guide him away from Charlotte and back to our cruel, cruel world.

"Of course, there is still the question of the identity of the killer. In this, we are faced with two paths, both leading to a particular truth. You will likely prefer the first. In this scenario, the killer is nobody.

"We will call this the Albany Scenario. Your former investigation will continue with little direction. The Terrance Martins and hackers of the world will remain suspect. Wherever this investigation leads, honestly, I do not think will matter. Youtopia will be gone, and I will already have started my work of bringing Oscar's vision to the world.

"The second option we will call the Dakota Scenario. The murderer, in this case, is you.

"Please relax. The flush in your cheeks is a good sign, but the sensation in your chest and hips is only the beginning. You must hear my final words before you choose which two hundred people will die.

"No one received your messages this morning. Excuse me for the insult, but your personal phone is painfully unguarded. So, no one besides you and Mr. Tramel and this VikkarAll know why you're really here.

"As to VikkarAll: for years now, he has been able to elude me. He's been the proverbial thorn in my side. He held the CNN video, the final piece I needed to bury my secret. But in his haste to get it to you, he made a fatal slip. For that, I must thank you. My people will have him within hours. The Senator's Immersion speech will be no more. Only you and I will know its secret.

"People will, of course, know you came here tonight. Your phone's location tracking, flight and rental car records, will all prove it. Your version of the story will be an interesting one, surely. You came to confront me, to get the truth of a video no longer in existence. You will recount a conversation I will deny, a conversation detailing a devoted CEO's plot to sabotage her own company. You will cite a paralyzing toxin that is no longer traceable in your system. You will try to connect the digital dots, but I hope you recognize by now that I am far superior to Sergio Morales, or James Peterson, or the VikkarAlls of the world.

"Remember too that this fanciful story comes from Anabel Downer, disgraced FBI Special Agent. The investigator who pored over videos of her estranged husband. Who had more access to our information than most upper-level employees. Who may have been working with, or for, the infamous hacker VikkarAll, and could cover his tracks. Who, when dismissed, did not return the baton we assigned her, but instead used it to break into our facilities tonight. Who accosted me and my colleague, drugged us, and murdered hundreds of innocent people more, all in revenge against Youtopia. Revenge against her very husband Paul, who abandoned her when she needed him. The man who rests now just stories beneath our feet, his life in fatal peril.

"Miss Downer, I ask: who do you think the world will believe?

"I am happy you are calming. You can see that the Albany Scenario is the only clear path, a path on which we are conjoined together. Our future is providence, the prodigious push of a celestial hand.

"I wish Youtopia had been what I initially intended. If so, all of this could have been avoided. But rare is the perfect first attempt. Without Youtopia, I could not have seen what I have seen. We could not be here. Now, I see the future with full clarity. It begins with Oscar. It begins with you and Paul, together again.

"It begins now."

JOSEPH REIN

Chapter 11

A cool air danced about the building. Across refurbished hardwood floors rolled the wheels of cushioned chairs. The music was trendy, soft but with deep bass, as though they sailed on a cruise ship, or lounged in a teenage clothing shop. White wainscoting ran the length of every wall, in the halls and each bedroom suite and here, in the conference room large enough for three hundred. Above the divide, at eye level everywhere, hung artwork of professionals and patients side-by-side, Raque Fords and Tom El-Saiehs next to the watercolors and still life fruit bowls of current residents. The chandeliers were immodest and contemporary, the finishes perfect. The place radiated money, the kind that suggested the speedy and fortuitous success of Abundant Life and all Youtopia Reintegration facilities of its kind in less than a year.

Ana sipped coffee flown in from Seattle. She placed her cup on the empty chair next to her—Paul's chair. On its other side, Lonnie sat stoic, her hands in her lap, her bouncing leg the only thing betraying her stony façade, the only thing showing her true animated self beneath. In a circle around them sat similar groups who remained mostly silent. It was Thursday, meeting day with visitors, with spouses and parents and devoted friends. These visitors were, for many Reintegrators, the only lasting connection to the world. Observers of a different kind.

Paul was taking too long in returning from the restroom. Ana fought the impulse to check her phone, to open a browser and find something, anything, that would take her away. Instead, she focused on the first person to receive the group's attention, Candace, the newest Abundant Life resident. Candace sat alone, had nobody to make the weekly Thursday visits, a fact for which she immediately apologized. Her mother would come, she said, but this was the same woman who'd flogged Candace when she mentioned Immersion in the first place.

"Well, okay. So, like," Candace began, stumbling her way into her story. She wore beaten corduroy pants, an oversized sweatshirt, and the droop of consistent shame. She explained her every action, as though she could only be understood by disclaimer, eliciting from Ana both compassion and weariness. "I was depressed. Like, so-hoooo depressed. I'm sorry, I don't mean before Youtopia. That shit was nothing! I'm talking right after the thaw."

"It's great to have you here, Candace," Gloria, the group leader, cut in with her unflappable calm. "But please, let's steer clear of derogatory slang here."

"Christ. Sorry. *Reintegration*, I meant to say. I can't even do this right."

"You're doing great," Gloria said. "Better than great. I can't tell you how happy I am that you are here." As leader of this group, Gloria was great herself. Her husband committed suicide just days after Reintegrating, a story she shared with all newcomers. "We must remember that we come to this place with no judgment whatsoever, with an understanding that we *all* know how difficult this is, and that we can only help one another."

"Help. Right." Candace pinched at the crown of her nose, knocking her rimless glasses to the floor. "Fuck! I can't..." She picked them up, examined them for cracks. She stared at them, through them, until her eyes welled up. She cried. She cried and cried, and the group, as per policy, sat quietly and absorbed it. They allowed her to mourn. They acknowledged her pain.

After a minute, Lonnie broke, saying, "Oh for fuck's sake, give her a tissue." She stood and offered a plastic package of her own.

Ana wanted Paul to return from the bathroom badly, if only to occupy the empty seat between them, to offer her his hand to hold. In this place, here in the circle, only in these meetings would he give that much to her.

Then he strutted in, his hair cropped short, his body trim but strong, his stride confident. He beamed his extravagant smile, the one that won him undue trust from strangers. He wore the collared shirt she'd bought him that final Christmas, azure to bring out his eyes. His entire body sheened with newness because, after all, he was at heart a sweatshirt-and-jeans guy, more flannel than formal. The room warmed to him. Even Candace stopped sulking, caught for a moment in Paul's kindliness.

But the image was, of course, a fantasy. It was not Paul these last months, or even Paul in the mirror of his Youtopia Feeds. It was a Paul who existed only in her own distant memory.

"I'm sorry," Candace said between her final sobs.

Gloria reached an arm out, though she was halfway across the room. "You have no reason to apologize."

"I mean," Candace said, waving her glasses, "I didn't even *need* these fucking things in there. Twenty-twenty. Better! Oh, but that's nothing compared to my allergies, sinus infections, migraines." She rocked a hand against her temple, then lashed it in the air. "And goddamn hemorrhoids!"

Gloria sat back in her chair. The group looked to her, but she said nothing.

"I hate this world," Candace said. "Hay-fucking-tuh."

In the ensuing silence, Ana stood. Lonnie shot her a scowl of disapproval, but Ana didn't care. It was time to go.

***

In the prior months since Paul had returned, Ana had found herself — as Sonya predicted — in a role well beyond wife. She served as hospice nurse, caretaker, lifesaver. First, she had to tend to Paul's body. His atrophied arms and legs had been reduced to skeletal proportions. His chest, once full and defined, the pride of his body after daily push-ups, was a sunken hollow. His insurance covered full physical therapy, but like anything medical, the cure only worked with a willing patient, which Paul was not. Even regular eating proved too much. Never before discriminate in his tastes, Paul now scoffed at anything with a strong smell, his gag reflex acute and immediate. He ate with a toddler's fussiness, often in his bed, where he spent days watching television, news and sports and infomercials, anything on public access — the program didn't matter. Ana drifted farther from the Bureau, taking on only consulting roles so she could stay at home to help Paul heal. Whenever she left his side, she returned only to find the same channel, the same volume, the same deadness in Paul's eyes. He grew a beard flush with gray even though, before Youtopia, he was a habitual morning shaver. He spoke only when Ana initiated conversation, and sometimes not even then. The only topic he had any interest in was her apartment — he hated it, and took every opportunity to tell her so.

She eventually tried intimacy. After a time, when his body had gained back some of its weight, Ana touched him again, small at first — a hand on his elbow here, a half-arm hug there. The first time she touched his inner thigh he twitched like a teenager. But when they finally took off their clothes, when he finally entered her again, he did so with closed eyes and fists against the mattress. He didn't seem to breathe. He seemed not to want to have sex *with* Ana but *through* her, to some indeterminate beyond — to Youtopia, perhaps. He pushed harder and harder. When he did open his eyes, Ana saw in them the aggression of Youtopia-Paul in his living room mirror, and her body instantly flexed and froze. She stopped him. After she was clothed, after she had already left the room, she heard his throat utter a guttural, deep moan of pain that she could do nothing to alleviate.

The next afternoon, she came home from the grocery to find all her kitchen knives laid out in strange ceremony on her island. She tensed in reflexive defense, as though Paul would pounce on her from some shadow. Then she saw the small puddle of blood he hadn't bothered to conceal running from the sink's edge, and knew the knives were not for her.

She removed them, and the scissors, the letter opener, the corkscrew, anything with a pointed edge. She hid them in a place he found immediately the next day, and then the next. In this he was surprisingly dogged. Ana considered a large safe, but then there were belts, and household cleaners and bottles of Excedrin, and any other hazards Paul could enlist. He could just open a window and jump. It was then, six months in, that Ana finally broke down and called Lonnie.

To her credit, Lonnie did not castigate Ana. If she was angry with Ana for shutting her out of Paul's Reintegration, she didn't show it. Instead, she came right over and tried to nurture Paul. She chuckled at his morbid jokes, made and bussed his meals, even read Facebook posts of former acquaintances to him in bed. She encouraged him to paint. Her visits brought to his days an optimism that Ana herself couldn't muster. But one night, a bottle of wine down and Paul asleep or brooding in his bed, Lonnie admitted to Ana that she couldn't do it anymore. Even she saw that Paul needed something neither of them could provide or understand. The next day, Ana called Abundant Life.

***

She found a male attendant, who entered the men's restroom and confirmed that Paul wasn't there. She tried the recreation room where, according to his doctors, he spent hours in silent contemplation. This was healthy behavior, they assured Ana, healthier than when he was at home watching TV, healthier than the many residents who spent entire days on their smartphones, attempting to again exchange their reality for something different. In order for the mind to recalibrate to the world, it needed to process their world, they told her. Each doctor said in frustrating concert to, "Give Paul time." He could Reintegrate, like everyone could.

Ana didn't find him in the rec room either. Aside from a man playing solitaire, the room sat empty. She went outside, searched along the three-acre walking path that cut through dense brush and imported maples, where Paul sometimes sat with his sketchbook. Halfway down the path, she interrupted a young couple kissing. She apologized, though once they saw she was not a worker, they dove back in, groping with a desperation unashamed and admirable. Ana wished it were Paul and her. Or even, she was willing to concede, Paul and some other woman, a worker or a secret mistress. Paul and Lonnie. At this point, any passion would do.

She ultimately found him, of course, in his room. It was a small but well-furbished space, decorated with consoling intent. Volunteer-made, hand-knit afghans lined the couch. The desk and dressers were real oak. A staff member turned over Paul's bed once a week, on Thursdays during the meetings, but Paul had already unmade it, had untucked the corners and bunched the sheets. He sat now looking out the patio door that led to his small but private outdoor space, his legs crossed before him. On the bottom of his right heel, Ana noticed his tattooed number, S217720, stark against his pale skin.

"Another minute of Gloria, and..." Paul drew in a long breath, something he did reflexively, without recognizing how agonized it made him seem. "You can go now."

He turned to her. Beneath his whiting beard his face looked thin, pale, but it hadn't exactly aged—no new scars, no freckles enhanced from sun. It looked paradoxically both older and younger.

"You could come home," she said.

Paul harrumphed with such force he alarmed even himself. "That's not home."

"Then we can make a home. We can go anywhere."

He sighed again, his sunken chest rising.

"Look, Paul, I want to help. I really do. But at some point, we have to face—"

"Did that one this morning," he interrupted, pointing at one of a number of charcoal drawings strewn across his desk. On the floor, even more accumulated like dirty laundry. There were so many that Ana stopped noticing, each one worse than the next, full of heavy, maudlin lines, full of unabashed nostalgia. The one he referred to, the one he slid atop the others, showed an idyllic park taken straight from his Youtopia memories. The only thing missing was Charlotte. And color. Though he used to bemoan dark art—he called it *blank and white* with his characteristic smirk—now Paul only painted in shades of gray.

"I like it," Ana said. "You should hang it somewhere in the building."

This time Paul laughed, a deep-throated, harrowing thing, as though Ana had just asked for a finger, for some body price to be excised and never returned, leaving him deformed. As though she wanted more than he could ever give.

"Paul, you need to live. *We* need to live."

With a flick of his wrist, he tucked the painting with all the others. "That's what they keep telling me."

***

Her phone dinged a notification. She poured her third glass of wine, or maybe her fourth. Tonight, like many nights, wasn't a good one for counting. After the meeting, Lonnie had hounded Ana with voicemails and texts, asking how she could just up and leave, why she felt it was Lonnie's responsibility to help her husband come back to life. Ana didn't reply. For all the time they'd spent together in the past months, something about Lonnie felt like a relic, a face in the yearbook. Someone who would reject Ana's offer to come with her to Andalusia, her beloved Andalusia, even if Ana were inclined to ask, which she wasn't.

One-way flights were going for relatively cheap. She could bring little along. In almost every respect, this would be the best time in her life for such a move. Her career had stalled, might stay afloat or drift downward but never again upward, never nearing the prestigious skies of her past. She had no furniture or land for which she held sentimental reminiscences. She had no one whom she would gravely miss, who would gravely miss her. She had little reason not to go.

The ding didn't come from Lonnie. It showed a photo of a tie-dyed teddy bear with the black print, I COLORED THE ATLANTA ZOO, across the stomach. The text read:

> *Pandas BETTER than advertised. Lun Lun in love with me.*
> *Competition!*

It was from Evan.

The day Paul entered Abundant Life, Ana had abandoned all subterfuge and called Evan. In a message, she offered to pay him, not for his sperm, but for the time he spent in Racine while she wavered. He called back immediately, and after she sent him the oversized sum, he dropped any umbrage, became again the cheerful confidant he had been at the start. He had given up FamilyMatch work and took a position in one of his family's hotels out West. "I know, a nine-to-five sucker. But it pays. Boy, does it pay. And I've got a pretty sweet in with the boss." He still traveled the country, now for the hotel, and mentioned his visits to the Midwest often. He would be spending two nights if she would like to grab a drink, no strings attached; or he was just connecting at O'Hare but would gladly bump flights if she was available. Every time, she had an excuse at the ready. She had no intention of seeing him again, of making any further amends, of developing some bastardized version of her and Paul's relationship with Evan. But unlike Paul, or Lonnie, or anyone else in her life, at times Evan gave Ana reason to smile.

To this new message, her phone offered autoreplies she had sent in the past, and she recognized the strange jubilance in them, the schoolgirl giddiness, the exclamation points. She chose one anyway and sent it. Then, before Evan could reply, she shut down her phone.

***

Two nights later, Ana found the perfect flight. Direct from O'Hare to Málaga via Aer Lingus. A window seat in first class. To her cart she added the flight and her amenities—no rental car or hotel, not yet. She could play that by ear. She agreed to terms of service and entered her sign-in information. She was a click away from booking when, on the television she'd turned on for noise, a familiar voice rang out.

It was a national evening news spot. As always, Sonya Young looked stark, serious. Her lips were pulled taut, as though she had never smiled and never would. She was another relic from Ana's recent past, and yet she felt so far away. The time since Ana had left the original Youtopia facility, shaky and crestfallen, seemed stretched infinite, like a waking dream. Like part of some other life. Then again, it was only a matter of time before Sonya reemerged into her—and everyone's—world.

Sonya wasn't the headline, but an interview on another story. It seemed that last night, in a hospital in Kentucky, Oscar Haskins died from cancer complications. His mother Jeanne declined an interview, but the anchor was pleased to speak now with someone who was as close to another mother as young Oscar had.

"No, no," Sonya said. "Jeanne is his mother. Our hearts go out to her now." She trailed a hair behind her ear and her eyes gave a cloying squint, gestures made to humanize her. Like all of Sonya's moves, they worked. "I only helped Oscar, in the way I knew how."

Ana grabbed the remote and hovered above the green power button. She shouldn't watch. She should — like she had instructed Paul inestimable times over — just move on. Yet something stayed her finger.

Sonya and the anchor discussed Oscar and his time in Youtopia. Sonya gave only pieces, but it was enough to move Ana, the anchor, the audience — enough to shift the ever-moving tectonics of their current world.

"Oscar far outlived his prognosis in Youtopia," the anchor said. "Presumably, he would still be alive today. Do you wish Youtopia hadn't been forced to close?"

Sonya looked down in faux-contemplation, even though Ana knew she had an answer ready for this. "That is a difficult question. On the one hand, of course, I wish the ending was not so abrupt. I feel for those who were murdered. I feel for Oscar and Jeanne. For all those hurting people who are trying to Reintegrate into the world."

She indulged in a drawn-out pause. "But I am, at heart, a forward thinker. For better or worse, Youtopia could not continue. Instead of wondering what could have been, we must now focus on what could be."

"And what do you see?"

"I see some very important changes. Not just to the way we live, to the way we interact with the world, but to our conception of what the world *is*. What is possible."

"That sounds very, dare I say..." The anchor relished in dramatic pause. "Youtopian."

"It is, and yet it is not."

Sonya didn't break eye contact. Ana remembered this stare well, the feeling that behind those eyes rested something deeper, something unsaid, something that Sonya wanted to reveal but never would. The difference now was that Ana knew what Sonya wished to say. She knew her secret.

The anchor looked beyond Sonya, likely to some producer signaling to wrap up the segment, but he ignored it. He wanted to know the secret as well.

"Does this mean, then, that you have been working on another project? Youtopia 2.0?"

Sonya smiled. "I am always working. Whether or not my future involves something of that nature, it is too early to say. But I will never stop trying to help the Oscars of the world. He is the key to my future—the key, perhaps, to all our futures."

THE END
...but please keep reading for our Bonus Content.

JOSEPH REIN

Book Club Guide

1. Youtopia presumes a world where people can live within their own minds. How close do you believe we are to this in real life?

2. Many of the novel's chapters are written in a "found documents" format—a television script, a magazine article, a blog post. In what ways does this affect the reading experience?

3. In the novel, Ana discovers that Youtopia causes Immersers to enact their basest, most deviant desires. They all "fall prey to a deeper lust." Do you agree that this would happen? Why or why not?

4. Ana is released from the case for watching her ex-husband's Youtopia Feeds. Do you think the Bureau was right to do so? In her situation, do you believe you could have resisted?

5. Given the choice, would you enter Youtopia yourself? Would others in your life? Where do you think your Youtopia would take you, and why?

6. Which character do you identify with the most in the novel, and why?

7. The novel first introduces us to the Senator, a character who will become integral to the rise and fall of Youtopia. Why do you think the author chose to name this character "the Senator" and nothing else?

8. What other books does *Youtopia* remind you of? Movies? Why? If you were to cast actors for the movie version, who would you choose and why?

Interview with the Author

Q. Where did the idea for *Youtopia* originate for you?

A. As with most novels, the book idea started years before any of the actual words met these pages. The idea for "youtopias" started as a small chapter in a larger work, a simple conversation between my protagonist and his pot dealer, actually. The dealer was spouting this farfetched idea of people living in their own brains, and at the time, I was probably exploring the idea in a safer space, through a person we weren't necessarily meant to take seriously. But as the years passed, as I saw more and more people living in their phones instead of the world before them, the more I realized the idea was serious, and that I should treat it as such.

Q. Why did you choose to write the book with some "found documents" chapters?

A. In part, I wrote this way because I've always admired works that play with form in fiction, works that take something like website excerpts or press releases and ask, can this contain a story? Where do the forms and stories intersect? In part, I also like the worldbuilding aspects: as a reader, you're not just hearing things from the narrator, or a particular character's point of view. But more for *Youtopia* specifically, I wanted the reader to encounter clues as Ana would encounter them. For example, the reader is introduced to Terrance Martin through his *Rolling Stone*-style article, as Ana would be. Same with Jeanne Haskins' blog: we read it, and then Sonya references her in conversation. I think it helps the reader become a complicit investigator in the story.

Q. Ana is a lead FBI agent, and yet she struggles with her own demons throughout the novel. Why did you portray the character this way?

A. For me, Ana came to life when I started seeing her as more than her job. The more I researched the life of an FBI agent, the more I realized, hey, these are people too. They go home at night and have a drink. They socialize. They have desires for family and friendship and work-life balance just like anyone. To me, thrillers based on crime can be painfully one-sided if the characters aren't given space to be an actual human — to get angry, to have migraines, to make mistakes and want to give up. I'm always more interested in the human side of things than the procedural, because procedures can be pretty static, whereas humans are ever-changing. Also, the twist regarding Paul's Immersion was a key plot point for me, even in the early stages. I knew that I wanted the protagonist's spouse to be an Immerser, to add that layer of complication to her path, but also to show her strength and resilience. In having the trauma of Charlotte's death hang over Ana, I wanted to show that she was struggling with grief, as so many of us do, but that she didn't take the easy road like Paul did. Entering Youtopia, where your deceased child can come back to life, seems pretty tempting. Life is the harder route.

Q. Terrance Martin and his ReaLife Church represent a religious reaction to Youtopia. Why was that aspect important for you to include in the book?

A. I grew up with religion, and so it's always interesting to me to see how organized religions react to the speed of our increasingly technological world. But more, if something like this were real, and affected hundreds of thousands of people, then certainly we would try to frame it in religious contexts. Is this our purpose as humans? If we created it, does it mean it fulfills some larger destiny? For the book's purposes, Terrance and ReaLife represent a counterpoint to a lot of what Youtopia stands for. Since this is a novel and not a work of theology, Martin had to remain primarily an antagonist, a driver of conflict. I believe, were this real, there would be far more nuance, especially regarding already established religions. How would the Catholic Church encounter Youtopia? Or Judiasm? Islam? Those would be interesting questions to tease out, given the time and space.

Q. Was Sonya Young always going to be the antagonist?

A. Yes. In fact, in early drafts, she was far too suspect. I revealed her devious ploy to ensnare the Senator right away; Ana looked at her with great suspicion. I realized: I'm giving away my ending! There's no mystery there. A good mystery has red herrings, has an ending that both surprises but also makes you say, "Of course, that makes sense." Hopefully this novel achieves that.

Q. Some portions of the novel seem eerily close to happening in our world. Do you believe we are on a path similar to the one in the novel?

A. Yes and no. I'm scared by how appealing something like Youtopia would be, to all sorts of people, myself included. That's what fascinated me most about writing this, be it with Terrance or Jeanne or Paul: it's not just one type of person who might want to retreat into their own personal paradise. Our true reality is ambivalent, and my hope is that we can embrace it, can recognize that the perfect world isn't something we can create, even as we strive to improve and better the world around us. It's the proverbial idea of life as a journey, not a destination.

Q. What is your writing process like?

A. All over the place! I wish it were otherwise. I used to be fairly routine, but then my job as a professor, my family obligations — not to mention just trying to enjoy life! — all disrupted that routine. Now I find pockets of time, usually an hour here or there, and just hammer it out. I tend to think things through well before they see the page, and I know I need to be efficient with my time, so the nice part is I rarely experience writer's block. Also, I try to get the full draft out before going back to significantly revise — the word processor makes editing-while-writing far too enticing, and it can lead to stagnancy. For example, Lonnie wasn't even in the first two-thirds of the book until I realized Ana needed someone to confide in. So I just wrote her into the end of the book as though she always existed, and then went back to fill her in. I also like to reward myself: I always save chapters as different files, instead of having the novel be one giant file, so I can feel that sense of accomplishment moving from one to the next. An added bonus is that it makes the novel easier to navigate, if ever I need to find something.

Q. What is your own personal Youtopia?

A. A great question! I think, if I follow the premise of the book, that I actually have no idea. I'm pretty afraid of my — or any — mind that is left to run free, that receives nothing but positive reinforcement. On the one hand, we thrive on rewards and successes, so I like to think that my Youtopia would include things that I find rewarding in my own life: writing and reading, knowing and raising my wonderful four kids, spending time with my wife, teaching. I love exercise and a good vacation on the water. On the other hand, there's that deviant side to all of us, the one that looks for instant gratification, that pushes the boundaries. If that side were perpetually rewarded, look out.

Acknowledgements

This book, like all books, made it here because of the help of so many others. I am eternally indebted to all those who knowingly or unknowingly supported its creation. This goes to all the authors of the utopian and dystopian fiction that influenced my early thinking on this book many years ago, and to the indispensable books that influenced Ana's character: Ronald Kessler's *The FBI: Inside the World's Most Powerful Law Enforcement Agency* and *The Secrets of the FBI*; David Sanger's *The Perfect Weapon*; Kate Fazzini's *Kingdom of Lies: Unnerving Adventures in the World of Cybercrime*; Candice DeLong's *Special Agent: My Life on the Front Lines as a Woman in the FBI*.

Thanks to the University of Wisconsin–River Falls for awarding me the sabbatical during which I accomplished most of the rewriting on this novel. To former instructors and mentors of mine: David Treuer, Liam Callanan, Jonis Agee, Gerald Shapiro, and countless others. To Kevin Morgan Watson, for recognizing the value in my short fiction. To Greg Peterson, for his council on the opening chapters. To Dave Yost, the best reader (and writer) I could ever hope to know.

Thanks to Dave Lane (AKA Lane Diamond), an excellent editor, and Kris Norris for a beautiful and haunting cover.

To my parents Bill and Barb: my deepest gratitude, for never saying I couldn't or shouldn't. This book is for them, and also for my kids, Colette, James, Johnny, and Olivia, who each day simultaneously keep me young and age me considerably. And finally, it is for my wife Jessica, my best friend, my most avid reader, and the reason this and all of my books are possible.

About the Author

Joseph Rein is the author of the short story collection *Roads without Houses* (2018), which was nominated for numerous literary prizes. His short fiction has appeared in over twenty journals, magazines, and anthologies worldwide, and has twice been nominated for a Pushcart Prize. He is also a screenwriter and critical essayist. His second feature-length film, Who Killed Cooper Dunn? (2022), was featured on Showtime and other streaming platforms. He wrote, produced, and acted in multiple other short festival films, and has two feature-length projects in pre-production. He is currently a Professor of Creative Writing at the University of Wisconsin-River Falls. When not writing or reading, he can be found hiking with his wife Jessica, playing cribbage, or recovering from various small injuries inflicted by his four children.

For more, please visit Joseph Rein online at:
Website: www.JosephRein.com
Facebook: @JosephReinAuthor
Instagram: @joseph_rein1
X (Twitter): @joseph_rein1

What's Next?

Watch for the second book in this series to release in late 2024.

YOUTOPIA REBORN
Youtopia – Book 2

Youtopia is dead — long live Youtopia Reborn.

Limited now to minors, the expanded mindscape worlds of Youtopia Reborn cater to the ill and unwanted, the children left behind by society. When Youtopia creator Sonya Young goes mysteriously missing, her abductor leaves a harrowing message: "Reborn for All."

Lane Samson, a former Youtopia Immerser and local reporter, receives a strange voicemail from an old friend who claims to have secrets about Sonya Young's abduction. The tip leads Lane to the one person more familiar with Youtopia investigations than anyone — former, disgraced FBI Special Agent Anabel Downer.

Together, Lane and Ana must piece together the mystery of Sonya Young's disappearance as the abductor escalates his attacks, as all of the Youtopia children, and Lane and Ana themselves, face perilous danger.

More from Evolved Publishing

We offer great books across multiple genres, featuring high-quality editing (which we believe is second-to-none) and fantastic covers.

As a hybrid small press, your support as loyal readers is so important to us, and we have strived, with tireless dedication and sheer determination, to deliver on the promise of our motto:
QUALITY IS PRIORITY #1!

Please check out all of our great books,
which you can find at this link:
www.EvolvedPub.com/Catalog/

Thank you!

www.ingramcontent.com/pod-product-compliance
Lightning Source LLC
Chambersburg PA
CBHW031229260626
47169CB00007B/2207